FREEFALL

A Divine Comedy

A NOVEL BY

LILY IONA MacKENZIE

First Edition
Printed and Bound in the U.S.A.
Pen-L Publishing
Fayetteville, Arkansas

ISBN: 978-1-68313-196-0
Library of Congress Control Number: 2018942152

Cover and interior design by Kelsey Rice

FREEFALL

A Divine Comedy

BOOKS BY LILY IONA MacKENZIE

POETRY

All This

NOVELS

Fling!
Curva Peligrosa
Freefall: A Divine Comedy

For Michael,
always my first and best reader

Midway in this mortal life I found myself
astray, in a dark wood. Ah, who can
say how terrible it was!

– Dante Alighieri

When a writer calls his work a romance…
he wishes to claim a certain latitude,
both as to its fashion and material,
which he would not have felt himself
entitled to assume, had he professed
to be writing a novel.

—Nathaniel Hawthorne,
Preface to *The House of the Seven Gables*

SAN FRANCISCO, CA
1999

Tillie deconstructs her fears

Tillie woke to another overcast morning in San Francisco, rattled by the dream image of her old friend Daddy wasting away in a jail cell. Burrowing deeper under the covers, she tried to ignore a tiny flicker of panic in her stomach. She'd lived with this low-grade anxiety for years, a tiger prowling the edge of her consciousness, ready to pounce. Her cash wasn't flowing—her latest artist grant hadn't come through yet—and the rent was due in a few days. She needed to find a new roommate or else get a smaller place. Her golden years didn't look promising.

No wonder she was thinking more about her youth, longing to reclaim it. Almost sixty, she'd sooner look backward than forward. Even her dreams offered up images of her late teens and twenties. The latest was an image of her friend Daddy in trouble. Daddy's original name was Darilyn, but her friends renamed her because Daddy had more zip. She and Daddy talked on the phone and exchanged letters now and then, but they hadn't seen each other all that much over the years.

Tillie dreamed of her often, though. It was always a variation on the same theme: her old friend was in the clink and it was up to Tillie to get her out. She was savvy enough to realize that the imprisoned Daddy could be some facet of Tillie that was locked up and wasting away, but she hadn't figured out why she was imprisoned or how to free her.

Tillie threw back the covers and climbed out of bed, bending and stretching to loosen her limbs. Pretending to draw a sword from its sheath on her hip, she parried with unseen foes on the way to the bathroom, refusing to let her fears get the best of her. She reminded herself she still had good health, she loved life, and she was resourceful. Something would turn up. It always did.

Bladder emptied, face washed, teeth brushed, and ready to meet the day, Tillie turned on her favorite jazz station and danced her way into the kitchen, stopping to make coffee. She poured it into a mug, added milk, dropped in two teaspoons of sugar, stirred vigorously, and glided over to her favorite perch, a burgundy brushed-velvet wingback she had picked up at the Salvation Army. Her command center, the phone sat on the table next to the chair, her sketchpad nearby so she could jot down ideas for her installations.

How the later stage in life got labeled "golden" remained beyond her. Pewter made more sense. All that dull drabness. So far her current phase had been anything but golden. Tillie was poor. She didn't have a permanent partner. She was still a nomad. And her work as an installation artist hadn't given her the prominence she'd sought. She also seemed to be experiencing the identity crisis she had skipped in her teens.

Yet Tillie didn't color her hair. There was no point. In spite of everything, she'd still be in her late fifties. Trying desperately to fool the world, she couldn't say sixty. That fast-approaching milestone weighed her down. What she wanted was a completely new body.

It was why she refused to try things some women did to fend off age: Botox, face-lifts, body tucks. There was always something the doctors missed; she couldn't remove all of the evidence. Tillie had read they even could give new life to a sagging vagina, the first giveaway, unless you had sworn off men. Even now, they were the only game in town—that is, when she could find an available one who could still get it up.

A late bloomer in all ways, Tillie also might be late for her own death. If she were lucky.

The phone shattered Tillie's reflections. Whenever it rang, she feared the worst: her mother, May, had croaked. At ninety-four, she was still feisty—her arms dripping with multi-colored bracelets, face powdered and rouged, lips painted bright orange, earlobes drooping under the weight of gold earrings, white hair tinted with blue streaks. So far, May could care for her one-bedroom triplex in Calgary on her own. She did the laundry, cleaned, and cooked her meals, as independent as she ever was. Most days she took the bus uptown and hung out at the Canadian Legion and other haunts that Tillie hadn't quite sorted out.

Tillie picked up the phone. "Mother?"

"I'm lonely. It's no fun being on my own. I miss Fred. At least he was a warm body to sleep with. I don't even have a cat anymore."

"I know what you mean. I didn't think I'd miss Frank."

"That jerk! You're lucky he's taken a powder. Permanently, I hope."

"Jeez, Mum. I thought you liked him."

"He wasn't my type. Too arty."

"If you're lonely, visit me. I'll scrape up airfare."

"You're always busy with your work. Anyway, the things you make give me the creeps."

"Thanks. I *love* your honesty."

"Well, I won't lie to you. That's why I won't visit."

"Maybe it's time to move to an assisted living place."

"Maybe it isn't."

The phone went dead. Tillie stared at it. May always had a way with words.

Their relationship wasn't flooded with love and goodwill. If it overflowed with anything, it was resentment and hostility, on both sides. The more guilt Tillie felt for having such responses to her mother, the more she resented her. She couldn't get away from the voice that hammered at her daily: *You should be spending more time with your mum. She's ninety-four. She could go any minute.* But there had been too many abandonments. Too many hurts. Too many unspoken words that were now irrecoverable and barred better communication.

The word "bar" reminded Tillie of Daddy being in the clink. The dream image intruded on her thoughts, blotting out May. Perhaps talking to her friend on the phone would shake loose some ideas of what the dream meant. She set down her coffee mug, looked up Daddy's Miami phone number in the dog-eared address book, and punched in the numbers on her blue Princess receiver.

While she waited for the phone to ring, Tillie thought of Sibyl and Moll, two other friends from the late '50s. They had all called themselves the Four Muskrateers. Naming themselves after a close relative to Canada's beaver made them feel patriotic.

Daddy answered the phone and Tillie asked, "What's a muskrat have that a beaver doesn't?"

"Tillie! I was just thinking of you," Daddy shrieked.

"You didn't answer."

"Softer fur!"

"You've won the first round in Double Jeopardy."

"It's great to hear your voice—where are you?"

"Not sure. Getting older has me in a tizzy. You know, all of us Muskrateers will be sixty in 2000?"

Daddy laughed. "Should we go into mourning? Or celebrate lasting this long? There's something to be said for endurance."

"I don't know. My mum's endured. She's ninety-four, you know. But lonely."

"May is ninety-four. Wow!"

"Yeah, that's what I say. I just wish I liked her better."

"It ain't easy having a mother."

"No kidding. But we've survived. Do you think Sibyl and Moll have?"

"Got me, babe," Daddy said. "Haven't talked to Sibyl for ages—she isn't dead because I get these weird Hallmark cards every Christmas."

"You too? No message."

"I know," Daddy said. "Just a bloody stamp that says 'Raleigh & Sibyl.' Fucking eerie."

"I've called her a few times to catch up."

"What about Moll? Haven't seen *or* talked to her since Toronto. Can you believe it's been forty years?"

"Haven't seen her either," Tillie said. "We didn't part on the best of terms. Remember? She thought I was a bad influence on you guys."

"Moll? Who's she to talk?"

"Sibyl's kept in touch with her. She's mentioned seeing her now and then. They both still live in B.C."

4

"Wouldn't a reunion be a gas?"

"A reunion?" Tillie stared at the overcast sky. The cloud cover seemed to shift, allowing a few shreds of sun to seep through. It might not be a bad day after all.

"Why not? We aren't getting any younger."

"Don't remind me. I'm game."

You should go visit your mother instead.

Get lost, Tillie said to the voice in her head. *I'll see her after the reunion.*

WHISTLER, B.C.
AUGUST 1999

TILLIE CONFRONTS THE PAST

Sibyl Pitt offered her funky cabin at Whistler for the Muskrateers' reunion. Tillie vhad visited the ski resort in her early twenties—before it became yuppified; before it was a resort. A tiny village in the cradle of two mountains, it wasn't named Whistler yet, and the houses *were* funky. So she expected Sibyl's place to be rustic and quaint. Made of logs. They would use candles and kerosene lanterns, cook on a wood stove, rough it. She came prepared, her rolled-up sleeping bag and stuffed backpack sitting on the seat beside her. Tillie also brought dried food. A tarot deck. Even a candle or two.

A sign said "Whistler," and she slowed down, watching for Ridge Road. Tillie's stomach gurgled, and it wasn't hunger. Fear, her old friend, was never far away. She was afraid to see these women again. What would they think of her? Tillie's life had taken a one-hundred-eighty degree turn from theirs. She didn't have a big house to show off. Or rings. Or a husband. What *did* she have to show for the last forty years? Most of her installations only existed in videos and photos. Nothing tangible. Nothing real. She was driving a '67 VW van, held together by faith and a mechanic who loved working on old vehicles. What would she have in common with the others except for their shared histories?

Tillie almost made a U-turn in the middle of the road, but then she recalled the empty apartment in San Francisco. It was still filled with unpleasant memories of Frank, her latest live-in, so she quickly shut *that*

7

door. She needed a break so she could get her bearings again. Find a new direction.

On the radio, Peter, Paul and Mary were singing "I'm just a poor wayfaring stranger." Tillie joined in, her voice off-key: "I'm going there to me-et my maker, I'm going there no mo-re to-o roam."

Folk songs were a welcome break from the hip-hop music that had taken over the airwaves, plaguing her since she left San Francisco. Tillie had tried listening to rap, wanting to be "with it." But she felt beaten-up by the words and blunt, monotonous rhythms. Though she hated to admit it, she knew she must be getting old when she couldn't relate to the new generation's music.

When Tillie pulled into Sibyl's driveway, her jaw dropped. The cozy, rustic cabin she had imagined, nestled among the pines, turned out to be a bloody three-story mansion, clinging to the side of a mountain. Definitely not what she'd expected. Feeling out of place already in her old van, her home away from home, she parked under some evergreens, between a new SUV and a Chrysler Jeep Liberty.

Glancing at herself in the rearview mirror, Tillie wondered how she would appear to these women, sorry now she'd never invested in a facelift. Her short spiked hair gave her a startled appearance, like an aging Orphan Annie. She had trouble reconciling how she appeared in the mirror—somewhat of a ruin—with how she felt, not much older than when the Muskrateers lived together in Toronto all those years ago.

Time and reality check. It wasn't the '50s. It was almost four o'clock PM on a Friday in August, near the end of the millennium. Reluctantly, Tillie left her van, approached the double front door, and rang the bell.

Sibyl appeared, wearing tight-fitting jeans and a skimpy red top, holding a glass of white wine in one hand, a cigarette in the other. Tiny breasts and not much meat on her bones. More waif-like than how Tillie remembered her. Short brown hair a thatched hut perched on top of Sibyl's head. Eyelids drooped, and the skin sagged under her eyes. Tillie noticed that one eye still wandered. Sibyl always appeared to be half-gazing at something just to the right.

She wasn't a pretty sight.

Smoke poured from her lips and nostrils—one long stream of it—and into Tillie's mouth, making her gag. When Sibyl saw the backpack and sleeping bag, she laughed, which started her hacking. She stood there, partly bent over, coughing and laughing and choking, wine spilling over her hand and onto the floor. She finally straightened up.

"You look like a refugee. You bring a tent, too?"

Tillie smiled, gritting her teeth, practicing restraint. She had to get through the next few days with Sibyl, her hostess. Like her mother, Sibyl had been drawn to Tillie's men. Believing sisterhood was powerful, Tillie had decided her relationship with women was more important than the men in her life. Still, it puzzled Tillie at times that she hadn't severed her bond with her mother *or* with Sibyl. Over the years, she certainly had reason to. But May was her mother. She couldn't just dump her. It wasn't Canadian. And she grudgingly admired Sibyl's chutzpah. She always did what she damn well pleased, unconcerned about the consequences.

Tillie needed all the friends she could get, especially at her age, so she said, "No, dear, my pig refuses to sleep in a tent. Pink satin sheets. Nothing else."

Sibyl was smiling, too, lipstick smeared, her lips pulled taut against her teeth, stretched to their limit. Her mouth had always been small, and Tillie remembered that smile. Cocky. Daring. A little angry tilt to it. But Sibyl's teeth seemed more widely spaced than Tillie remembered, and she hadn't seen a dental hygienist for a while. Nicotine gave her choppers an antique look.

Sibyl didn't seem to realize Tillie was joking and kept sneaking worried looks at her van, as if Tillie really did have a pig with her. Tillie actually had considered a pig as a pet after Frank moved out a couple of months earlier. She'd read they are smarter than humans. Better company, too. But she hadn't warmed to the idea of sleeping with one. She had some pride.

Tillie dropped her backpack in the front hallway and clomped inside, feeling like a klutz in her scruffy, ankle-high hiking boots and khaki shorts. She'd thought they all would be hiking and exploring, hanging out, not fussing with clothes or makeup. Just being their basic, back-to-the-earth selves.

She should have known better. Whenever two or more women are gathered, Venus—goddess of beauty *and* love—would be in their midst, causing them to compare, to pose, to compete with one another.

Tillie's boots sank into the white plush carpet. It felt about three feet deep, reminding her of quicksand she'd run into on the farm when she was a kid. She hadn't known it was a bog until she began to sink. Luckily, it was only a foot deep. Still, since then, she never quite trusted the earth to be constant and stable.

Family pictures filled the hallway. Sibyl's two sons at different ages, dressed in baseball uniforms and holding bats, snow skiing, water-skiing, wearing graduation hats and gowns. It all looked so middle-class. So normal. So bourgeois. Something else Tillie had avoided. She had feared she would die if she got stuck in a conventional nine-to-five life. She'd tried it for a time, and it did almost kill her.

"Pete's a wrestler, eh," Sibyl said proudly, pointing at her son's picture. "Or used to be. Could've gone to the Olympics if it weren't for his dad."

She took a swig of wine and puffed on her cigarette, shaking her head. Staggering, she aimed herself determinedly for the living room.

Tillie could see why Pete would take up wrestling. He must have wrestled with a lot in that family.

Strains of Rompin' Ronnie Hawkins and the Hawks singing "Hey! Bo Diddly" poured out of the living room. Daddy and Moll's laughter climbed hysterically and then stopped. Daddy shouted out "Hey! Bo Diddly" in counterpoint to Ronnie's voice, the way the Four Muskrateers had done in Toronto when they were on the prowl, hanging out at the Le Coq d'Or, the club where the Hawks had performed.

Sibyl tottered on her pink high-heeled mules fringed with feathers, yakking between drags on her cigarette and sips of wine.

"Listen to the racket, eh! The girls are kicking up their heels already." A cloud of smoke and Tillie following her.

Tillie had smoked herself when she was younger. Until she started wheezing all the time and had trouble breathing. Terror was a great teacher. She quit fast, and living in California had spoiled her. Non-smokers reigned.

Gagging, Tillie walked hunched over, trying to duck under the smoke, hoping to find purer air near the floor. Then in a flash she saw the title of her next installation: DEATH IN MENACE. Now she needed to figure out what it meant. Death was menacing enough, though life seemed more frightening at times. You never knew what was coming next. Losing a breast. A womb. A lover. It must be the menace of post-menopause that made Tillie's current work so dark.

Tillie visualized a walk-in meat locker, torsos of women hanging on hooks. Of course, she wouldn't use real women; that would be too raw. A row of women's legs emerge from the opposite wall, all of them wearing garters and doing the cancan. She'd have to rig up a way to animate the legs. Make it seem like they were really kicking. Maybe she would have the torsos in motion too, turning slowly like meat on a skewer. Contrary motion. Maybe the legs should all be kicking in different directions, giving a pinwheel effect. Not like the traditional cancan where all of the legs point one way. It could add an interesting dimension to the piece.

Tillie bumped into a pair of *real* legs.

"Hey, Tillie, bad back? Mine gives me trouble, too."

Tillie straightened up. Daddy. Hair still bleached a straw color. Wearing green tights that showed off her shapely calves. One hip thrust out. The old Daddy. Always posing, watching herself. Lips outlined a darker red than the interior. Same smirk. And the eyes—green, too, highlighted with metallic green eye shadow. Tillie recalled lynxes in the Calgary Zoo staring at her as Daddy did, coolly appraising, withholding. Something untamed trying to break free. In high school, it had been jarring for Tillie to glimpse something primitive rippling under the pleated skirt and white blouse that Daddy wore to school.

They hugged, tentatively, Sibyl and Moll looking on. Tillie could feel Daddy's curves, her body lacking muscle, soft and squishy. Like the Florida Everglades, near where she lived.

"We did it, girl," Tillie said to her. "Wow, I can't believe we're all together again!"

Daddy's perfume clung to Tillie when they separated, the same old cat smell now mixed with Chanel No. 5. A mass of gold and silver bangles clattered each time Daddy moved, dancing up and down her arm, matching the big hoops in her earlobes.

Moll screamed, "Tillie, you're a sight for sore eyes!"

11

The last time Tillie had seen Moll, her large breasts and shapely but-tocks had attracted all the guys. She had the best build of the four of them—and she knew it. She still had the breasts, but they were even bigger now, and her body was matronly. Tillie felt trim in comparison; her shape hadn't changed much over the years. Taller than the other women by several inches, Moll's dirty-blonde hair—caught up in a ponytail—blended with gray strands. *Très sportif*, she shunned makeup.

Tillie held out her hand to shake Moll's, wary, remembering the last time they saw each other at a party in Calgary, a couple of years after the Muskrateers had broken up in Toronto. Moll wouldn't speak to Tillie then, still blaming her for being led astray. *Bullshit* was what Tillie had thought then, and it popped into her mind now. *Bullshit.* You can't be led astray unless you want to be. It wasn't Tillie's fault that musicians and football players and married businessmen laid Moll. Tillie hadn't tied her to the bed and insisted that she have sex with them.

But apparently Moll had forgotten the way they parted—or she was willing to consider a truce. She threw her arms around Tillie and almost smothered her in an embrace. Tillie got a musky whiff from Moll's under-arms and from between her breasts; the sweaty black jersey she wore stuck to her skin. Surprised by this enthusiastic welcome, Tillie peeled herself away.

Outwardly, the women appeared different. Age had carved up the flesh and added its own fickle dimension to their bodies. They all looked at one another shyly—eyes a little misty, feeling the shock of viewing their own aging selves reflected in the faces of friends.

Tillie and the other Muskrateers might not have seen each other much over the years, but they continued to hang out together. Whether they were aware of it or not, their lives merged in some underground den, surfacing at times in dreams. Forty years soon fell away, as swiftly as snow melted on a sunny day. They were inextricably woven together through shared histo-ries, experiences, and intimacies—the woof of relationships, good or bad.

The CD had changed, and now the Beatles were singing, "It's been a hard day's night . . ."

"Good stuff, Sibyl," Tillie said. "So much better than rap—"

Daddy snapped her fingers and tapped one foot in time to an imagined beat: "You don't like rap, girl? It's the poetry of the people who don't have a voice."

Tillie shook her head. "Any wine for this poor wayfaring stranger?"

The Four Muskrateers
Revisit Their Youth

From Sibyl's living room window, a wall of glass framed a ravine filled with pine trees. Slanted rays from the late afternoon sun filled the room, turning everything inside gold before it disappeared behind the nearby peaks. Water bubbled over rocks from a stream winding past the house. The women sat on black leather couches and chairs, staring out the window, catching glimpses of themselves reflected in its surface, each grasping a flute of champagne. They took frequent sips, avoiding each other's eyes, not quite ready to dive into the waters of their youth.

Tillie feared they wouldn't have much in common after so many years. Her previous conversations with Daddy and Sibyl suggested everyone except Tillie lived a pretty standard life. That was strange for Daddy, who was a radical feminist in her early twenties and had never married. She'd been active in the extremist group "Students for a Democratic Society." Guerilla theatre. The works. She was even to the left of Tillie herself, who'd been far enough out there at times. They had lots of catching up to do.

According to conversations Tillie had with Sibyl over the years, of the four only Moll devoted herself fully to being a housewife. Though Tillie and Sibyl also had kids, they worked outside of the home and never were strictly housewives. Tillie could hardly boil water, which made it tough when she had to prepare her dried food. According to Sibyl, Raleigh did the cooking in their household. But maybe Moll wasn't strictly a housewife either. Maybe there wasn't any such thing if it meant you were married to a house. Or maybe you could be the wife of a house—and that was what so many women resisted. Houses didn't talk. Nor did they make love. But they did require a lot of care.

As for houses, Sibyl had obviously done all right for herself. Five bedrooms. Matching bathrooms. Skylights all over the place. Walk-in fireplace. Working in her dad's two-bit corner store as a kid had given Sibyl a nose for business. Her dad was malleable, and she could get her way with him, practically running the store herself before she was fourteen. She had told him what products would sell, reorganized window displays to attract customers, and made bank deposits. Sometimes her ideas were right on. Other times they had cost her dad money. But they were a team. She had the reins and knew when to use them. The store had never made much money, but at least it didn't operate in the red after Sibyl's input. A few cents profit was better than none at all.

Sibyl and Raleigh were the same age and high school sweethearts. But he had her father's pliant nature *and* his failings. He wasn't a good businessman, and Sibyl ran his life. Sometimes she made good recommendations. Often she didn't.

Sibyl jumped up. "Almost forgot. Have a surprise for you. Remember Ben, one of my old boyfriends in Toronto? The amateur filmmaker, eh?"

"Ben? Yeah," Daddy said. "He filmed us for a class he was taking."

"I remember," Tillie said. "He appeared when we least expected it. Like candid camera."

Moll set her glass down on the coffee table. "Didn't he call the film *The Four Muskrateers*?"

"Voila!" Sibyl said, grabbing the cartridge from the coffee table and jamming it into the VCR. "That's the surprise! He turned it into a video for me."

"You're kidding!" the others screamed in unison.

"How'd you get it?" Tillie asked.

"Ran into him at a bar in Vancouver. He said the Four Muskrateers launched his documentary film career. Won an award for it at film school."

"Far out," Daddy said. "We're stars."

The sun had set. They sat in the dimly lit room, munching popcorn that Moll had popped, sipping wine, laughing raucously, and staring at their younger selves on the screen.

Tillie laughed when she saw Sibyl wearing her signature bowler hat, puffing on a cigar, some man's overcoat draped over her shoulders and dragging on the floor. Nothing underneath. It was her Marilyn Monroe calendar shot, except she didn't have Monroe's equipment.

Daddy shrieked: "What a pair of knockers! That hat . . ."

"Jesus, look at you, Sibyl," Tillie said. "I remember that hat. You wore it everywhere."

It was quite a trick keeping it on during sex. She just had to make sure she was on top. Not a problem for Sibyl.

On the screen, Sibyl's tiny breasts dissolve into car headlights that blink on and off. Tillie's image materializes out of Sibyl's headlights.

"Hey, Tillie, when were you dressed like *that*?" Moll asked.

Tillie had trouble remembering and wondered if she had hit one of her black holes. Did she ever own that '20s-style dress, ballooning out in the back and tucked in at the buttocks? It looked like a parachute. She didn't recall being so style conscious. Now she avoided anything that looked predictably stylish, throwing together her original outfits from thrift shops, the weirder the better.

Unaware of being filmed, Tillie strolls over to a bench at a Toronto bus stop and sits down, yawning, her long hair pulled back into a chignon, face pale against the dark hue on her lips. Very chic. And ladylike. Until her head falls forward and her lower jaw drops, head jerking up now and then, eyes fluttering open for a moment, knees spreading wide. The camera zooms in on the spot between her legs, probing the darkness, the front of a bus rushing out of there, heading for the "Downtown Garage."

"Christ, Tillie," Daddy said, "I've heard of giving birth to strange things, but a bus?! Holy cow—weird."

The bus melts into the entrance of the subway station on Yonge Street. It's night, and the Four Muskrateers pour out of the opening, pushing their way through the crowds, laughing and yakking, neon lights flashing all around. High-spirited. Young and pretty and on the prowl for men and action. The scene switches suddenly to the zoo, the girls replaced by chimps picking fleas off themselves, and then back to them standing in front of a storefront, staring at their images, preening, and then back to the chimps grooming each other.

"The bastard's a real misogynist! Comparing us to primates."

"You're right, Tillie," Daddy said. "Turn off that bloody thing—the sonofabitch really used us—we should sue him."

Sibyl slurred, "Too late, eh? Statute of Liberation has passed."

Tillie said, "A Statue of Liberation might make an interesting sculpture."

"The Statue of Liberation *has* passed," Daddy said. "We need a new wave—another women's movement. How about it! Ready to lead the charge?"

Face flushed, waving her wine glass and cigarette around, Sibyl ignored the others and kept on talking. "Been involved in enough lawsuits. This house could go any day, so enjoy it. We're being sued."

"Sued? Shit," Tillie said. "That's rough."

"I kid you not. Raleigh inherited his dad's construction business, you know. He didn't sign a construction contract. A major contract. So fucking trusting. Left himself wide open." Sibyl scowled and sucked on a cigarette. "The guy sued him and won. Raleigh lost our business—couldn't come up with the bonding. Had a seventy-million-dollar job pending. Declared bankruptcy. Now *I'm* being sued too, and this house is in *my* name."

For an instant, both of Sibyl's eyes focused before one went off wandering again, searching for something that always seemed beyond her field of vision.

Tillie wondered if their money problems were all Raleigh's fault since Sibyl was so involved in managing their financial affairs. Tillie had always liked Raleigh, a warm, easy-going guy. On the surface, at least. She sipped her wine.

"I'm surprised you haven't left him—it's not the first time he's screwed things up for you guys."

"Don't remind me. I wake up in the night screaming. Can't sleep more than an hour or two. Believe me, I've thought of taking whatever money's left. Just disappearing. Go to Italy."

"Why Italy?" Daddy asked.

"Took a vacation there years ago. First trip to Europe. That was it. Love at first sight."

"I'm hungry. Any food around here?" Moll asked, trotting off to the kitchen. A counter connected it to the living and dining room areas.

Sibyl's voice droned on: "Can't make myself do it," she said. "Let *him* leave. He won't. Too scared. Spaces out on grass. Blows our savings to prove he's a man."

"Sounds like denial," Daddy said. Her cell phone beckoned from the bowels of her handbag, playing "The Battle Hymn of the Republic." Daddy reached inside, clicked it open, and inspected the screen. "Isn't that music a gas? The office—to hell with it—I'll call later."

Sibyl continued talking, ignoring Daddy: "Not so easy to just walk away."

Tillie never could figure out Sibyl's relationship with Raleigh. They had started going steady in high school. Of course, steady for Sibyl didn't mean being exclusive. She expected Raleigh to be a straight arrow, but it didn't apply to her. And for some reason he went along with it. Raleigh must have known she was screwing around with other guys, but it didn't seem to bother him. Maybe he got off on it. It reminded Tillie of Harold, her stepfather. If anyone asked for cuckolding, Harold was it. He begged to be abused—had sought it by marrying May in the first place.

Sibyl and Raleigh had gotten engaged when they were seventeen. A diamond ring *and* an engagement party. The works. The party financially wiped out Sibyl's mum and dad, but being affianced didn't stop Sibyl from doing *her* thing. She went to Toronto with Tillie, Moll, and Daddy, leaving Raleigh in Calgary. No regrets. Wearing his engagement ring. It seemed to drive men wild. They were more interested in her with a ring than if she hadn't had one.

Maybe Sibyl knew the ring was an aphrodisiac; maybe it was why she nailed Raleigh. She realized, even then, that many men don't want commitment. Since she was already taken, they could have all the fun they wanted without paying the consequences. Some sucker would pick up after them. The ring made her safe.

It all seemed connected to Sibyl's discovery that she was adopted. One night in Toronto, Sibyl had told the Muskrateers she'd been twelve when she found out about it. While she confessed to them, she huddled in a bucket chair, hugging her knees to her chest, and blurted out, "I'm certain my adoptive parents stole me." No wonder Sibyl's wandering eye was always looking for what she'd lost. She was convinced the woman she called mother—a mousy little thing who deferred to her strapping husband and did housework to support the failing grocery store—had taken Sibyl from one of her wealthy employees.

Years after the Muskrateers had split up and left Toronto, Tillie passed through Vancouver and met Sibyl for dinner. She and Sibyl got pretty chummy after a few glasses of wine, and the talk turned to sex. Sibyl seemed eager to brag about the affairs she was having. It didn't surprise Tillie that Sibyl still was on the make. But she was shocked to hear that Sibyl always blabbed to Raleigh about the men she slept with—and according to her, she had plenty.

Tillie asked how he handled it.

"You kidding? Turns him on, eh? Improves our sex life. He loves all the details. What positions we've tried. Even what size cock the guy has."

At the moment, Tillie had other things to think about. "What's this about Italy?" she asked, her antenna on high alert.

"Inherited the family house when Mum died. Used that money to buy a two-bedroom apartment in Venice. Prices were rock bottom. Can't get a place in Venice anymore for what I paid. The pad's all mine, eh? I rent it out."

"Venice," Tillie said. "Wow! My favorite city. Spent a few days there once. I loved it." She was already sitting in a Venetian plaza, near a fountain, listening to a gondolier in the distance serenading his passengers.

Venice itself reminded Tillie of a huge installation. In process. Parts appearing and disappearing. Depending on the light and time of day. So much expressed in reflection, the water both a mirror *and* the source of the city's life. Ghostly. Neither totally real nor imaginary. Like all great art. Inviting viewers to participate and reconsider their basic assumptions about cities. Making them more conscious of themselves and their relationship to Venice.

Approaching the city for the first time, all she had seen from the train window was water. She had asked another passenger where they were, amazed when he had said "Venice." She hadn't realized it floated at the edge of the Adriatic, immediately feeling at home in that surreal world, neither here nor there, gateway to the West and East. She had always felt in limbo, an inhabitant of some liminal realm, not belonging to either Canada or the United States. Or anyplace else for that matter. Except maybe Venice. Since that visit, she had wanted to return for an extended stay.

And then it hit her: the Venice Biennale would be happening in the fall. She had always wanted to show her stuff there. Crashing the event could give her exposure and publicity. If nothing else, she'd get her name in the papers and maybe find a wealthy sponsor. Now she needed to convince the others that Venice was in their future.

"That city scares me," Moll said. "It's going to sink any minute. And all that stagnant water in those canals."

Tillie and Moll had been best friends before they moved East with the other Muskrateers. Tillie had even stayed at Moll's parents' place for a few weeks before they'd left. Of the four of them, Moll had the most normal upbringing. Her folks had enough money to live in a nice house and buy new clothes and drive a late-model car. The rest of the Muskrateers lived in hand-me-downs or things found at rummage sales. In contrast, Moll's father was a VP in the Royal Bank of Canada. Not a big shot but a responsible position. A closet queer. Not unusual. *Everyone* was in the closet in those days, their real selves hidden.

Moll's mum didn't work, but she was always busy serving on some committee and helping with the PTA. She wore wire-rim glasses, her hair a mix of faded blonde and gray, resembling someone's granny even when Moll was just a kid. She went around with a kind of worried, hurt look on her face, like a goldfish.

"You're wrong," Tillie said. "Venice isn't sinking. It's rising out of the ocean like Venus. On the half shell."

Tillie was having another vision. Instead of Venus rising from the sea on a half shell, the Muskrateers were surfacing on a huge fake one. At night. Lots of spectacular lighting and fireworks. She could tie this in with Death in Menace and other installations she would plant around the city, featuring the four of them. She knew something would shake loose if she got away from home.

"Swell," Moll said, ambling back into the living room. "Venice rising scares me even more."

Daddy, sprawled on one of the sofas, moved over, making room for Moll. She said, "Ever wonder how different your lives would've been without these men? Hey, Tillie, what if you hadn't gotten pregnant so young?"

Tillie was staring at the darkened wall of windows, envisioning rockets as they snaked through the Italian night over the Venice lagoon, illuminating the Four Muskrateers. They were celebrating their sixtieth birthdays on a huge artificial cake in the bay, a slight variation on the earlier image of a half shell.

"Hey, Tillie, wake up," Moll said. "Think your life would've been different without a kid?"

Reluctantly, Tillie returned to the present. Part of her was still in Venice, dazzled by the fireworks display she'd conjured up. Turning sixty might not be so bad if she could welcome it in that city.

"I would've gotten pregnant anyway. I didn't know any better. No one told me about birth control. Making babies and being a good little housewife were my choices."

"You didn't stay married long," Daddy reminded her, eyelids at half-mast. "And you weren't a good little housewife! You told me you rotted all 'what's-his-name's' white shirts—put too much bleach in the water!"

Tillie and Daddy had hung out together in high school, before Tillie dropped out. Daddy's natural hair color was black, and she had worn it straight then, a kind of cap cut. The little hook in her nose had given her a slightly witchy appearance. A few years later she became a blonde—permanently—and paid a plastic surgeon to give her a Zsa Zsa Gábor nose.

Tillie poured herself the last of the champagne and watched the bubbles surface and burst.

"I needed a name for my son, Valentine. Didn't want him to be illegitimate, like me. How else could I get it? Anyway, I don't think love is the reason most couples get together. There are forces stronger than love."

"Grim," Moll said over her shoulder, pattering to the kitchen area to check the water.

"It *is* grim," Tillie said. "Fate's in charge. Picks us up and discards us. Controls our lives."

"Terrific!" Daddy said.

"'Life's but a walking shadow, a poor player that struts and frets his hour upon the stage and then is heard no more. A tale told by an idiot, full of sound and fury, signifying nothing.'"

They all stared at Tillie as if she had a deformity.

"Wow," Daddy said. "*Macbeth*."

"One of your husbands?" Sibyl asked.

Sibyl hadn't attended college and wasn't a reader. The classics didn't exist in her world, in spite of her middle-class trappings.

"A character from Shakespeare," Tillie said. "Scottish king. I had to memorize a passage and recite it in the Shakespeare class I took. Our prof thought we'd lost the art of memorization. I've been memorizing poems ever since."

"Everyone knows Lady Macbeth had the balls," Daddy said, "but he became king."

Daddy never had attended college either, but she *did* read. Voraciously. Her father had passed on his love for books. As Tillie recalled, Mr. Duff spent most of his time in the basement, brewing beer and making dandelion wine, reading Robbie Burns' poems, and reciting them from memory. Periodically, he'd surface. Short, like a gnome, always wearing a fedora, lines of poetry drifted out of his mouth like riffs on a guitar. He lived, ate, and breathed poetry. He also liked guzzling his malt.

Daddy's father may not have amounted to much—after all, what were poets good for?—but at least she had one. Tillie didn't even know her dad.

Tillie laughed at Daddy's comment. "Without men, we're nothing. The medium is the message."

"Good old McLuhan," Daddy said.

"What're you guys talking about?" Sibyl downed her wine and poured another glass. "Want more wine? Plenty in the cellar, eh. I won't go down there, though. Never know what you'll find."

"Buried somebody there?" Daddy asked.

Sibyl snickered. "Some old boyfriends."

Daddy leaned her head to one side. "What if you'd been born in the twenty-first century—no Raleigh? What would you have done?"

"Traveled. Been the CEO of a circus. An animal trainer. A jockey. A gondolier."

"Not a mother?" Tillie asked.

Moll interrupted. "Someone set the table, please. Pasta's ready. I'm throwing a green salad together. Jesus, Sibyl. We need groceries. I feel like Goldilocks. The cupboards are bare."

"Wrong story," Tillie said. "Goldilocks was mixed up with bears, not bare cupboards."

"What's it matter? Our cupboards *are* bare."

"No kidding," Sibyl said. "I'm feeling bare, myself." She stared at the window. Its glass held back the night.

"I always identified with Goldilocks," Daddy said. "The bears were a smug bourgeois family—real '50s setup—I was glad Goldilocks broke into their house and shook things up—but after she was afraid to face the music."

"Okay, okay, I'll face the music!" Sibyl said. "Didn't have time to shop before you arrived. Barely made it up from Vancouver as it is."

"Great pun on 'bear,' Sibyl," Daddy said.

Sibyl wobbled into the dining room and grabbed four place mats and some silverware, dropping everything onto the table. "Help yourselves."

"Come on, Sib," Moll said. "Let's light some candles. It's a celebration."

After dinner, they sat around the dining room table—cheeks flushed, reminiscent of hormones flashing off and on like neon lights. Night now, the windows had turned inward, candlelight and the women's reflections flickering on the glass. Black swallowed the pine trees, the mountains.

Tillie opened her backpack and pulled out a tape recorder. "You guys mind if I tape our conversation? I'm working on a new installation. I need some women's voices."

Sibyl looked blank. "An installation?"

"I'm an installation artist."

Tillie had never explained to them what she did as an artist. She avoided mentioning this part of her life. And no wonder. Tillie's mother and step-father didn't have a clue about art—about culture. When Tillie discovered she was an artist, she'd always felt ashamed of it. Just saying that word sounded pretentious, as if she were acting superior to others.

"What in hell's an installation?" Sibyl said.

"I create spaces you can enter. Interiors. You know?"

Sibyl nodded. "You always had a knack for decorating."

"I'm not an interior decorator! I find a lot of different stuff and put it into a new context—empty rooms, sometimes museums or galleries."

"Jeez," Sibyl said, "I haven't been to a museum since I can't remember."

"Me neither," Moll said. "Museums bore me. Old art and furniture."

"I usually find abandoned buildings or other structures and play with them. Transform them. Create stories with objects I find or make. You walk around inside these places and become more conscious of where you are. What you're seeing."

Sibyl and Moll looked a bit dazed, but Daddy was listening intently.

"Sounds more democratic," Daddy said, "more available and less elite."

Both Daddy and Tillie went through their "'60s Civil Rights phase" together. Daddy went farther in bringing down the system than Tillie had, getting involved with Students for a Democratic Society and other radical groups.

"I know," Tillie said. "Not everyone understands the art in museums. And not all people get to see it. Installation art breaks down those barriers a little bit."

"That's radical," Daddy said.

"Maybe. Anyway, the art isn't something plopped on the floor or hung on a wall. It's rooms. Spaces. It's what's around you."

"What's the point?" Moll asked.

"To make people think about their environments, their actions. Every situation—even when I'm working at ordinary jobs to earn money, you know, waitressing, cleaning houses—all of that feeds me. I want to get that heightened feeling into my work. Make discoveries about things we take for granted."

"Cool," Sibyl said.

"Watch out, though! I use a lot of everyday things in my art. I'm a great collector."

Moll yawned and stretched, letting out a healthy growl. "Mountain air always makes me sleepy." She rose, stacked the plates, and zipped them into the kitchen area.

Tillie followed, carrying some dishes herself, surprised that Moll had no interest in art or culture. Of all of them, she had seemed the most likely college candidate. Though Moll always was athletic, it wasn't until she left Toronto that her strong interest in the outdoors had surfaced. In high school, she had taken up track and field, winning lots of medals. She also wielded a mean tennis racquet, beating everyone in sight. And she had been a star player on the softball team.

But she also had been pretty chaste—the boys used to call her the Virgin Mary—in contrast to her skinny younger sister, Rosie, who was something else. A pushover, Rosie had severely round heels, and she hung out with all the hoods. The cops picked her up along with the Leblanc brothers when the four of them broke into Sibyl's parents' store and stole bottles of booze.

Moll compensated for Rosie by being extremely good at everything she did, and that included moral superiority. It was as if she had to be the best so she could make up for her sister *and* her father's deviant behavior. Tillie never heard Moll talk about her dad's other life. He seemed to be a good father, taking Moll skiing (her mother wasn't *sportif*), teaching her how to ice skate, helping her with homework, especially math and science.

After hearing so many rumors about Moll's dad wearing his wife's clothes and lurking in men's toilets, Tillie had been curious to see what a queer looked like. But she either had visited at the wrong times or the stories were false. He seemed like a normal father, sitting in the front room before dinner, reading his paper, sipping a martini. Nothing appeared queer about that. He even had helped Tillie with her lessons when she was still trying to make it in school.

While they were cleaning up after dinner, Tillie learned that Moll and her family lived in Nelson, B.C. She managed to cram raising kids and cooking for bake sales—and all the rest—between skiing, climbing mountains, swimming, hiking, and biking. Moll took her three boys along on her adventures: backpacking, camping, exploring the great Canadian outdoors. Her husband, Curtis, liked to fish, but he was more of a stay-at-home type. Going on camping trips with them was the extent of his involvement. Moll also whispered in Tillie's ear that Curtis had prostate cancer and Sibyl and Raleigh had already gone through several near financial disasters.

The two of them returned to the dining room table.

"You didn't answer me," Tillie said. "Mind being part of my next artwork? I won't identify who's speaking. You'll be anonymous."

"Okay by me," Daddy said.

Sibyl nodded her head. "Yeah, I don't care."

"As long as I don't have to go to a museum," Moll said.

Tillie turned on the recorder and grabbed soiled knives and forks. She stopped at Sibyl's place, her food almost untouched. "You finished?"

Sibyl lit up another cigarette and blew smoke in Tillie's face. "Yeah."

Still a rat.

The call of the wild

In the night, crashing and banging noises woke the women. They tumbled into the hallway, scrambling for bathrobes, screaming, turning on lights, pounding on Sibyl's door. She opened it, still dressed, still smoking, and still sipping on wine. The sounds seemed to come from the basement.

"What's going on?" Tillie asked. "Is someone trying to break in?"

Sibyl laughed. "Relax. Just the grizzlies. The best garbage collectors and they don't charge."

Tillie felt disoriented. Now it was the bears that wanted inside Goldilocks's pad, not the reverse. Actually, Goldilocks and Sibyl had a lot in common. They both were nervy as hell.

Having the grizzlies foraging outside brought up all Tillie's old fears of bears. Her mother had scared her when she was a kid with *her* fears about them. It was contagious. She remembered being parked in the family car with May in Banff; Harold had gone to buy some smokes. Her mother locked all the doors and visibly shivered with fright, certain a bear was lurking outside. Tillie thought she'd gotten over those terrors, but the minute her guard was down, there they were, bigger than ever.

Everyone returned to their bedrooms, but Tillie was unconvinced by Sibyl's explanation about the grizzlies and decided to stay awake so she had a better chance of finding a hiding place when they broke in. Nothing to shoot the bears with but a camera, one of Frank's old castoffs. She was still getting over the trauma of him leaving. Actually, Frank's exit didn't bother her as much as what he took with him—parts of herself.

A photographer, he'd used her for a model, making artsy photos, putting her in convoluted poses, naked. Yes, he was naked, too. He believed the photographer also had to be vulnerable, and he wanted nothing to come between himself and his subject. He tried every angle he could imagine, doing intense close-ups of her eyes, ears, scalp, crotch, breasts, under-arms—every inch of her body. He also experimented with x-rays and x-ray techniques. Really getting under her skin.

At the time, she didn't question it, giving her all for art, though she began to feel fragmented, chopped into pieces by the precision of his camera techniques. An eye here, a toe there. It was creepy, like living with a killer whose preferred method was chopping up his victims. It was an aspect of art she hadn't noticed before, the bond between artist and subject and the created object—the damage that could be done in the process.

One night, after a particularly grueling photography session that includ-ed listening for hours to another of his endless monologues, she finally blew up. She pointed out he only talked about himself and his photogra-phy. He didn't give a damn about her work. She asked him to pack up and leave. Never a love relationship, it had been a convenience. That was all.

But after he moved out, it was a shock for her to wake up to bare walls, the pictures of her various parts gone. She'd gotten so used to viewing her-self in that way, she felt raw, traumatized, the images no longer there to clothe her. Overwhelmed with loss, it wasn't for Frank.

Once she got used to living alone again, she did nicely without him around, and she definitely didn't miss his harangues. But she also began having nightmares about being in a totally dark room, hundreds of glow-ing eyeballs staring at her. In reality, Frank's photos hung in people's homes and in galleries. So did Tillie. She felt freaked out by all those strangers' eyes invading her.

The dreams reminded her of how scary it had been to enter the place she and Frank had once shared. He had turned the whole apartment into one big darkroom, using a red miner's lamp to find his way around and to inspect the images he hung up everywhere. Half the time the windows were covered in black fabric. Not an inch of light showed through, as if they were under attack. Knowing she feared the dark, he took real pleasure in her discomfort.

After experiencing so much derangement, Tillie's visit to Whistler was essential. She hoped getting away would stimulate new ideas for her next installation. Having so few productive years left made her anxious. And if she was anxious, her imagination contracted. She also feared she couldn't keep up much longer with the demands of creating installations. Doing them was physically exhausting. Still, art was her life. She'd be lost if she weren't working on something.

If she could finally gain more recognition as an artist, she might put some money in her pockets. In the past, she had managed to ignore her financial status. She usually made enough to get by, picking up a temporary job when necessary teaching a class or as a waitress. She also received grants and commissions here and there to pay the bills. She even used food stamps when things were really tight. But with sixty approaching like a bullet train, she realized old age was bad enough. An impoverished old age was hell. So she hoped the reunion would offer more than renewed friendships, important as they were.

Determined not to sleep, she kept thinking of the video the Muskrateers had watched earlier. So strange to see herself as a young woman, through someone else's eyes, caught unaware. She was hungry for those images. Hungry for that younger self. Hungry to see herself immortalized on film and put back together again after Frank's dissection.

She headed downstairs, but Moll and Daddy had beaten her to it. The two of them were slumped on a sofa, wearing bathrobes, faces shiny with night cream, eyes fixed on the screen. The dim light gave them a ghostly glow. They didn't notice Tillie slink into the room, curling up like a cat in one of the big padded armchairs.

She joined them at the altar of their shared past: Toronto. The Four Muskrateers tramping up Yonge Street, hair swept back into bee hives, eyes designed by Maybelline, lips poppy red and swollen from so much kissing, dodging swarms of people. The Greeks were there. East Indians. Chinese.

Italians. Jews. Russians. Trinidadians. Japanese. Tillie had felt she wasn't in Canada any longer. She was in the world.

They had lived in a beat-up old neighborhood, front porches sagging, paint peeling. Cheap basement suites and bed-sitting rooms. Musty smells. Mildew. Fried onions and garlic. Winter slush. Penetrating damp cold slipping under sleek fur jackets. Tillie had sneaked over to Rosedale or Forest Hill sometimes, walking the tree-lined streets sandwiched between stately mansions, crunch of leaves underfoot, pretending she lived there. The well-kept houses, many made of brick, comforted her. They suggested permanence and stability.

The Muskrateers had their first taste of elegant dining in the Royal York Hotel, candlelight glinting off real silverware and china plates. They hung out on Bay Street with button-down businessmen out for a night of fun on expense accounts. The Town Tavern: Oscar Peterson and Mel Tormé. Honking cars dodging streetcars that clattered through the night.

In the movie, all of these images evaporate into a swirl of bees pouring out of the Muskrateers hairdos, buzzing around a hive. The bees growing, filling the screen, their bulging eyes staring out at the viewer, giving way to the women lounging inside the living room of the apartment they shared. A tilted Christmas tree filled one corner of the room, decorated with strings of popcorn and cranberries. No gifts.

Wearing bathrobes, they're yakking. Painting their nails, towels wrapped around their heads Turkish fashion. Fade to them dressed for a night on the town. Tillie had forgotten the sleek black dress she'd bought on credit, spaghetti straps holding it up, her dyed black hair teased into a puffy bouffant. They all had dyed their hair black at one point, pretending they were sisters. Sibyl's signature bowler hat hid her hair, brim pulled down over her eyebrows. Daddy before the Zsa Zsa makeover, nose a little hooked, lower lip stuck out in a pout. Moll showing her healthy, foxy white teeth in her best say-cheese smile. The Four Muskrateers, arms linked, dissolve into the camera lens.

Tillie wanted to dissolve into it, too, become one with that former self. Instead, she fell asleep on the chair, the film replaying in her dreams, the past revisiting her. *She's dismantling the beehive, pulling out bobby pins, combing her hair, untangling all the backcombing. One bee keeps circling her head, trying to dive-bomb her, stinger erect and ready to pierce the first opening it finds.*

She woke with a start, alone in Sibyl's living room, striking out at something invisible, the blue TV screen blank, feeling terribly alone, an ache in her chest. It was a feeling she had experienced a lot in Toronto.

TORONTO
1958

The Four Muskrateers
tackle Toronto

A little tipsy, the four women were sprawled out on couches and chairs in Moll's rumpus room in Calgary. Her parents were spending the weekend at Banff, so the girls had the place to themselves.

They'd been drinking beer and gossiping about the Calgary Stampeder football players. Tillie had a crush on Joe Kapp, the quarterback. Moll had something going with Tony Padricowski, a lineman. Sibyl couldn't decide between two halfbacks she liked, Jeff and Phil, both brothers, though she was already engaged to Raleigh. As for Daddy, she was dating a guy, Max, who was good buddies with the players.

The Stampeders had made it into the playoffs, the Grey Cup, for the first time in years, and it was being held in Toronto. The Muskrateers were caught up in Grey Cup fever, wanting to join the team there. The players were already talking about the bash that would follow the game, win or lose, not to mention all the smaller parties that people were planning to have around the city. The girls couldn't bear to miss the action, but they also didn't have the money to fly to Toronto and back *or* pay for their other expenses.

"Hell, let's just move to T.O.," Tillie said, slurping the foam off her beer. "Get jobs there. I've always wanted to see the East."

"Me, too," Daddy said, raising her glass in a toast. "To T.O.!"

It didn't take much to convince Sibyl and Moll to join them.

They even invented their own theme song, set to the music of Louis Prima and Keely Smith's "Robin Hood":

Many long years ago,
four beauties from Cal-gar-y,
traveled across the plains,
to fulfill their destiny.

Eager for adventure, willing to take risks, hoping to find rich men to take care of them: "Take from the rich and give to the poor" was one of their themes. Men held the ticket to their future, their only hope of moving up in the world.

College didn't exist for their crowd. It was the '50s. Women had better things to do. Have kids. Find a husband. Usually in that order. Moving to T.O. was their version of going away to college. Breaking with their roots. Trying out new things. Except Tillie had a head start on the others.

A high-school dropout, she had been on her own since she was fifteen. Unlike the others, she had already lived in another city—Vancouver—and thought she knew the ropes. She had always been a good actress.

Toronto the Good. Tillie didn't understand why it was called that. To her it was Toronto the Bad. It boggled her at first—vast, cold, remote. Staid. Reserved. A real city. Not like Calgary—the cow town. Not the wild, inno-cent, wide-open West, gateway to the other East: the peaceful Pacific. Not graceful Vancouver, that pearl of a city, part of the necklace of coastal mountains. Shimmering by the sea.

Toronto:
- Old World drab
- Old World values
- Other world to Tillie
- Lost world
- Her lost world

The 1958 Grey Cup came and went in a blur of booze and balling. The Stampeders won and returned home—heroes. The Four Muskrateers stayed in Toronto, stuck there indefinitely because they didn't have the money to return home. The East was new territory. They didn't have a rule-book to follow. They had to improvise.

Tillie tried to find an island in the midst of so much newness and change. She wasn't the only one. They all felt out of their depth, restraints discarded, leaning on each other for support and definition. Lost in possibilities, the swirl of new experiences, people, and places. Bars and parties, afloat on booze and grass, bennies keeping them awake during the day so they could party again that night. Hungry for any kind of action. Intoxicated with too much freedom—and with life and men.

They'd never seen so many different kinds: football players, hockey players, jockeys, artists, lawyers, actors, businessmen, musicians. Everything but dot-com men.

They were multicultural before PC was in: Blacks, Indians (Eastern and Western), Japanese, Chinese, Jewish. The men drifted in and out of their apartment, their beds, their lives. The ones with money bought the women meals in nice restaurants before going to bed with them. The others just slipped between their sheets, leaving grease on the pillowcasFes, ghostly presences, shapes in the dark the Muskrateers temporarily clung to.

It wasn't exactly the men themselves that they wanted, but some notion of maleness. Some quality that men possessed: status, stability, power. A ticket to something more. Men weren't afraid to try new things, take risks, stand up to conventions. Some men, at least. They blasted their way through life, breaking down walls if they got in the way, or leveling mountains. Men rocked. They rolled. They rhythmed and blued. The Muskrateers watched.

Tillie wasn't a stranger to rock and roll, but jazz and the blues *were* new to her. At the start, she felt disoriented by jazz. The first time she really listened to it was with Bif, a Black guy she picked up at a club. They went to his place after the bar closed, and Tillie felt like she'd entered the twilight zone. He only used colored bulbs in the light fixtures. Red. Blue. Green. When he turned them all on, they cast a mellow glow over the room, turning his skin and hers almost the same color. It was Christmas without the presents.

After putting on a record, he guided Tillie to the couch. Progressive jazz, he called it. Not like the harmonies she was used to. Not the country-western singers' simple songs of love and loss that dominated Calgary's airwaves then. Jazz was a cacophony of sounds and rhythms. She felt so dizzy, she almost fell off the couch. But she got hold of herself, unwilling to let on she wasn't as hip as Bif.

"You smoke?"

Tillie nodded. He lit up a joint and passed it to her. Imitating him, she sucked deeply, falling back into the cushions—sinking into the composition. The grass made the discordant notes seem like music. She nodded her head, with it, hip. Yeah, man. It was cool.

And it blew Tillie's mind. It was like entering a cave, into some primitive level in herself that the colored lights and the music stirred. You Tarzan, me Jane. Raw. Down to basics. Skin on skin, the contrasts fading. She had entered an installation then without knowing it. And it shook her good. It made her question everything. Here was the source of power, this dark, sensual realm. The mind-blowing music that spoke a language she hadn't heard before. Not music, exactly. She couldn't dance to it; she couldn't sing it. She could only hold it in her head like she did marijuana until it started pressing on the neurotransmitters in her brain, sending off sparks, putting her in a trance.

Just publicly being with a Black man was mind-blowing enough. In Calgary, Tillie had to sneak around when she went out with Blacks. Visit their pads at night, secretly. Or park with them out in the country.

Even Daddy had been critical of Tillie once when she had seen her with a Black football player. Daddy, judging her? Daddy, who was willing to try *anything*?

In T.O., it didn't matter who saw Tillie with Bif. Some people stared at them, but she liked it. She liked the attention. Liked being different. And she liked making out with Black men. They didn't seem embarrassed by sex or in a rush to finish. When she was with Bif, everything else fell away. She lost herself in the senses, in the flesh. Time stood still. All that existed was reaching for those heights.

Kinsey had been right after all. Women could get pleasure from sex.

Bif didn't work a nine-to-five job. He freelanced, operating a kind of import/export business. Traveling to Mexico and other exotic places. Bringing back clothes, jewelry, shoes, wallets, handbags, trinkets, a little dope. Quite a bit of dope, it turned out. He wore jeans and white peasant shirts and colorful ponchos, silver rings studded with turquoise circling every finger.

Bif transfixed Tillie. He created a fiesta atmosphere wherever he went, spreading his wares on the ground over a flowered tablecloth, clicking out a catchy rhythm on finger castanets. Drawing a crowd with his patter. A pied piper, he used his skin color as a flag he ran up a pole and displayed, doing anything he could to show it off. It wasn't something to hide or be ashamed of. His attitude made Tillie more bold and less inhibited.

Bif initiated Tillie into Toronto's underground. He introduced her to other refugees from the straight world. They followed their instincts, living subversively. Spouting poetry. Hanging out in coffee houses on Bloor Street. Pulling in just enough money to get by. Not interested in power or social status or success. Bohemians.

And it all started with jazz and jazz clubs.

Tillie followed Bif down dimly lit concrete steps to a back alley hole-in-the-wall in the financial district. The door had a bullseye in the center and a sign overhead that read "The Bull's Eye." A Black bouncer, bald head a gleaming bronze globe, stood outside.

"Hey, man," he said, giving Bif a high five. "Long time, no see."

Bif slapped him on the back. "Hey, buddy." He fumbled in his pockets. Turned to Tillie. "Got five bucks, babe? Left my wallet at home."

She dug into her shoulder bag and pulled out a crumpled bill, handing it to the bouncer. He opened the door and ushered them inside.

Tucked away in a corner of the room, three musicians jammed—a white bassist and a Black piano player and drummer. Eyes closed. Immersed in the sounds pouring out of them. Audience transfixed in wordless worship, nodding and snapping fingers, eyes meeting intensely in the dim light, communicating a deep understanding. They worshipped the god of music, the god of sound, the god of feeling.

Music was more than simple harmonies and melodies. Endless variations could be visited on a single tune.

What Tillie once had accepted as truth, she now questioned. There was more to know about life and world affairs than what *Time* magazine covered in its pages. Women's place in society could be redetermined. She didn't have to fit into some idea of what it meant to be an attractive woman. Blacks weren't to be feared. Rigid, stultifying rules could be broken. Complexities existed. Subtleties. Nuances.

Art had entered Tillie's consciousness, turning her upside down, inside out. Except she still had to support herself, and she couldn't do that without working in the very world she was trying to escape. She was a prisoner.

But she needed adventure and action. Pandora's box had opened, and the lid was lost. Hormones raging. Out of control at times. Nothing to counter her urges for excitement and fun and new experiences. No real family to turn to. Few inner constraints. Just the other Muskrateers. But they were in over their heads, too.

Bif had been a good teacher. Tillie dug his lifestyle. They didn't call it "lifestyle" then, of course. She dumped her nine-to-five job, the office work that made her feel like a machine. Sitting all day at a typewriter, pounding out letters and reports, plugged into a dictating machine. Falling asleep and slipping off to the bathroom to wake up. Splashing cold water on her face. Masturbating in one of the cubicles.

"Don't get caught up with the masses," Bif had said before he left on another trip.

He never did tell her exactly where he went on those excursions, and she had learned long ago not to ask too many questions—of her mother, of her stepfather. Of anyone. The answers could be too painful.

Tillie never heard from Bif again. Some friends said they saw him in Vancouver. He always claimed he wanted a more moderate climate. He had never made any promises to Tillie—to anyone. She knew he would be temporary: now you see him, now you don't.

Tired of the usual look, Tillie started experimenting more with clothes. She found a Russian-style fake black fur coat and hat. Silver slippers with stacked heels and platform soles. In thrift shops, she dug up '20s dresses and wore rings on every finger and some of her toes. Gold and silver glitter lit up her nails. Long hair dyed black and hanging to her waist, she resembled a Russian Gypsy.

Tillie even tried waitress work for a change of scene. At least dropping dishes and breaking them kept her awake. No way she could fall asleep, rushing from tables to kitchen to cash register, sometimes mixing up the customers and checks. Her boss felt sorry for her. Kept her on, for a while.

Then Tillie lost her job and got behind on rent. The other Muskrateers carried her for a couple of months, but they didn't have much money themselves. They got fed up because she was out every night and slept all day, not making an effort to find work. Toronto had much more nightlife than Calgary did. She hadn't learned yet how to juggle work and play.

Everything started to fall apart. She and the other Muskrateers began fighting. They picked on each other, sometimes two on two. Other times three on one, shifting alliances. They accused each other of leaving dirty clothes or grimy dishes or discarded men around the place. Money and other things disappeared. Sibyl got greedy, sleeping with the other women's guys—and not always behind their backs.

Moll blamed Tillie for just about everything, including her own debauchery. *Tillie* made Moll move to Toronto. *Tillie* was the one who turned Moll on to Blacks and clubs and musicians. *Tillie* made Moll fuck her brains out. *Tillie* stole her innocence. Moll called Tillie a whore and fled, returning to Calgary.

Tillie shifted from being a semi-responsible person—who managed to keep a job or two going—to a semi-bohemian, alienated from everyone, including Daddy and Sibyl, who stayed on and got a place together. Unanchored, Tillie drifted around the city from one room rental and job to another. The break from the Muskrateers was almost as traumatic as a family dispersing. The ground shook under her feet long before she moved to San Francisco and experienced a real earthquake.

WHISTLER, B.C.
AUGUST 1999

THE MUSKRATEERS
ANSWER THE CALL

It was eleven AM before Tillie appeared downstairs.

Sibyl was planted in front of the dining room table, wearing Raleigh's brown silk bathrobe, about ten sizes too big for her, so involved with a jigsaw puzzle she didn't notice Tillie. No sign of Daddy or Moll.

Tillie found a mug and poured herself some coffee.

"Where is everybody?"

"The store. Picking up groceries."

"Any cereal?"

Sibyl pointed to the kitchen. "Cupboard over the stove."

"You eaten?"

"Never eat breakfast. Coffee's all I have."

"You'll disappear. What's your doctor say about your weight?"

Tillie filled a bowl with Kellogg's Rice Krispies and sniffed at the milk she found in the fridge. It smelled okay, but the cereal had lost its snap, crackle, and pop. All it did was fizzle when she poured the milk over it.

"Haven't seen a doctor for over seven years."

Sibyl snapped a puzzle piece in place and lit a cigarette off one she had going in the ashtray.

"You serious? You don't get regular mammograms or paps? What about HRT?"

"What's HRT? Rapid transit?"

She bit down on the cigarette, clenching it between her teeth so she could use both hands to move the pieces around, resembling blackjack dealers Tillie had seen in Vegas casinos.

"Hormone Replacement Therapy. Women have hormones, you know. Estrogen. Progesterone. Don't you read the papers? Magazines?"

"No time. Got better things to do."

"You're a prime candidate for osteoporosis."

"What's that?" Sibyl set the cigarette in the ashtray and sipped her black coffee, matching up three more pieces and shouting with glee.

"Bones get brittle and break more easily as we age," Tillie said. "A real problem for thin women who smoke."

"Lets me out, eh," she said. "Gimme a break. No, don't. Doctors make me break out in hives. Ever had hives?" She didn't wait for Tillie to answer, and she didn't stop working the puzzle. "I get huge welts. My whole body swells up. My dad never went to a doctor. Lived to seventy-six and then just keeled over. Heart attack. That's how I wanna go."

"Makes me more anxious to ignore these things."

Sibyl shrugged her bony shoulders and the bathrobe slipped off one of them. On some women it might look seductive. On Sibyl, it was pitiful. All bones. She resembled a waif.

"Last time I saw a doctor, he told me I had a spot on one lung," Sibyl said. "They watched it for a while. Nothing happened. It didn't grow or shrink. So I've got a spot on a lung. So what? Some people have worse things." She picked up her cigarette and puffed furiously. "Finally stopped going. Figured I could've done without all the terror. Living from doctor appointment to doctor appointment. Not really living either. The fear was making me sick! I wasn't any better off knowing about it. That's why I haven't seen a doctor for seven years."

"And you still smoke?" Tillie was the one feeling terror now. A spot on the lung was nothing to mess with unless you didn't like life much.

"Cigarettes are my friends. Keep me calm, eh. Why give them up? Life's too fucking short." She snuffed out the cigarette she'd been puffing on and grabbed another. "Ms. du Maurier, meet Ms. Tillie." She flicked her red plastic Mickey Mouse lighter, dragging deeply and blowing a mouthful of smoke in Tillie's direction.

Tillie coughed. "Ever hear of secondhand smoke? Never mind. What's the puzzle?"

"Haven't a clue. Raleigh buys puzzles for me and throws out the boxes before I see them. More challenging. No fun putting it together if you know the ending." Sibyl gulped down some coffee and made a face. "Cold. Ugh."

"Want help? I do borders pretty well." Tillie sat down across from her.

"Borders are easy. Work on the sky. I hate skies. All that sappy blue. Give me gray any day. A good ol' gray sky." She glanced out the window and shuddered. "Another nice day. Shit. Too much blue. God has blue eyes and we're at the center, drowning." Sibyl almost looked at Tillie then, her wandering eye focusing elsewhere. It was gray and the other one was a grayish hazel.

"You *like* gray skies?"

"Yeah. Blue's so impersonal—distant. Gray makes the sky feel closer, like a blanket's covering it. It's softer than hard-edged blue."

"You have a point. Jeez, how many puzzle pieces are there?"

"Four thousand."

"Four thousand! You'll be working on this till doomsday."

"That's the idea. Keeps my mind off things. I'd have gone bonkers a long time ago without puzzles."

The dark circles and bags under Sibyl's eyes seemed more accentuated. Tillie felt sorry for her, even though Sibyl had burned her plenty of times. In junior high, at the weekly dances at Riverside Community Center, she would be her best friend to her face. But the minute Tillie went to the bathroom, Sibyl would ask her current beau to dance and then badmouth her, making up stories that Tillie had deliberately forgotten. It could've been Sibyl's way of punishing others because she was adopted. It certainly didn't get her many friends. But she didn't seem to care what people thought of her, and if she had a conscience, she kept it well hidden.

A few years later, Sibyl let everyone know she'd slept with Tillie's first love. Tillie didn't have any claim on him after they separated, but she still had some feelings for the guy. Sibyl knew that. After all, he was Tillie's first love, and Sibyl was supposed to be one of her best friends. Yet that was what she liked about Sibyl. She did what she wanted, to hell with the consequences. She refused to be cowed by all the "shoulds."

Sibyl rested her cigarette in the ashtray.

"Raleigh knows how mean I get without a puzzle to work on. Gives me something to look forward to. I get excited seeing a picture take shape. Hell, you should know what I mean. You're an artist."

"I guess."

Sibyl looked at Tillie's part of the puzzle. "Hey, you're good. Would've taken me a week to do that sky."

"What happens to these things when you're finished? Frame them?" Tillie checked out the living room in the daylight, expecting to see completed puzzles hanging on the walls.

Sibyl laughed. "You kidding? I take a picture of every puzzle. Got an album full of them. Then I burn the pieces."

"Sounds like a ceremony—a ritual."

Sibyl shook her head vigorously. "I'm not religious."

"You must have a reason for burning them."

"I just like fires. I save the ashes, like a cremation. See that huge jug over there?" Sibyl pointed to an urn that was almost as big as she was, its indigo background splattered with sunflowers. "That's where I put the ashes. The puzzles seem like old friends."

"Yeah. You've always had a way with your friends."

Moll offered to take everyone on a hike that afternoon. "Come on," she said, "I'm going stir crazy."

Tillie thought she heard the grizzlies prowling outside again. Daddy didn't have proper shoes and wasn't a hiker anyway. Sibyl looked longingly at her puzzle. An image was almost ready to emerge.

"Let's walk around town," Sibyl suggested. "We can look at the shops. Stop at the Chateau for wine."

"With all these great trails to explore?" Moll said. "Why not take the gondola to the top and pick up a trail there. Get a taste of mountain air. Great views. Come on, guys. Try something new. Challenge yourselves!"

Just the thought of wandering around in the mountains reminded Tillie of being in Toronto. Anything could happen there. She had no control. The thought both attracted and scared the hell out of her, bringing up all those feelings she had when they went East and left familiar ground behind. Lost. Frightened. Alone. Dependent on the Four Muskrateers, her new family. And they weren't exactly dependable.

Tillie said, "I read that the Whistler Valley trail's supposed to be the easiest. Paved."

"Too dangerous!" Moll said. "You'll get run over by rollerbladers if the runners and cyclists don't get you first. Much safer picking up a trail off the gondola."

"More likely to run into some men if we stay in town," Sibyl said.

Tillie wouldn't mind meeting a new man. She hadn't tried a Canadian for a long time. She always seemed between men. They either didn't work out, or they never stayed long enough to dig in and make a long-term commitment. For years, she'd concentrated on artists of all kinds, from performance to street artists. She spent a lot of time on the street herself, hanging out with them. A filling for a sandwich, unrecognizable without the bread that surrounded it—the men.

"I don't want men to determine where I go hiking," Daddy said. "I'd sooner pull a Medusa."

"New kind of car?" Sibyl asked, putting another puzzle piece in place.

"Get off it, Sibyl," Daddy said. "You know who Medusa is. Killed her kids to spite her two-timing husband."

"I've thought of killing my kids," Sibyl said, lighting a cigarette. "More than once." Her wandering eye got a strange glint in it.

"It's getting late," Moll said. "We'd better get with it."

She put on her hiking boots. Her blue eyes stared unblinkingly out of a face remarkably smooth for her age, no makeup masking it, her eyebrows not plucked. She'd become as plain-looking as her mother. Unflashy. Sexless.

Daddy said, "At least I stopped letting men define me."

45

Moll jabbed back, "Why the face-lift then?"

The two women were mud slinging again, a weekly ritual in Toronto. Flinging truths at each other. The shock treatment.

Daddy's face changed color, appearing scalded. "Real estate's tough—lots of younger women to compete with—I need to look good."

Sibyl piped up, "A face-lift? Boy, I could use one, eh. Can't stand looking in the mirror anymore. Scare the hell out of myself."

"Go for it, girl!" Daddy said. "Out of commission for a month or so and presto—a new woman—doesn't cost that much either—and they don't call them face-lifts any more—it's getting 'refreshed.'"

"I could use a little refreshment," Sibyl said.

"Let's go," Moll said.

Daddy asked Sibyl for a pair of walking shoes. She reluctantly pushed herself away from the puzzle. The central image was starting to emerge. A naked woman's torso had formed.

Tillie strolled over to the puzzle while the others gathered their things. "A black *Venus de Milo*, minus a head. Wow! Reminds me of the *Black Madonna*."

Daddy was bent over, tying her shoes. "Wrong mythology," she said. "Venus isn't the same as Jesus' mother."

"I think they're closely related. Venus went through a kind of virgin birth. Appeared out of the sea like Venice. Gave birth to Cupid, the god of love. Anyway, you don't have to be a virgin to be divine. I think *we're* divine!"

"Yeah, but I wouldn't call us godly," Daddy said.

"All the Bible stories claim Mary was a virgin," Moll said. "The authors must've been on to something."

"The men who wrote the gospel narratives had an agenda," Tillie said. "They were trying to control women *and* god. Their message? A woman can have power only by being pure and following Mary's example. They were trying to desensualize us." She strapped on her hip pouch.

"I agree," Daddy said. "The priests turned Mary into a paleface—where she's from, she would've been dark, not light skinned."

Sibyl puffed on her cigarette and took another look at the image she'd been working on. "Big hips." She tried a hula motion, but she was so skinny, nothing much moved. "Who's this Black Madonna?" she asked.

"I ran into her in Europe," Tillie said. "I was hitching over there, doing my grand tour. She's found mainly in Italy, Spain, Poland, Egypt. Even Germany and Switzerland."

"Gets around. Any connection to Madonna, you know, the singer?"

Tillie and Daddy looked at each other and burst out laughing.

"The joke?" Moll asked, shrugging into her scruffy backpack.

"Sorry," Tillie said. "The Black Madonna's another name for the Virgin Mary, only she's dark skinned—"

"Got it," Moll said.

"And she has turned up in churches. Usually as a sculpture. Some Black Madonnas started out white, but the soot from candles darkened them." Tillie slipped into the kitchen, filled a glass with water, and gargled a mouthful before downing it. "Those old churches were always catching on fire and turned some sculptures black. Others were carved originally from dark wood. I've even seen ceramic Black Madonnas glazed a chocolate color."

"How'd we get into all this Black Madonna stuff?" Moll asked.

"Sibyl's giving birth to one. Look at this torso."

The Muskrateers took the chair lift instead of the more protected gondola. The higher they climbed, the cooler it got. At first Tillie liked the wind on her bare legs, arms, and face. But the temperature dropped about twenty degrees the closer they were to their destination. She realized she should've listened to Moll. "Take a jacket, eh, Tillie. Wear your jeans. It can get cold up there." But she resisted being mothered, especially by Moll. Her moral superiority grated on Tillie at times.

Moll's cheeks had taken on some color, and she looked more relaxed than she had so far that weekend, almost beautiful, her sandy-colored hair, mixed with gray, turning gold in the sun. The younger Moll shone through—self-assured, in control. Tillie remembered that look well. She used to envy it. She still did. A look that had something to do with coming from an intact middle-class family and having a stack of neatly folded cashmere sweaters in her closet.

Tillie never seemed to be in control. Even when she was making art, she didn't know what was going to happen from moment to moment, the results always a complete surprise. Now she took out her camcorder and captured their ascent up the mountain, flipping back and forth between shots of the valley and the heights.

When they reached the top and disembarked, Sibyl fumbled in her purse, lighting up, heading towards the concession building. Moll took off in the other direction, to the trailhead. She called out, "Trail's over here, you guys."

"I need a glass of wine first," Sibyl said.

Daddy echoed Sibyl.

"Not now. *After* the hike. It's getting late."

If Tillie joined Sibyl and Daddy, it would be a mutiny. She figured, if they had come this far, they might as well go the full distance. Mold was growing on her from sitting around so much. She needed some exercise, too.

"Come on, you guys," Tillie said. "Do you good. Get some pure air in your lungs."

Sibyl moaned, reluctantly changing direction. Daddy followed. Sibyl sucked in some real air along with cigarette smoke and almost choked on it, setting off another coughing spell. The others stopped and waited for her to finish.

"Here, drink some of my water," Moll said, handing Sibyl a clear plastic container from her backpack.

Sibyl pushed it away. "I need something stronger than water."

They started walking again. Daddy and Sibyl tried to keep up with Tillie and Moll.

"Slow down, you guys," Daddy said. "What's the rush? You'd think something was chasing you."

"I'm just trying to keep warm," Tillie said, legs and arms covered with goosebumps. She did a few jumping jacks while waiting for them, her pack flopping around, hitting her back. Daddy and Sibyl were huffing and puffing already. "You were right, Moll," Tillie said. "I don't see any bikers *or* rollerbladers."

Moll shrugged. "Nor other hikers. That's what's nice about this trail."

Tillie hadn't had this in mind. Just the mountain and the Muskrateers. Scary. To be so alone. In the wilderness.

The narrow path wound back and forth, giving a view of the valley spreading out below and the Coast Mountains. If the jagged peaks weren't topped with snow, they'd look like a caravan of giant humpback whales. Something prehistoric—frozen. Tillie had never seen the mountains from this angle before, though while growing up in Calgary, she got used to the Rockies' sharp edges puncturing the western sky.

"Awesome," Tillie said.

Moll nodded. "I know. They never fail to amaze, eh? Oh, listen!"

Tillie heard a loud, high sound. "What is it?"

"Hoary marmot. 'Whistlers.'"

"You think Whistler's named after them?"

"Yeah."

"Why does it whistle?"

"It's warning its colony about us. Look, there's one. No, two! They're wrestling."

Moll and Tillie stopped for a minute, enjoying the animals' high spirits.

"They look like squirrels," Tillie said. "How do you tell the difference?"

"They're bigger, and they burrow."

They started walking again. Tillie tried to match strides, but Moll's height and long legs gave her an advantage. Tillie had to hustle to keep up.

"You wouldn't come up here alone, would you?" Tillie asked.

Moll was constantly scanning the area and frequently checked out the sky. "Oh sure. I've taken lots of solo backpacking trips. Nothing like hiking to a lake few people have seen. You just need to watch for sudden weather changes. Snow can fall in these mountains in July. You've got to be ready for anything."

Tillie was impressed. She'd always wanted to go backpacking. Get away from civilization. She even fantasized about doing it on her own, a kind of vision quest thing. But the thought of being alone in the wilds freaked her out. No Starbucks. No museums. No beds. She also hated being pestered by mosquitoes and flies. While she loved nature, she preferred it filtered and in small doses. Backpacking would feel like an overdose. A real ten-derfoot at heart, how could she become a Girl Scout now?

"It's not my bag, I'm afraid," Tillie said. She skidded on some pebbles, catching herself before she fell, and stopped, blurting out, "Wow, what a view." Then she recorded it, giving Sibyl and Daddy time to catch up.

Sibyl grunted and lit up again. "I hate scenery. All that pukey green makes me nauseous. Give me a smoke-filled barroom any day."

Tillie thought she had a point. Nature was one thing. But this wasn't just nature. It was too wild, too unruly, too unpredictable. Like life. And death. She hoped she could get this feeling into her new installation. The rawness. The tension. Anything could happen.

"I don't get it, Sibyl," Tillie said. "You don't like scenery, so why have a home in Whistler?"

"The skiing's great."

"You're a skier?"

"You bet," Moll said. "She's good. Never falls."

Daddy said, "You're so out of shape!"

"Don't have to be in shape to ski. Go up in the gondola. Ski down. Drink a lot of hot toddies after."

"Amazing," Tillie said.

They started walking again, single file, Moll and Tillie still in the lead, the ground under their feet pitted with animal and human footprints, some merging.

"Hey guys," Tillie said, "watch your step. I almost tripped back there."

Sibyl and Daddy nodded and plodded on, falling behind. No one spoke.

The trail dipped down into an alpine area, evergreens closing in on them, shutting out much of the light. Tillie felt as if she were drowning in the pungent pine scent, a smell she associated with Canada. She loved Canada and still had a deep connection to her homeland, but she never had liked pine trees. They were too much like church steeples, pointing one way. The message was clear: the Christian god or nothing. She could do without that kind of religion. She hated imperialism—or anything too pure. She would take palm trees any day, their curvy fronds and the balmy breezes that go with them. She wished she were below one right now, sipping on a margarita.

Tillie took advantage of this time with Moll to ask her about Sibyl. "What's up with her lung?"

"The spot? She refuses to see her doctor."

"I got that much. Is it cancer?"

"If it is, she's not admitting it. You know Sibyl."

"Not sure I do anymore."

"You guys are too quiet," Moll yelled. "Make some noise so the bears will hear us."

"Bears!" Daddy cried out.

Goosebumps ruffled Tillie's skin at the thought of grizzlies, and she turned her head to glance at Daddy and Sibyl. Daddy was looking around frantically, as if she had just awakened.

"Holy Christ," she said, "let's go back."

Tillie agreed. The wilderness really *was* fierce in Canada. It wasn't like tame Mount Tamalpais in Marin County where Tillie walked sometimes. There a hiker might run into an urbanized mountain lion out for a Sunday stroll—but not likely.

Moll laughed and tramped on. "They're shy. They won't bother us. Just give them some warning."

"If bears are so shy," Tillie asked, "why are they always attacking people?"

"That stuff gets exaggerated," Moll said. "It's more rare than being struck by lightning."

"Comforting," Tillie said. "I've always wanted to take a hit of electricity. Charge my batteries."

But Tillie wasn't convinced and peered into the darkening woods, expecting to see fangs coming at her. The sound of twigs breaking startled her, and she saw a blur of movement through the trees. A stag broke out into the clearing and stood there, staring at them, tense, ready to bolt. Tillie aimed at it, capturing its startled look before the stag sprang away.

"Let's pair off with the other two if you're worried," Moll said. "Get them talking *and* moving."

"Fine with me."

Moll was a little too Canadian for Tillie's taste—too noble, too good. The two women didn't have much to say to each other. Moll didn't dig art; Tillie didn't dig her wilderness. It wasn't that Tillie didn't like wildlife and trees. She just didn't like it in extremes or without some civilizing influence. Like people nearby who could come to the rescue. Mounties and tracking dogs.

They waited for the other two. Tillie and Daddy exchanged places, and Tillie dropped back with Sibyl. Walking loosened their tongues, and talking took their mind off the dangers as well as the boredom of no shop windows to look at. No glass for gazing at their own reflections. Tillie mused on her new installation and avoided thinking about what might be lurking in Sibyl's lungs. She planned to mix the women's voices with images from the trail, so the human voice became a background drone for the wilderness instead of vice versa.

Tillie glanced at her watch. They'd been walking for an hour. She called out, "Hey, Moll. I've had enough. Let's go back."

The others shouted "Yeah!"

Moll shrugged. "Okay by me."

When they started back, Moll took the lead again, Daddy joining her.

Tillie asked Sibyl, "What's the scoop on Moll? She's turned into a real loner."

"I think it's hard for her to sit around for too long, especially since Trevor died."

"Her son?"

"Yeah. Her youngest. Fifteen. Had leukemia."

"Shit. I'd croak if something happened to Valentine."

They started climbing, and Sibyl stopped frequently to catch her breath. Concerned, Tillie watched her struggle, unable to offer any help.

Sibyl lowered her voice. "Yeah. I'd lose it, too. Not Moll. Never saw her cry. Curtis did, though. Trevor was a lot like his dad."

They started walking again, slowly putting one foot in front of the other, trees and undergrowth threatening to take over the trail. Tillie got a whiff of mold from deep in the forest and asked, "She ever talk about it?"

"Nope."

"How do you *not* talk about it?"

"Got me. You know Moll. She's always been pretty closed, eh."

Tillie tried to recall their time together in Toronto and Calgary, remembering Moll as the sunshine girl, always joking and laughing. Carefree. Tillie never expected her to have any *real* troubles. Moll had too much going for her.

"I'm amazed she hasn't said anything about it."

"Just the way she is. She'd lose it if she opened up about her troubles. You know, Curtis lost his job when he was fifty after twenty years at the same place. Not easy to get work at that age."

"Tell me about it! Where'd he work?"

A rabbit scurried across the trail, chased by a bigger animal. The two went by so fast that Tillie couldn't make out if it was a fox or a coyote in pursuit. She tried to capture them on the camcorder.

"Local hardware store. Went under new management. Curtis didn't get along with the new boss. Pretty rough on them for a while. Curtis was depressed. Moll had to keep it all going. Managed to pick up something, answering phones in a real estate office. First time she'd worked for pay since getting married. It killed her, being indoors all the time."

"And I thought she lived an uneventful life!" Tillie was revising her view of her friends as being conventional.

"There's more. Curtis had prostate cancer. Bad. Almost didn't make it. Hardly a blip from Moll, though. It amazes me she doesn't bitch more. I don't know how she puts up with Curtis. A real procrastinator. It took him ten years to finish building their deck."

"You could build ten houses in that time."

"I know. Raleigh has his problems, but that isn't one of them. Moll's got the balls. Made her sons stand on their own two feet. Not like Raleigh. He spoiled our sons rotten. Now I'm paying for it."

"How'd he spoil them?"

"Forking out money right and left. Dirk, the oldest one, is okay. Married. Got a couple of kids. Hey, I'm a granny! But Pete, the youngest, is still living at home. A real mess. Can't keep a job. Was working for Raleigh but he had to fire him. Pete's too unreliable. Run-ins with the police."

Tillie asked, "What's Pete's problem?"

"Cocaine. All he lives for. Getting high." Sibyl coughed.

"You getting a cold?"

"Fresh air must be getting to me."

"Me too."

Sibyl's concerns reminded Tillie of *her* own messes, something she'd like to forget. She'd made enough of them over the years. And cleaned up a few, too. Art is nothing if not messy. So is life.

"Ever try one of those drug rehab programs?"

"Oh, sure. 'My name is Sibyl, and my son's a drug addict.' I've got it down pat. What's the use? I'm not an addict. Pete is, and he won't admit it." She dug into her cigarette pack and lit up again, sucking the smoke into her lungs like someone who was drowning.

Tillie suddenly felt chilled again, legs covered with goosebumps. Living in the States had made her forget the things that constantly threatened Canadians. The extreme cold and long winters. The wilderness so close. Survival a main theme in Canadian lit. But wasn't survival the name of the game, no matter where you lived?

Daddy and Moll had gotten way ahead, but now they were slowly backing up, drawing closer to Tillie and Sibyl. And then Tillie saw what had put them in reverse. She tried to run, except her feet felt as if they were encased in concrete.

A grizzly stood on its hind legs in the middle of the path, about fifty yards ahead of them, sniffing the air. Then it matter-of-factly turned towards the Muskrateers, bared its teeth, and roared. Frozen in place, in time, Tillie's heart knocked around in her chest like a jumping jack.

But she couldn't take her eyes off its fangs or its claws—the color of bone and bruises. They could do a little damage. Time stopped. Cocaine. Cancer. Spots on the lung. All these things seemed trivial compared to being devoured by a grizzly. Tillie imagined its massive jaws closing over her head, crushing it while she was conscious the whole time and listening to the bones crack. No anesthetic. No reassuring words as she left this life. Just the bear's heavy breathing and throaty growl.

Tillie turned on her camcorder, its familiar whirring sound reassuring, and focused it on their visitor. If she was going to die, she wanted to leave a record of what killed her. The viewer framed the bear, made it seem less threatening, the camcorder itself trapping the animal and limiting its motion. Tillie watched, fascinated, her voyeur self standing back and absorbing the spectacle.

Still, Tillie's legs had become jelly, and she expected to collapse right there, a quivering mass of succulent, aging flesh. The bear wouldn't care about the wrinkles or reduced elasticity in her skin. He might even like the chewiness.

Moll and Daddy were directly in front of Tillie and Sibyl now. Tillie had forgotten about Sibyl and glanced over at her. She looked like she already had passed over to the other side, her face the color of a fish's underbelly, a pool forming between her legs.

Without turning her head or taking her eyes off the bear, Moll whispered urgently, "Stay in a tight group. Don't make any fast moves. Keep backing up—slowly."

Tillie wasn't sure her legs would obey. She felt hypnotized, under the bear's spell, its intense gaze. Double bear: the one in the viewfinder and the actual one. She'd do anything it wanted, even walk into its open arms. Except those furry appendages weren't arms exactly. Tillie thought maybe it was a dream and she'd wake up any minute, relieved, the danger over. She'd had lucid dreams like that where she was sure she was awake, that it wasn't a dream.

How many times had she heard your whole life flashes past when you're near death? She hoped those earlier memories would appear, something to take her mind off the terror. But all she could remember was a book she had read, *Bear*, by a Canadian author. Lou, the main character, becomes a bear's lover on a tiny island where she's staying. Tillie had been envious as hell of Lou by the time she finished the book. Except Lou's lover is an old, broken-down black bear. The Muskrateers' bear was a young, virile grizzly.

Tillie wondered if it was male or female. She shouldn't be thinking of such things when she was about to die, but animals had always been a sexual turn-on for her. A totally uninvolved part of her that was observing the whole thing from a great distance looked for the bear's dong. Maybe it was just horny, not hungry. Maybe it was a real stud, aroused by women.

As if reading her mind, the bear dropped onto all fours and gathered its bulky body together, moving in their direction. None of the fairy tales she had read came close to capturing the terror she was feeling. She looked at the ground, surprised that a pool was forming between *her* legs, too, a tiny rivulet joining her puddle with Sibyl's.

Tillie looked into the viewfinder again and freaked herself out even more by zooming in on the bear's face. She told herself she was just seeing a big bear rug. A Mountie would come riding out of the woods any minute, raise his rifle, and hit the grizzly between the eyes. After all, it *was* Canada.

But the bear kept ambling towards them, in no hurry. Tillie wondered about making a deal, sacrificing one of the others so the rest could go free. The bear couldn't eat more than one woman at a time, and she was glad Moll and Daddy were in front, running interference. Tillie planned to run like hell as soon as the bear attacked. It couldn't chase down all of them.

Abruptly it stopped, rising on its hind legs again, sniffing the air and growling. The four women inched backward in sync, resembling a giant centipede. The bear glanced in their direction once more before turning, dropping on all fours, and sauntering off into the trees, crashing through the undergrowth, making a path for itself.

Tillie was almost sorry to see it go.

DEATH IN MENACE

It hadn't been a dream, though when the Four Muskrateers talked about it later, it seemed like one. The surreal quality. The heightened danger. The terror.

The four of them had sprinted all the way back to the gondola, Daddy and Sibyl not having any trouble now keeping up with the other two, certain the grizzly would pounce at any moment. Even Moll was shaken. She'd seen bears before in her rambles, but none had come so near, and this was the first grizzly she'd experienced close-up. They all hoped it was their last.

Panting, they clambered onto the gondola, feeling humbled, aware of just how helpless and vulnerable they were. At the mercy of the elements. Completely unprotected in some profound way.

Sibyl laughed nervously. It was contagious. Soon they all were laughing, tears pouring down their cheeks, unable to stop. The gondola swayed and lurched its way down the mountain, finally depositing them at the bottom. Moll drove them to Sibyl's place. After showering, they drank wine till they were past tipsy, united again as they once were forty years earlier, linked by this near-death experience.

Though they had made it safely back to civilization, Tillie wondered if they would ever feel completely safe again, the grizzly's image burnt permanently into their brains. The teeth. Its claws. Eyes dark and impenetrable as the backside of the moon.

Tillie, who had a videotape of the whole thing in color, played it for them over and over, a kind of ritualistic cleansing of looking death in the face. Could death be as frightened of them as they were of it? Not likely. It had time on its side. Humans didn't. Time was the enemy, the bride of death. Or the husband. Depending.

That night, while the bears made their usual raid on the garbage, the women slept deeply, like the dead. Even Sibyl. Tillie dreamed she had left the women on the trail, facing the grizzly, and run off into the woods by herself. Before long, she was lost and wandered around, seeking a way out, the dense undergrowth barring any exit. She could hear the other women's voices and tried to call out, but she couldn't quite make herself heard. The forest closed in on her, and she woke up crying "help," her own garbled voice finally breaking through the membrane of sleep.

Tillie had the covers over her head, but the other women's muffled voices and laughter were coming from somewhere. Then she heard the bedroom door open and Sibyl call out, "You okay?"

At first Tillie thought she was still dreaming, still lost in the woods, and cried out, "I can't see. Help!"

Sibyl pulled the covers off her head and laughed. "Geez, Louise, come up for air. You could suffocate like that. Coffee's on."

Sibyl drifted out of the room, leaving the door open, the tantalizing aroma of brewing coffee taking her place. Cautiously, Tillie eased out of bed, putting one foot, then the other, on the bear rug she hadn't really noticed before. Now she did become aware of it and screamed.

Sibyl came running back. "What happened? Break a bone or something? Don't sue, for chrissakes."

Tillie sat on the bed, legs drawn up to her chest, arms wrapped around them, her eyes closed. "There's a bear in this room!"

Sibyl screeched with laughter and stumbled out the door. "It's a bear rug. One of Raleigh's treasures. Won't bite, honest."

Tillie recalled that Sibyl had said Raleigh liked to hunt, his trophies all over the house: moose and elk antlers and heads, as well as a stuffed grizzly head. No wonder the place was under siege every night. She'd seen squirrels and birds mourn the death of relatives and chatter furiously at the slayers. Why not other animals? They had spirits, too. Why wouldn't they seek revenge?

Tillie stepped on the rug again but quickly hopped onto the wood floor and stared at the hide. Indians saw bears as animal gods, embodiments of unconquerable power, symbolic of potency itself—sexual potency. Maybe Freud was right. Sex and death do hang out together, orgasms being little deaths. What a sneaky thing to do, pair up sex and death. No wonder she felt turned on by the grizzly they'd run into. Maybe at the moment of death she would exit on the waves of one final major orgasm.

Tillie had heard that bear cults were some of the earliest known forms of religion. Some people once viewed the bear as Bear Mother, the life-giving Great Goddess, and women had a long history with bears. Maybe the Great Mother and Death were bed partners, too.

It was getting crowded.

Then Tillie thought of how grizzlies and black bears dig in the ground, grubbing constantly for food, single-minded, the plowed earth getting renewed and fertilized from the animals' droppings and leftovers. They literally didn't leave a stone (or log) unturned in order to fill their ravenous appetites. Was this behavior contagious? Had the bear spirit invaded her? Had she been initiated?

Tillie pushed away these weighty thoughts and flopped into the living room, dodging Raleigh's treasures, wearing a shapeless red nightshirt over her jailbird tights, black stripes alternating with white circling her legs. Her zebra look. After having her own run-in with a wild animal, she could understand a hunter's impulse to kill one, to capture something so elusive and mysterious, so other. To turn it into a trophy. It was almost as if humans could overcome death if they made it visible in a stuffed bear or elk's head. It was like saying, "Hey, death doesn't claim everything." These animals still lived on in an odd kind of way, their presence palpable in their absence.

Sibyl was back at her puzzle. There was something reassuring about the precise motions she went through, plunking pieces in place, the satisfying snap of one part fitting into another. The final picture was certain, even though Sibyl might not know until she was finished exactly what the image would be. Assuming she finished.

Tillie wished she had more certainty in her life. She always felt as if she could take off into orbit any minute. Actually, the orbit part wasn't accurate. If she *were* in orbit, she'd have nothing to complain about. It was the *lack* of orbit that worried her, especially at her age. She drifted from grant to grant and side jobs in-between. No definite pattern to follow. No roots. Little property. Just the installation pieces she inhabited for a while and then left. Everything was temporary. Except death. She couldn't shake the image of the grizzly coming towards them, swerving at the last minute.

Moll and Daddy were sprawled on the sofas. Moll wore gray sweats. Daddy was in her favorite tights, white this time with a flowered hip-length tunic. They were sipping coffee and reading some old *Maclean's* magazines and *National Geographics*.

"Hey, Tillie," Daddy said, "sleep okay?"

"Pretty good. Weird dreams, though."

"Know what you mean," Daddy said. "I thought the grizzlies had gotten into the house—this place was rockin'!"

Tillie went out to the kitchen, poured herself a cup of coffee, and shrieked with laughter. Then she sauntered back into the living room, holding a bear claw in one hand, coffee in the other. "Fess up. Who's the comedian?"

Sibyl coughed and snapped another puzzle piece in place. "Thought we could use a laugh, eh?"

Tillie took a big bite. "I'm glad we're eating bear claws and not the reverse. You stayed pretty cool, Moll. I'm impressed."

Color flooded Moll's face, like an instant sunrise. "Yeah, well, you guys were amazing. If anyone had bolted, it would've been all over."

Tillie shivered, unwilling to imagine what might have happened.

"What's on the agenda for today? Another hike?"

"I'm game," Moll said.

"No way!" Daddy and Sibyl shouted. "We get a vote this time."

"I was joking, actually," Tillie said. "I'd sooner get run over by roller-bladers than have a bear devour me."

"Yesterday really shook me up," Daddy said. "We could've died!" She put her plump bare feet on the glass coffee table, her toes pressed into the surface, leaving blurry imprints. "Makes me realize my life's become a dead end. I'm as good as dead—all I do is sell houses and condos—meet friends for a drink after work—go home—look at the tube—maybe read a little before I go to sleep—smoke a little dope. I'm wasting this incredible life trying to get rich."

The other women nodded sympathetically.

"I'm on a treadmill," Daddy said. "Same old, same old, every day—let's join the Peace Corps or something—they take older people—do something useful before we die—we were going to change the world once. Remember?"

"I know," Tillie said. She put her coffee cup on the glass table and stared into it, scowling, as if she could see her future there, mixed in with the grounds. "I feel I *am* doing something useful as an artist. But I'm still trying to break through, for chrissakes. Almost sixty. There, I said it! And waiting to be discovered. I need to *do* something before it's too late. Maybe it *is* too late."

Sibyl clattered out to the kitchen and poured herself some coffee, almost drowning in Raleigh's bathrobe. It trailed behind her like a bridal train.

"What's the big deal about being an artist? Shouldn't you get a real job?" She lit a cigarette and blew the smoke in Tillie's direction.

"Thanks, Sibyl," Tillie said. "You're a big help. You sound like my mother."

A puzzled expression on her face, Moll held up the *National Geographic*. "I've been reading this article about the San, these Bushmen artists. They do rock paintings. It says the paintings don't just represent life. They also contain it."

Sibyl said, "I don't get it."

"I don't either," Moll said, squinting and reading from the magazine: "'When shamans painted an animal, they weren't just worshipping a sacred creature. They also harnessed its essence.' What's a shaman?"

Daddy said, "Shamans are kind of like a priest, except they have magic powers—some people think they're healers."

"They have visions and do other bizarre things," Tillie said. "Maybe it isn't bizarre to them."

"I need a shaman!" Sibyl said, settling in front of her puzzle again. "Are they good lovers?"

"Let me finish," Moll said, turning back to the magazine. "'The Bushmen put paint to rock and open the way to the spirit world.'"

"Jesus, Tillie," Sibyl said. "You do *that*?"

Tillie shook her head and laughed. "Afraid not."

"You still haven't told me the big deal about being an artist," Sibyl said.

Tillie shrugged and jiggled one of her feet. "It isn't a big deal. Just my path, I guess."

"So how'd you get on this path," Sibyl asked.

"I try to give life to my imagination."

Sibyl scratched her leg. "So?"

"I think artists are kind of tour guides into our 'image-nation.' They show us stuff we wouldn't be aware of, like the Bushmen painters."

"Huh?" Sibyl sipped her coffee.

Tillie fiddled with each of the rings circling her fingers and thumbs. One had a Minnie Mouse image. Another a skull and crossbones. She had picked it up during her "Memento Mori" period. She'd attended a retreat led by a monk who claimed he and his brothers constantly repeated the mantra "remember that you must die." He said it kept them more intensely focused on the present moment—on life. Sibyl was having that effect on Tillie.

Tillie also had adorned her toes with rings and looked at them now for inspiration, each one given to her by a former lover, all artists of one kind or another. Then she looked at the women, trying to sense their response to her words. "Most artists give life to things that wouldn't exist otherwise. I don't mean artists are some big deal like god or anything!"

"You're like a medium," Sibyl said. "I can dig that. I've been to a few séances. Got any pictures of your stuff?"

"Might have some in the van. I'll look later if you want."

"Cool. I'll become an art connoisseur." Sibyl looked down at the puzzle pieces and let out a whoop, grabbing two and snapping them into place.

Daddy said, "You just do installations?"

"I've done a lot of different things over the years—drawings, paintings, collage, construction, photography. I bring them into my installations now when I need them."

Moll yawned. "So what are your pieces about?"

"My themes? They've stayed pretty much the same—mainly political. Feminist. Autobiographical."

Daddy said, "Sounds like you should be better known. Ever show your work in Canada?"

"Been in the States too long. Can't apply to the Canada Council for the Arts. It pretty much controls the art scene here."

"Must be other ways to get known," Daddy said.

Tillie spread her arms wide: "Well, I'm *dying* to go to Venice this fall for the Biennale. There's a wilderness for you, Moll. You can't *not* get lost in that city."

Sibyl's eyes never left her puzzle. "What's a Biennale?"

"Venice's major art show," Tillie said. "Happens every other year."

"Oh yeah," Sibyl said. "I saw something about it once. Posters."

"Countries from all over the world have pavilions for their artists," Tillie said. "Even Canada."

"Ever show your stuff there?" Sibyl asked.

"Not yet. I'm working on something—the piece I told you about—and I have a lot of ideas percolating. If I were in Venice, they'd start to gel. It's like putting one of your puzzles together. Don't know till I'm finished what I have." Tillie clasped her hands behind her head and leaned back, staring out the window, picturing herself on a vaporetto, cruising the Grand Canal.

"You going to apply to the Venice gig?" Daddy asked.

"Don't have enough of a name. I'd have to crash the show."

"We used to be great at crashing parties," Daddy said. "I could get into that—lend you my expert crashing *and* marketing skills. I'm a good saleswoman, you know."

"Hey, you guys can be part of my installation! Literally."

"Swell—disembodied voices," Daddy said.

"I'd like you to be physically involved in it, too."

"What a blast!" Daddy said. "Let's live it up—the Four Muskrateers on the road again."

Tillie said, "We were going to start the first female rock band. Remember? It's not too late."

"Venice will never know what hit it," Daddy said. "Sounds better than the Peace Corps—muskrats are aggressive as hell, you know."

Sibyl's hand hovered over the puzzle. "You serious? You *wanna* go to Venice?"

"Why not," Tillie said. "Let's have a pre-sixtieth birthday bash *and* crash the Biennale."

"We should book plane reservations right away," Daddy said.

"Yeah, while Venice is still afloat," Tillie said.

Sibyl had forgotten the puzzle. "You guys *are* serious. I'm game. Are you, Moll?"

"I don't know." She fanned her face with the *National Geographic* and avoided the others' eyes. "I need to check with Curtis. I can't just take off. And flying to Venice is costly."

"Everyone can stay at my place," Sibyl said. "For nothing."

Daddy turned to Tillie. "Can you come up with the bucks to get there?"

"Should be able to. All I'll need is a cheap flight and spending money. I can always pick up work there if I have to. Get paid under the table."

Moll said, "I guess I'm not as unhappy with my life as you guys. I don't need to get away."

Daddy said, "There's more to the world than a kitchen and nature."

Moll crossed her arms over her ample bosom. "I like my life. I love the outdoors. Being a wife and mother—grandmother, actually. I don't have anything to prove."

"Maybe, but you need *some* action," Daddy said.

"Hey, you've never really spent time in the wilderness. That's a *real* action-filled trip."

"I got a taste of it yesterday," Daddy said. "No thanks."

"That's how I feel about Venice. No thanks! Crowded with tourists. Rotting. Old. Give me something uplifting. Anyway, what's the point of us all going to Venice?"

"To launch Tillie and shake up our predictable lives."

"I don't want to shake up my life."

"Come on, Moll. Let's live it up while we can," Daddy said. "We might never have this chance again."

"We're not *that* old," Tillie said. "You make it sound like we're going to croak any day." She avoided looking at Sibyl.

"Never know," Daddy said. "Death's a real menace at our age—anything can happen."

Tillie slapped her leg. "That's the name of my new piece: DEATH IN MENACE!"

"Couldn't you guys go without me?" Moll said. "I mean, it's great to see everybody again, but . . ."

"So you're breaking up the gang," Sibyl said.

"How long are we talking about?" Moll asked, fiddling with a loose strand of hair, glancing over at Tillie.

"I don't know. Two to three weeks," Tillie said, pretending to cough and returning Moll's look, hoping she got the message: this could be their last chance as the Four Muskrateers. "What about Raleigh, Sibyl? Will he mind you going?"

"No sweat. We don't keep tabs on each other. It's my place anyway. He doesn't have any say about it."

Tillie couldn't believe they were seriously considering a trip to Venice. It reminded her of when they all had decided to move to Toronto. This time in their lives actually resembled their late teens and early twenties. Their identities were shifting; a major change was occurring. As she'd heard others say, when one door closes—in this case, their fertile years—another opens. In fact, it felt as if the floodgates had been unfastened and water was rushing through, carrying them into the soggy delights of Venice. Tillie pictured herself being tossed around by the deluge and searched for something to hold onto. Once again, as in Toronto, it was the Muskrateers and her identification with them that offered a temporary refuge in the midst of these major shifts. She needed the other three at her side as she made this major transition.

Moll stood up and brushed the crumbs off her clothes. "Three weeks! That's a long time. Curtis might not want me to spend the money."

"You don't have your own reserves?" Daddy asked.

"We're married. Everything's joint." Moll gathered up the empty coffee cups and took them out to the kitchen. "Anyone want more coffee?"

Daddy frowned: "What a drag—no wonder I never married—I only go for two kinds of joints—the ones you smoke and the places where you listen to music and booze it up."

"I'm with you, Daddy," Sibyl said, lighting up.

Moll took her coffee out to the wooden deck, leaving the door open. She sat on a green Adirondack chair and took deep breaths.

"When should we go?" Sibyl said. "I have to see if the apartment's available and get time off work."

"What work are you doing these days?" Daddy asked.

"Keep books for a few companies. Do it from home, mainly. I have a friend who might fill in for me."

"September would probably be the best time," Tillie said. "Weather's still good and the tourists thin out."

"Okay by me," Daddy said. "I've got some vacation coming." She picked at the chipped polish on her toenails.

"I'll make some calls later," Sibyl said. "What about you, Moll? September work?"

"I don't know. I need to call Curtis."

"Near the end of September would be best for me," Tillie said. "But I'm between men. Doesn't really matter when we go."

Tillie always had sneered at bourgeois life, except when she was married to Don, her second husband, the ex-jock, who was willing to be Valentine's stepfather. He'd anchored her then. Offered some stability. The only guy she'd ever lived with who actually worked a nine-to-five job, a salesman of orthodontic supplies. She'd reined in her wilder impulses—her need to travel and explore—to give Valentine a stable home for a while, and she'd used that base to develop her skills as an artist, taking classes, learning the craft. But she thought she'd suffocate from the sameness, the boredom.

Now she'd settle for some of that dullness again after living like a vagabond since Valentine had set out on his own. She thought she'd be relieved to be free of her mothering responsibilities, not a role she'd chosen willingly, but she missed the stability it gave her. Now she took off when the spirit moved her, traveling when she could come up with a plane ticket or enough money for gas, working her way from place to place. Unencumbered by furniture and other belongings. Avoiding the middle-class mentality. She hadn't realized how much of an anchor Valentine had been.

Just give her a husband with a steady job. She'd grab him in a minute. Give up being a bohemian. She even envied Moll's relationship with Curtis. Except that attitude put Tillie right back where she'd always been: dependent on men to define her *and* to support her financially and emotionally, a trap she'd tried to avoid.

As if reading her mind, Daddy said, "You've never talked much about your second husband."

"Number two? Not much to say. Don checked out permanently a few years after our divorce. Cancer."

"Rough," Moll said, strolling back into the living room and plopping onto a chair.

"Yeah, especially for Lucille, his widow. Valentine and I went to the funeral and hung out with her after the services. Strange. I'd met her once before they married. Don brought her to see me. I think he wanted my approval, like a mother or something."

"Or maybe he was rubbing it in—showing you that other women found him desirable," Daddy said.

"Maybe. Anyway, Lucille and I felt like sisters. This dead man united us. I didn't even *know* this woman, but we were telling each other all these intimate details. Comparing our experiences with him. What he was like in bed. Everything!"

"Don't you guys want to do something?" Moll said, standing up. "It's a gorgeous day. Let's have a late lunch in the village."

"When are you gonna call Curtis?" Sibyl asked.

"I dunno. He won't go for me taking off for three weeks. Not if I know Curtis."

"I won't go without you," Sibyl said.

Tillie and Daddy exchanged glances. Familiar ground, Sibyl and Moll forming an alliance. Tillie watched her plans crash around her and Venice float away, towed by Moll and Sibyl. It reminded her of Bogart dragging *The African Queen* behind him, only in this instance it was a whole city being pulled.

Sibyl took a puff off a cigarette and started coughing. This time Tillie and Moll's eyes locked in mutual concern.

"I'll go only if you don't make me visit a bunch of art galleries," Moll said. "Art's not my bag."

"Terrific," Tillie said.

"I'll bring a life jacket, just in case," Moll said.

"And a good compass and maps," Tillie said.

All for one, and one for all

It was the last day of the reunion, and Tillie felt something had shifted between them. They were the Four Muskrateers again: all for one, and one for all. They'd picked up the threads of their shared past and woven them into the present. And they had looked death in the face and survived. For now.

What big teeth you have, Grandma.

Excited about Venice, Tillie had been typing up notes on her laptop, ideas for her new work. The video of the grizzly definitely would have a place in it. She played it repeatedly for the women. They sat there now, in the safety of Sibyl's living room, waiting for the plaster to set that covered their torsos and legs. Tillie needed the casts to take with her to Venice for the installation. They all watched the bear approach them again, reliving that heart-thumping moment just before the animal turned away and lumbered off into the woods. This time, they whooped and hollered, voices rising. Tillie fast-forwarded and rewound the tape, in control of the grizzly's movements, certain of the outcome. It helped them all digest the trauma and contain the terror it stirred.

The experience would already have taken on the quality of legend or myth, except for the images Tillie captured on her camcorder. They showed what actually had happened, though not necessarily what *did* happen. One day, when the Four Muskrateers were telling their families and friends about the incident, they would embellish it, creating a larger truth.

Heroines all, each would find her own way to revise the incident, making it even more frightening, reducing the distance between bear and women to just a foot or two.

Tillie was now thinking of ways she could manipulate the tape and transform it for her installation. She'd bring in more sound, not just her labored breathing and Moll's whispered instructions to back up slowly. Perhaps she'd include a ticking clock. A grandfather clock amplifying the measured tick-tock sound and the chimes calling attention to the passing minutes, their lives eaten away by time, more dangerous than the grizzly. The grandfather motif could represent the patriarchy and how *its* time was running out.

She'd make it appear as if the bear was retreating from the women rather than the reverse. Maybe she'd splice her video with some images a friend of hers had captured recently when she was boating on a lake in Glacier Park. A grizzly dove into the water and chased the woman and her companion until a moose wading near the shore distracted it. Earlier, the woman had been filming the bear devouring a carcass on the beach from a safe distance—she'd thought.

"Isn't this damn stuff hard yet? I'm getting claustrophobic, and I need a smoke."

Tillie handed Sibyl a cigarette, lit it for her, and tapped the plaster. "Another twenty minutes should do it. Hang in there!"

"Christ, Tillie," Sibyl said, "get me outta here! I feel like a mummy."

"You *are* a mummy," Daddy said.

"Don't remind me."

Moll also was squirming around on her chair. "Yeah, this plaster's starting to itch, and it's clammy as hell. Hasn't it set enough?"

"Another few minutes. Can I get you something? Bear claws? Road kill?" She glanced at the tape recorder, checking to see if the tape had run out.

"Not funny," Sibyl said.

Moll thumped the plaster. "What'll you do with these molds?"

"You'll see."

Tillie started cutting through the plaster, carefully removing the casts, each one bearing the distinctive imprint of the person wearing it. She stacked them on newspapers, not sure herself how she'd incorporate them into her piece.

The other three women—wrapped in gauzy white protective cloth—began to unravel it. Bits of plaster fell to the floor like snow. Nearly naked, they glanced at each other's bodies, trying not to appear curious. Moll's large breasts sagged, resembling gourds, and she'd lost her waistline. Sibyl's breasts seemed in retreat, her body almost boyish. Daddy's white flesh looked spongy, like a marshmallow.

Moll grabbed her robe and threw it over her shoulders. "Yuck. I need a shower." She headed for a bathroom, Daddy and Sibyl following.

When they returned to the living room, Moll was dressed in her sweats. Daddy was in her usual calf-length tights, coral colored this time, with a floral top. Sibyl wore jeans and a yellow t-shirt. Tillie had already moved the casts to her van and was sweeping up the plaster bits.

Moll clapped her hands. "Who wants to take a walk?"

She was greeted with a chorus of "No way, José" and ducked, pretending to defend herself against their assault. "Okay, okay, I get the message. You guys want wine coolers?"

No disagreement this time. They all nodded, and Moll retreated into the kitchen.

Sibyl wandered over to her puzzle, standing over it, staring at the torso of the Black woman. "So what about this Black Madonna?" She picked up a puzzle piece and plunked it in place, starting now on the background.

"A lot of people worship her," Tillie said.

Moll appeared, carrying a tray of glasses, ice cubes tinkling. Tillie took two glasses from the tray and handed them to Daddy and Sibyl.

Daddy sipped her cooler and looked thoughtful. "It's a real drag not having a religion at my age—I mean, I'm spiritual in lots of ways—"

"I know," Tillie said. "I'd like to think there's some meaning to all this." She waved her arms.

"Yeah, meaning," Daddy said. "That's the word."

"I'm turned on by ideas, I guess," Tillie said. "Anything that expands my vision of the universe and us. Art's my religion!"

"I'm all for expansion," Sibyl said, pushing out her chest.

"Ever hear of string theory?" Tillie asked.

The other women shook their heads.

"It's mind-blowing. Some physicists think particles—matter in its smallest form—are made of vibrating strings."

"Like violin strings?" Moll asked.

"I don't know. It gets really complicated. Tied up with unified theory and eleven space-time dimensions. Except we can't see these extra dimensions. So the reality we're aware of is only a sliver compared to what's actually out there. Think of it! There could be other worlds nearby, brushing right up against this one."

Moll glanced around the room and shuddered. "I don't like that idea."

"That's a blast," Daddy said.

"You talking about spirits?" Sibyl asked. "I'm into spirits."

"Who knows? But it has me thinking about this life *and* our perceptions. How limited we are. Even time doesn't travel in a straight line. Our past could be still in the future or happening right now."

"You mean I'm not really almost sixty?" Daddy said.

"I'm not saying we don't age, but maybe our physical body can only exist in this one element. It could prevent us from entering these other dimensions or even being aware of them."

"And here I've been hoping my body will be resurrected when I die," Moll said, "good as new."

"Maybe our consciousness lives on and travels to another level once it's free. It blows my mind to think all of these different worlds might exist side by side, and we're unaware of it."

"You making a case for UFOs?" Daddy asked.

"I'm not into that stuff, so I don't know. But we're a speck in the whole scheme and our vision's extremely limited."

Daddy nodded. "I dig it—we're so focused on life here, we may be missing the big picture."

Tillie had spent so much time in the last couple of years listening to Frank's monologues that it was a relief to express her own thoughts for a change. She continued. "Maybe death allows us to make the shift to one of these worlds. Maybe the body prevents us from getting there. Maybe this life *is* a preparation for something else, not just a dead end—a hole in the ground."

Sibyl yawned. "Sounds Christian."

"I'm just blown away by how much mystery surrounds us," Tillie said. "There's so much that's invisible to the naked eye. So many ways of seeing. That's why I love art. It can open us to new experiences."

"We're just a bunch of vibrating strings, eh?" Moll said.

Sibyl lit a cigarette. "Suppose that's why vibrators are so popular?"

"You use one of those things?" Moll asked.

"Only in a pinch."

"Hey, gals," Daddy said. "I've got something that'll vibrate your strings. Ever try Ecstasy?"

"Ecstasy?" Sibyl said. "What's that?"

"Something amazing—a lot different from grass or LSD—you don't realize you've taken anything—won't freak you out."

"So what's the point?" Sibyl said.

"It makes you feel terrific—blissed out and super loving towards everyone."

"I don't *want* to love everyone," Sibyl said.

"You'll never feel so great again—believe me."

Moll shook her head. "I'm not into drugs. You guys do it if you want. I'll pick up the pieces after."

Sibyl found five puzzle sections all at once that connected and looked as if she'd struck nirvana. "Why not sop up some more wine? That's one thing we have a lot of in this house. Wine and puzzles."

"Alcohol's a downer, not an upper," Daddy said.

"Suits my personality. I've seen you put away enough booze. Don't preach to me." Sibyl grabbed her glass and drained it.

Daddy flicked on the video and fast-forwarded it, pressing pause when she reached the part where the grizzly had risen on its hind legs again and was facing the women, teeth bared. Tillie and the others couldn't take their eyes off the screen, mesmerized by the creature, ready to follow it anywhere. The image reflected off their eyeballs, eight grizzlies in the room.

And then Daddy pressed play. The animal turned, ambling off into the trees, the moment lost. The women let out a collective breath—a sigh of relief or despair—that something so pure had bypassed them. Surely that would have been ecstasy, terror turned inside out. Pushed into its opposite.

Daddy turned off the VCR, and the living room came into focus once more, the bear rug in front of the fireplace a laughable alternative to the real thing. No one frolicked on it—a mockery of what they'd lost and gained.

"Last chance for Ecstasy," she said.

Tillie had heard of Ecstasy. She just never got around to checking it out herself. "Hey, I'll give it a whirl. Hell, it's our last night together for a while. Come on, you two. It'll prepare us for the weird stuff in Venice. What've we got to lose?"

"I've never done any serious drugs. Just doesn't turn me on," Moll said. "I get high enough on the outdoors. Anyway, it's against my religion."

"Your religion?" Tillie said. "When did you get religious?"

"About five minutes ago."

"Believe me, taking Ecstasy's a real spiritual trip," Daddy said. "We can drink some red wine too—a communal thing—you'll love it—promise— it'll change your life!"

"That's what I'm afraid of. I like my life fine, just as it is," Moll said.

"I don't mean you'll end up a different person," Daddy said. "You'll just appreciate even more the things that turn you on—you'll get stronger feelings for nature—everything."

A real saleswoman, Daddy said what you wanted to hear. Leaned on the soft spots. Knew when to apply pressure, when to back off. It was a true skill. She was an artist too, but at making others do her will.

"That's what I'm afraid of," Moll said. "I might get addicted to the feeling."

"No way—it's just the key that opens the door—once the door's unlocked, you don't need the key anymore—it's safe, believe me."

Even Moll couldn't stand up to the peer pressure, still a powerful force at fifty-nine and three quarters. Eventually, they all yielded to Daddy's wishes and sat on the floor cross-legged around the bear rug, each cradling a tiny white pill in one palm.

SAN FRANCISCO
LATE '50s & EARLY '60s

TILLIE TAKES A SIDE TRIP

In the late '50s, Tillie ended up in San Francisco with her new friend, Gwen. But that episode ended badly, and Tillie returned to Calgary, penniless. She reignited her relationship with Robert Doucet, her first lover, got pregnant, married him so her son wouldn't be illegitimate, gave birth, and left Robert six months later. She couldn't bear a future trapped with a guy who had no prospects or interest in anything but hanging out with his buddies on Friday nights in local beer parlors.

When she entered the '60s, Tillie hooked up again with Daddy, and they eventually moved to the States together—once more to 'Frisco, as they called it then. Mrs. Duff, Daddy's mother, kept Valentine in Calgary until Tillie started working and found an apartment. She had to work two jobs to keep them going, but Tillie didn't mind. She was living in the most beautiful city in the world. The sacrifice was worth it.

After being chained to a typewriter all day in the financial district, she left behind her daytime self, shooting across the Bay Bridge to Oakland and stepping into her night job as a receptionist at the Fred Astaire Dance Studio. Daddy already was a dance instructor there and had turned Tillie on to the gig.

"It's a gas," she said. "Better than plunking away at a typewriter."

The elderly men and women who hobbled through the doorway were snatching at anything to push away death, hoping to become Fred Astaire and Ginger Roger clones, twirling in a perfect romantic dream for the rest of their days. Tillie ushered them into the inner sanctum—a maze of dance floors, mirrored walls, and tiny offices where the instructors closed their deals.

She sometimes felt a twinge of guilt about participating in this sophisticated form of prostitution, but it never lasted long. Though she felt sorry for them, these desperate men and women would have to fend for themselves, just as she herself did.

Daddy was always game to rub shoulders with other free spirits, pushing boundaries, creating new ones. And San Francisco had lots to offer, a mix of people from different ethnic groups, not white-bread Calgary. North Beach—Enricos, the Jazz Workshop, the Black Cat, the Purple Onion. The Condor, where topless originated. Tillie and Daddy thought it was a gas, the ultimate in women's lib. Free of bras.

San Francisco released Tillie from the restraints of growing up in Canada. She had a lot to shed. Her niceness. Her politeness. Even her inhibitions. Daddy had grown up in Canada, too, yet she seemed way ahead of Tillie. The word *inhibition* didn't exist in her vocabulary. Or maybe it was so deeply rooted she had to go overboard in everything she did to deny it. She got into group sex and whatever drugs were making the rounds (bennies, LSD, grass). Neither did *nice* exist for her. She didn't mind being a bitch, picking fights with anyone she disagreed with, including Tillie.

One minute Daddy rode the feminist bandwagon, pouring over *The Feminine Mystique* and *The Second Sex* as if these books were Holy Scripture. The next minute she was hanging out with her latest sugar daddy. And she went through several. A guy she met at the Iron Horse, a visiting businessman from L.A., paid for her nose job, her apartment, her I. Magnin clothes, and her professionally coiffed bleached hair. He shaped her into a stereotypical Hollywood sex symbol, something he could relate to.

Tillie was confused. She still couldn't figure out Daddy, who seemed to be rehearsing for a bourgeois life, becoming a beautiful and bewitching sexual partner to her high-profile, wealthy husband. But Tillie couldn't imagine her ever being tamed by marriage or a conventional world. Trashy, wild, and unpredictable, Daddy always seemed driven by some invisible force. And it may have been her mother, that diffident Mrs. Duff.

Daddy once confided in Tillie that her mother had always been highly critical of her. Mrs. Duff was never satisfied with her daughter's looks, intelligence, behavior, or goals. But her father thought she was a princess. A leftist, he nurtured Daddy's love for reading and for social causes. But Mrs. Duff had more influence over her daughter, and Daddy couldn't shake her mother loose. That critical voice never gave her any rest.

Tillie wondered if that's what drove Daddy to extremes. Tillie couldn't keep track of who her friend was. Nor could she keep up with all her gigs. One of Daddy's angels liked sex with multiple partners—all at one time. He especially liked watching two women going at it together. Daddy was game. She seemed ready for anything, needing to extend boundaries, especially her own.

Tillie might have joined her and been more experimental with drugs and sex if it weren't for Valentine. He kept her grounded. Just six, he didn't know what had hit him. In a strange country, he totally lost what little security he'd had in Calgary, thrown out into the world, bewildered by starting school, attending daycare centers.

Tillie didn't know it then, but you don't have to be Medusa to destroy your kids. You can do it just by ignoring their needs. Benign neglect. Something in her didn't want to be a mother. Not then, anyway. Pushing away her son allowed her to revolt silently, to get back at Valentine for disrupting her life and taking it in a direction she wouldn't have chosen, even though he didn't have any choice in the matter. To punish his father for getting her pregnant and fucking things up in the first place. For putting a roadblock in front of her. She wanted to blast through that barricade.

At the time, Tillie didn't understand any of that. In her mid-twenties, she wanted to see the world, have fun, and be free of responsibilities. After trying to protect Valentine from his dad, a petty thief, Tillie finally had to admit she wasn't much better.

Daddy eventually dropped out of what she considered the mainstream just as suddenly as she did everything else. She dove headfirst into the counterculture and moved to a commune in Oregon. At first, Tillie got breathless letters or postcards going on about Daddy's latest adventures.

Trippie Tipsy Tillie—
Excuse all the coffee marks and who knows what else on this paper I've been up all night stoned on the moon it's so big here tonight you'd think it grew in the trees it's every-where a big silver bowl filling up the sky no I'm not on dope at the moment mescaline's the big thing and LSD you should get hold of some Tillie it's the greatest high ever what's so great is not having schedules to meet you know what I mean

> up at 7
> off to work by 8
> lunch at noon
> finish work at 5
> have dinner at 7
> screw at 10
> go to sleep at 11

Ugh I'll never do that to myself again I've thrown away my watch and we don't have a clock in the house fourteen of us are living together people are coming and going all the time and everyone's in and out of everyone else's bed it's cool meeting people from all over the world we had a cou-ple from Germany here for a week but they couldn't stand the disorder and took off after trying to organize us there was a full scale rebellion almost a third world war so they vamoosed a cool chick from France moved in yesterday and has been teaching me French parley vous francaise we're all collecting welfare I'm getting it under three differ-ent names cool eh the system is shot anyway and needs to be ripped off they're always ripping us off telling lies and keeping us in the dark about what's really going on the corrupt government has TOO MUCH POWER I'm reading a lot of Marx and other lefties and I'm really getting into tantric yoga WOW is that powerful stuff sometimes we go on for days one long orgy and climax got to go now and watch the sun come up it blows my mind!

After Daddy left the Oregon commune, she sent Tillie a few letters from L.A., raving about a guy she was living with who was a big honcho in SDS. Seriously chummy, they were working together to change the world, putting on consciousness-raising and reading groups, pushing civil rights, a lot of the stuff Daddy and Tillie had talked about when they had lived together.

The next Tillie heard from Daddy was a couple of years later. She had broken up with the SDS dude. The women in the movement had separated from the men and started their own commune. Got involved with radical feminism. They wanted *real* change, not mainstream feminism, and attended demonstrations all over the country. They were against marriage and the family unit—a patriarchal institution. In the last letter Daddy sent, she went on and on about how great sex was with women, more erotic than with men—fully out of the closet.

Several years after she'd left the Bay Area, Daddy showed up one day on Tillie's doorstep. Tillie was just out of her second marriage with Don, finishing up her BFA and managing apartments so she and Valentine could get their place rent-free, trying to live a respectable life until Valentine got launched. She got financial aid and a student grant or two. Student loans. Food stamps.

Lots of people stopped by the complex, responding to the vacancy sign, looking for a place to rent. So when the bell rang, Tillie opened the door and quickly sized up the person standing there. Not someone the owners would want as a renter; not someone Tillie would want as her neighbor. Stringy black hair hung to the woman's shoulders, a black kerchief was tied pirate fashion around her head, and large gold hoops dangled from her ears. Teeth covered with moss. Hairs on her upper lip stained brown from smoking. Decked out in dingy white harem pants and a shapeless, blousy top. Everything looked slept in. A dusty, banged-up VW was parked in front, fake tiger skin covering the seats, the back full of yelping dogs. In the passenger seat, a younger woman waited.

"Sorry, no vacancies." Tillie closed the door.

The bell rang again. *Fuck. A fair-housing vigilante.* The woman probably had half a dozen kids in the back seat, too. Tillie would have to take her application. She opened the door again.

"We don't take animals."

"Tillie, it's me, Daddy!"

She couldn't believe it. Her old friend looked like a refugee from a garbage dump.

Daddy pointed at the car. "Sammie and I are passing through—on our way to a demonstration in L.A.—thought I'd look you up—got an extra bed for an old friend?"

Tillie didn't. She and Valentine had only two bedrooms. They used them both. She wasn't going to put her son out of his room. But what could she do? She and Daddy went back a long way, and her mum had sheltered Tillie and Valentine when they were homeless. How could she shut the door in her friend's face?

She decided to give up her bed and sleep in the living room so Valentine didn't have to watch the two women make out. "Bring in your friend. The dogs have to stay outside."

Tillie's neighbors peered out from behind their curtains, making her nervous. She definitely couldn't afford to get booted out, and she didn't want complaints to the owners. She was close to getting her degree, and Valentine just had a year left in high school. Sammie and Daddy's visit needed to be short.

Neither woman had seen a shower in days. Sammie wore a soiled white Nehru top with similarly stained white harem pants that ballooned out at the knees. Tillie showed them the bathroom and gave them a couple of towels. The smell of stale grass, sweat, dog hair, and stinky feet filled the small apartment.

Daddy and Sammie were on a macrobiotic diet and couldn't eat anything Tillie cooked, which suited her fine. Taking over the kitchen, they hauled in an ice chest from the VW and pulled out moldy-looking vegetables, rice, grains, and their own blackened pots.

After eating, Sammie floated around the place, fondling the loop of blue prayer beads she was wearing around her neck and muttering "Om mani padme hūm." Tillie hadn't been around Eastern religions much then, and she didn't know what was going on. Sammie plopped in the middle of the living room floor, sitting cross-legged, eyelids half closed, arms outstretched, thumb and middle finger touching, chanting "OM."

Daddy sprawled on the sofa and said, "Hey, let's kick back. Light up a joint."

Tillie frowned. "Sorry. I have to set a good example for Valentine. No dope in the apartment."

Daddy glared at her and said, "You've become an uptight bourgeois!" Then she slammed out and took off in her car with the yapping dogs.

Sammie just kept chanting and sitting through it all. When Valentine came home from school, he almost tripped over her.

"Hey, Mum," he said, "is she for real?"

Tillie nodded, hustling him off to his room so she could explain who their guests were.

A week went by and the two women didn't show any signs of leaving, though they were seriously disrupting Tillie's life, sleeping half the day, carrying on much of the night. It was hard for her to convince Valentine he couldn't just flake out, too. He still had to get up, go to school, and do his chores around the apartment complex.

Tillie finally told the two women the owners had a policy that guests could only stay for one week—maximum. She didn't tell them it was a new policy she had just invented. Since she was manager, she had to set an example and enforce the rules. Daddy grumbled something about rigid Republicans. Sammie said a few Hail Mary's before resuming "OM." And the two of them slipped out while Tillie was at school the next day, leaving behind some dried up cabbage, a couple of roaches, and a bed full of fleas. The apartment had to be fumigated.

The next time Tillie heard from Daddy, her old friend had done another abrupt shift. She had moved across the country to West Palm Beach and had earned her broker's license. She said selling houses was like selling dance lessons—you go for the soft spot. Find the weakness and lean on it. She had never tried to sell higher than the bronze level ($2000) at the Fred Astaire Dance Studio because it was easier to sell. The gold and silver levels scared off people. It was too much of an investment, thousands of dollars. Daddy didn't seem to have a problem selling condos and houses either. She even made enough to buy her own home and more.

Yet here was Tillie, still having trouble finding two coins to scrape together.

WHISTLER, B.C.
AUGUST 1999

THE MUSKRATEERS TRIP OUT

Sibyl poured everyone a glass of red wine to help them slosh down the Ecstasy. Tillie almost panicked, images of the dead Heaven's Gate cult members flashing through her mind. What if the Ecstasy was laced with cyanide? But it was too late. Tillie turned on the tape recorder and the camcorder. At least she'd leave a record.

They had Chinese food delivered so they didn't have to drive anywhere. Spicy orange scallops dotted with chili peppers, chicken smothered in black bean sauce, bok choy and black mushrooms, egg rolls, and rice crammed their plates. They sat in the living room, eating, drinking wine, voices interweaving with the food odors, the two getting mixed up at times.

The elixir took effect gradually, imperceptibly. Tillie had never been so aware of each texture and flavor, her taste buds bursting—mini-orgasms. She felt she could go on forever, just chewing, extracting each strand of flavor from the food. She remembered a meditation retreat at the Green Gulch Zen Center. They had eaten their meals in silence. She came close to this sensation then. All distractions stripped away, she experienced things directly, intimately. Bare attention.

One by one, her senses expanded to their fullest, combining to heighten her appreciation of everything. It reminded her of lucid dreams. She seemed more awake than when she was actually awake, highly conscious of what was going on in and around her, everything intensified.

She didn't want to wake up from this feeling.

"Hey, you guys," Daddy said, "you hear that?"

"What?" Tillie asked.

"Gurgling. Sounds like a grizzly's stomach growling."

Sibyl laughed, the sound unusually melodic, running up and down the scales. "It's our hot tub. I just turned on the jets. Thought we'd have a soak."

"Okay by me," Moll said.

She set down her plate and stretched out on the bear rug in front of the fireplace, wearing shorts, rubbing her exposed legs and arms against the fur. She appeared ready to start purring, her back arched, fingernails running through the pelt, looking vulnerable, relaxed.

Daddy picked up Moll's plate and carried it, along with her own, to the kitchen. On the way back, she stopped at the aquarium, watching the tropical fish, her face pressed against the glass, sticking out her tongue and licking the smooth surface. The fish—flashing fluorescent orange and yellow and green—darted towards her, placing their mouths against Daddy's lips on the other side of the glass.

It was love at first sight.

The other women floated out to the deck, dropping their clothes in flowering heaps, the pink-blue-green-purple petals of their underwear blooming against the rough wood. The women melted into the long Canadian twilight, suspended outside time, sinking into the steaming water. Hovering on the brink of old age, they still seemed lit by the glow of youth. Jets exploded against their skin.

"This is great! A thousand massaging fingers," Sibyl said.

They all nodded in agreement, smiling blissfully.

Their nakedness seemed normal, the years falling away. Toronto, the four of them running around the apartment nude. Unselfconscious, buoyed by youth and the firmness of their flesh. Nothing to hide from each other. Each body a variation on a theme. *Their* theme.

Tillie was surprised that their bodies still had a girlish quality to them, even in late middle age. Breasts slung low but alluring, each woman's different in size, shape, and nipple color. Moll's full and flirting with her waist. Sibyl's like fried eggs. Tillie's somewhere in-between. Gravity exerting its pull, changing their shape. Gravity. The enemy. That oppositional force. Working with time. The two cronies.

San Francisco. Late '60s, early '70s. Tillie remembered stopping by a party on Greenwich Street, walking into a living room full of men and women. They were all naked, strolling around, sipping wine, guzzling beer, chatting in clusters, acting as if it was normal to be at a party nude. Their protest against conventional ideas didn't fool anyone. Protests always felt phony. Staged.

Tillie had felt out of place then with clothes on, but she wasn't ready to unzip. Not yet. Daddy did. She had stayed.

"It was a blast," she told Tillie later.

Tillie almost believed her.

This time it wasn't a protest.

"Daddy," Tillie called out. "Bring the goldfish into the hot tub and you won't have to leave them."

"Cool idea," Daddy said. They heard cupboard doors opening and closing inside the house. A minute later, she stepped onto the deck, carrying a water pitcher in one hand, a Pyrex measuring cup in another. The fish fluttered against their new limitations, reminding Tillie of Sibyl, walleyed, restless. Trapped.

"Don't worry, my babies," Daddy crooned, "you'll soon be free."

Daddy—who never wanted to be a mother. Daddy—who avoided kids whenever she could. Babies?

She stopped at the hot tub and tipped the containers, emptying the contents into the water. The women shrieked, fish brushing against them, nibbling, darting between legs and through the forest of pubic hair.

"Move over," Daddy said, tossing off her clothes, slipping into the water. Cupping a struggling fish in her hands, she brushed it with her lips. "Wow—their mouths are like tiny vaginas—I didn't know fish could be so erotic."

Tillie stared at the pine trees, etched against the darkening blue sky, and didn't hate them anymore. They still reminded her of church steeples, but they were also themselves. She was the one who gave them the churchy connection. Almost sixty, and seeing trees for the first time. Like being born again. The God of Love compacted into a tiny white pill. Amazing. She had swallowed god! She hoped S/He didn't mind.

Tillie settled into her euphoria, embracing it like bunting, awash with warm thoughts and feelings. She even loved the sagging, ravished skin of herself and the other Muskrateers. It was a map, the arc of their lives traced in it. As if blind, she reached out and touched each woman, sketched with her fingertips the delicate patterns, the planets of liver spots, the variations of color and tone. The women didn't recoil, her explorations sensual, not sexual. Non-threatening.

"Don't stop!" Sibyl moaned. "I didn't know I had skin before. No one ever touches it."

Never touched? Tillie might not have had lasting relationships with men, but they did touch each other. Artists, they lived in their hands. Massage. Stroking. Immersed in the flesh.

Tillie watched an army of ants carrying their booty across the deck surrounding the tub. Moll sighed, turned over onto her stomach, and placed one of her arms in their path. The ants changed direction, marching up her triceps, evoking shrieks of delight.

It started to rain. Tillie had never been so aware of water, each drop vibrating on the roof of the house, pinging, tittering, the sound expanding like a bubble, her mind fully focused on it. A symphony of raindrops. She watched the patterns the rain made on the water's surface. Then she closed her eyes, let her head drop back, mouth open, and swallowed the sky. She gargled, the rain entering her, impregnating her.

Later, they moved into the house slowly, drying off, dressing reluctantly, putting on the restraints that go with clothing. Sibyl turned a couple of lamps on low, most of the place in shadows. The night suddenly surrounded them, the windows throwing back their images. It was both comforting and scary to be enclosed in this way, caught in the web of their own reflections.

Moll lowered herself onto the bear rug again and nuzzled it. The others sprawled on the sofas and chairs, bodies super relaxed from the hot tub and drug, floating between sleeping and waking. A single purplish-blue fish, tinged a deep burgundy, undulated in the aquarium, moving constantly through the water, fins fluid as silk, stopping periodically to stare at them. It reminded Tillie of an elegant woman in a floaty diaphanous dress.

Tillie said, "You think we're in a big fish tank, being fed, observed?"

The other women nodded their heads in agreement.

Sibyl said, "Goldfish can't grow any bigger than the tank they're in."

"Makes sense," Daddy said, running an ice cube up and down her arm, moaning with pleasure. "People can't either."

"What if we're in one that's too small?" Moll asked, suddenly looking frightened, drawing her knees up to her chest and circling them with her arms. Moll, the strong one, crumbling.

"Break out—or find someone who'll help you," Daddy said.

"We broke out of a really small tank when we left Calgary and went to T.O.," Tillie said.

"Yeah," Daddy said, "but we fell into another one."

"Always another one to bust out of," Tillie said. "If we don't, we live out our lives in a tank that's too small."

"I'm happy with my fish tank," Sibyl said, lighting a cigarette and taking a deep drag, watching the smoke rings she had blown until they dissipated.

"You think death's a way to get into a bigger fish tank?" Moll asked.

"Depends on what you believe," Tillie said.

"I believe there's something after death," Moll said. "If I didn't, I couldn't stand living."

"Unless you think this is all there is," Daddy said. "Make every moment count—be ecstatic."

"Sounds very Buddhist," Tillie said. "Buddha didn't know all the answers either."

"Who does?" Sibyl asked.

Tillie shrugged. "I wouldn't want to know all the answers. Just some clues. It's like creating a work of art. We discover what we need to know as we go along. Enough to go to the next stage. At least, that's how I work. If there's something divine, I'm sure it's constantly improvising."

"That's the scariest thing I've heard," Moll said, shivering. "Not knowing anything for sure. Making it up as you go."

"Just go with the flow," Tillie said. "Take it as it comes."

"I would've gone crazy after Trevor died if I hadn't believed in an after-life. In god. My faith kept me going. And my minister. Sometimes I wake up at night, thinking I hear Trevor calling for help. If I gave birth to him once, why can't I bring him back to life?"

Moll's voice broke and she started to sob. Ignoring their stiffening joints, the other women lowered themselves onto the rug and circled Moll, patting her back, stroking her hair and arms, allowing her to unload.

"I feel like I killed him or something," she choked out. "Gave him bad genes. I should've been able to save him," she wailed, a plaintive sound like a wild creature.

Soon they were all crying, Moll's deluge triggering their own unshed tears, even Daddy, who'd never given birth. Tears merging, melting into each other, creating a salty ocean they floated in. Water and words got mixed up, the women confessing to one another their fears, their failings, through the long hours of that night.

Moll told of her sexless marriage, no intercourse with Curtis for years.

"One night I found him making out with a young guy from work, a drifter. I guess he'd been doing it for a long time, off and on."

She told of the Anglican minister who'd helped her through her son's death—and also had helped himself to Moll, taking advantage of her defenselessness, distracting her from grief with the sexual desires she'd submerged for so many years.

The women shook their heads at his brashness, knowing that they too would have succumbed to the word of god become flesh, that their flesh was just as weak as Moll's. Of course, he had received a call to another church, in Eastern Canada. Of course, he didn't intend to divorce his wife for Moll. Of course, he had left her shattered heart behind, a triple wham-my: she had lost her son, god, and a lover.

"Why don't you leave Curtis?" Tillie asked.

"Where would I go? Besides, we're a family. We're grandparents! Anyway, it's too late to start over, and I don't want to grow old alone."

They all nodded at that, too. They understood loneliness. They under-stood the fear of growing old, the fear of death—no longer able to push away its reality. They knew that a relationship could offer some solace, even if the couple wasn't well matched.

Their talk reminded Tillie of Black churches she'd attended, the call and response, the nodding and amens. All in it together. All caught up in the same net, pulled in by the same fisherman—death. Everything fades in the face of it. Or becomes super exaggerated.

Daddy told of *her* lack of interest in sex. "Bed death the lesbians call it—no desire—been years since I've wanted to make out with anyone, male or female."

"Hormones," Tillie said sagely.

"Yeah—who knows—maybe I should've been analyzed—maybe it's all mental."

"Bull," Tillie said. "Sex changes for women. Some women anyway."

"Most women," Sibyl said. "My friends all say it's different now. Slower to orgasm. The need not as urgent. Fantasies less frequent, if at all."

"I haven't lost my desire to be with a man," Tillie said. "I just don't want the focus only on my genitals. My whole body's a vagina. A lot of men don't get this. I go crazy from being stroked all over! My sexual response has been diffused."

More nods.

"The old things don't hold much zing for me any longer," Daddy said. "But I don't know where to go next." She stared at the one goldfish left in the tank, hovering near the surface.

Tillie talked of her guilt over Valentine, her worries about his addictions, her negligence as a mother, her inability to control how he turned out. "Maybe that's why I love art, something I can control a little at least."

"That's why I do puzzles," Sibyl said. She told them of Raleigh's father's blindness, how excruciating it was to watch this once vital man try to navigate, and her fears about Raleigh's sight. He was going blind in one eye from a hole in the retina. "It's as if that fucking hole is swallowing both of us."

Another black hole. Tillie realized they *all* had one that wanted to suck the life out of them.

"A real Greek tragedy," Tillie said. "The bloody Greeks knew it all. They just didn't know how to blow up the planet. That's our job, I guess." She spilled out all her fears—of aging, of never making it completely as an artist, of growing old alone and poor. Of dying.

United by their stories and a shared past, the women drifted off to bed, one by one, the words tapering off, leaving a chasm behind them that they'd have to fill again and again.

In the morning, in the light of a sunshiny Whistler day, they folded back into themselves, like tulips, the sun closing rather than opening them up. The previous night seemed like a dream, their confidences dissolving in the sun's rays. Embarrassed by the intimacies and emotions they'd revealed, they ate breakfast mainly in silence, avoiding each other's eyes. Like a one-night stand. Wash-up. Pack. Clear out.

Tillie didn't even notice when she tucked a couple of monogrammed towels into her suitcase, images of Whistler embroidered in each corner. Just a keepsake. When she found them there later, after she unpacked, she would laugh at her absentmindedness, forgetting the other things that had shown up in her handbag or suitcase from various travels. Souvenirs, she called them. Mementos. Something for her artwork.

Later, they all stood on the deck, surrounded by suitcases, embracing briefly, reminding each other that they'd meet again in Venice on September thirtieth.

"Don't forget to make your plane reservations," Sibyl said.

The others nodded, that mysterious city already exerting her charms, claiming their attention, drawing them into her maze.

Sibyl was staying on at the cabin for a few days. Moll drove off alone. Tillie offered Daddy a ride to Vancouver to catch her plane.

The last Tillie saw of Sibyl before they met again in Venice, she was standing over the hot tub, puffing on a cigarette, staring forlornly at her fish. They floated there like deflated balloons. Tillie aimed her camcorder and shot.

VENICE, ITALY

"Darkness precedes Light and She is Mother."
(Inscription in the altar of Italy's Salerno Cathedral)

TILLIE CRASHES VENICE

Exhausted from traveling for twenty-four hours, Tillie drags her suitcase to a nearby dock and waits for the vaporetto. In the dark, the Italian signs are unreadable, and she wonders if she's in the right boarding area. Lighted boats glide back and forth on the canal, leaving gentle ripples in the impenetrable water.

Alone on the pier, eyes closed, knees bent, arms outstretched, she passes the time aligning herself with Venice's energy. First she focuses on harmonizing her root chakra with the earth's core. Then she concentrates on her second chakra, hoping to awaken her female power and creative force. She needs all the help she can get to crash the Biennale. It's her last chance to become an internationally famous installation artist.

Even at fifty-nine and seven-eighths, Tillie is burning with ambition, though she still has to fight the Canadian ethos of avoiding the limelight and pursuing mediocrity. For many Canadians, third place is better than number one. "Who Do You Think You Are?"—the title of an Alice Munro short story—says it all. Who do you think you are trying to be better than others? No wonder Canada's national emblem is the beaver, a shy creature that spends most of its life out of sight. Tillie also used to feel invisible. But living in the States all these years and becoming a U.S. citizen have made her less modest.

Shifting her attention to her third chakra, the source of her personal power, she wonders what the difference is between personal and female power, but the yogis will have to figure it out. Other things currently occupy her attention. Tillie watches a grizzled old man wearing a seaman's sweater and carrying a plastic bag shuffle towards a spigot at the other end of the dock. Then he approaches her, speaking Italian, poking the middle finger of one hand into the circle he makes between the thumb and index finger of the other one. She backs away, dragging her suitcase, her rucksack weighing her down. He follows, yelling and tugging at his zipper.

She can't believe this is happening in her favorite city, a dirty old man wanting to show her his shriveled bud, *and I'm ten and back in Calgary after dark and a man wearing an overcoat whips it open under a streetlight he isn't wearing anything else his thing limp and pitiful dangling between his legs it sends a thrill through me and I curse you fucking shit cocksucker bastard and lift my skirt wiggling my ass and scare the hell out of him he takes off down the street and I run home laughing all the way.*

But this isn't Calgary. It's Venice. She trips on a loose board, catching herself before she pitches forward into the canal, picturing the headlines: UNKNOWN ARTIST WASHES ASHORE AT THE LIDO AND MAKES A SPLASH. Furious, Tillie whirls and almost falls into the old man's arms. He smells like rotting fish. She calls him a perverted old fart who should be ashamed of preying on female tourists. Retreating, raising his hands as if in apology, he gets the message.

A crowd is waiting on an adjacent dock, and a waterbus pulls up. She runs—lugging her bags, just making it before the boat pulls away—and collapses onto a bench. She asks the woman sitting next to her if this vaporetto will reach the San Stae stop. The woman nods.

Relieved, Tillie sits back, watching gondoliers snake through the canal, paddles soundlessly cutting into depths. Water laps against ancient piers. Sea smells and other pungent odors drift by. Lights flicker in the passageways. The dreamy slow speed limit suspends her in time. Many buildings appear only partially inhabited, shuttered windows a stark contrast to glowing interiors and lights shimmering on the water. Tillie glimpses elegant parlors featuring Moorish columns and tapestries. A woman steps out on her balcony, silhouetted against the light, and Tillie imagines *herself* standing there watching the boats go by, flashes of light in the dark.

The next morning, snoring—not the soothing sound of gondoliers crooning to their passengers—awakens Tillie. Forgetting where she is, she thinks Frank is in the other twin bed, and she's forgotten her earplugs. Turning onto one side, she finds herself staring into Daddy's wide-open mouth.

Relaxed in sleep, Daddy's skin sags in spite of a face-lift, gravity pulling it downwards. She looks vulnerable, jaw slack, a little spittle gathering at the corners of her mouth, dark roots showing in her hair. What *are* Daddy's roots? Where would they take Tillie if she followed them? She tries to remember how Daddy looked before she started bleaching her hair. It had been almost black, and she recalls the hawk-like, pre-bobbed nose.

Years earlier, Daddy had told Tillie that when she slept with a guy, she wore everything to bed: false eyelashes, falsies, and anything else to bolster her self-image. Back then, she was still trying to attract men and be a glamour puss. Even in the sack. Though she's toned down her makeup, Daddy hasn't lost her need for razzle-dazzle.

Long ago, Tillie herself gave up on most cosmetics. Time-consuming and uncomfortable to use, they made her too self-conscious. She felt like a fraud, her painted mouth belonging to a stranger. She was always smacking her lips together and eating off the lipstick. So what was the point of using it?

Daddy's attachment to these things is something else that doesn't add up. A card-carrying feminist, why would she let herself be manipulated by the commercial culture? Exploited? Or maybe she just wants to be beautiful. Why shouldn't she paint her finger and toenails whatever color she wants? What's wrong with decorating her body? Tribal people—men *and* women—do it, following an impulse to alter their appearance. So Daddy adds another layer to her physical self *and* her personality in this way. But how many layers can she tolerate without collapsing under the weight?

Jetlagged, all of this thinking hurts Tillie's head. Too exhausted the previous night to do anything but undress and fall into bed, she didn't even brush her teeth. She runs her tongue over their gritty surface and looks around the room: a five-drawer cherrywood chest of drawers against one wall, a wooden-backed chair with an upholstered needlepoint seat under the window. Matching purple comforters. Prints of Venice above each bed. A large, tarnished oval mirror hangs above the chest, framed in pewter. Not her favorite color.

The city has begun to work its magic on her—Venice and her own fertile imagination. She can always count on the latter for entertainment and to provide material for her art projects. As a girl, she often entered this in-between world whenever she was bored, and as an adult she depends on it to guide her creations. Relaxed and in that state between waking and sleeping, Tillie sees a Black *Venus de Milo* hovering at the foot of the bed. She recalls seeing a similar image in the puzzle Sibyl worked on at their Whistler reunion. Except this one is pregnant. Very pregnant. Italy—where motherhood is still worshipped and viewed as divine.

Daddy says, "You look like you've seen a ghost!"

Tillie's reverie shattered, she screams.

"You *have* seen a ghost," Daddy says. She throws back the covers, yawning and stretching like a cat. She's wearing a thong, and a flimsy little turquoise silk top barely conceals her still-firm breasts. No babies to unhinge them. Her smudged eye makeup looks raccoonish. "Where in hell are we?"

"The old world," Tillie says.

"Puh-leese! I'm allergic to 'old.' You made it! What's the time?"

"Haven't a clue."

"Have a nightmare?"

"Sort of." Tillie glances cautiously around the room. "Must be the unfamiliar bed."

"Didn't even hear you come in. Hey, girl, we're in Venice—isn't that a gas?"

"A muskrat's delight. All this water."

That night, Tillie and the others sit on the balcony of Sibyl's digs, zonked after sightseeing all afternoon, at the moment not saying much. Sipping wine, they watch small boats weave in and out on their private canal, each woman in her own bubble. The light is soft and rosy, the sky clear and just beginning to darken.

Tillie loves the apartment's many Venetian touches, from the handsome tiled entryway to the dark wood beams marching across the ceiling to the large windows framed in lace. Sibyl bought the place furnished, and many of the older pieces retain the city's flavor, ornate with an overstuffed feeling. Tillie easily could never leave. As usual, Sibyl's eye for a great deal has served her well.

Now Tillie puts down *Death in Venice*, impatient with Aschenbach's pursuit of the young Tadzio and his lost youth. Impatient with his feeble attempts to alter the truth: coloring his hair, applying rouge to his cheeks and lips. The attempt to appear younger makes him look foolish instead.

As an artist, she's a fan of illusion, the use of light, pattern, color, texture, and shape to have an effect on viewers. But for her, art strips away falseness, forcing the participant to see the world more clearly. It uses deception to get at the truth. Aschenbach uses it to kid himself.

Twilight creeps up on them. A small motorboat passes below, steered by a young man. A gentle wake causes the parked boats to bob and dip and scrape against their moorings. A few outdoor lights glow and shimmer in the water. Ferns and ivy and geraniums tumble out of window boxes and balconies.

Sinking into a reverie, Tillie sees the pregnant torso materialize from a mist hovering over the channel. Tears gush into the canal from where the torso's head should be, giving Tillie an idea for a water fountain she could create. She's never tried to go commercial with her skills, but a fountain could be a great moneymaker if only she had the business sense to manufacture and sell it.

Tillie glances at Daddy and the others. Sibyl is puffing away between sips of wine, gabbing with Daddy and Moll. What would they think if she told them about her vision? She can hear Sibyl saying "Get a life, kid." Well, she has a life, and Venice is her muse. She expects mysterious things to happen here. The city hovers somewhere between heaven and earth, everything unstable and afloat, nothing as it appears to be, a place of many masks turning perceptions upside down and inside out. She herself feels like a modern-day Alice, plummeting through this crack between the worlds, lost in shimmering surfaces. Where will she land?

Venice—or maybe it *is* Venus—has started working its magic on them. Moll is wearing mascara, some rouge, pale lipstick. Unusual for her. She's always preferred *au naturel*. Though more subtle, her artifice reminds Tillie of Aschenbach. Or else Moll is breaking out of the box she's been living in. Tillie doesn't blame her for experimenting and testing the waters. In Venice, there's plenty of water to test.

Tillie glances at Sibyl, who also seems changed in this new setting, clothed in the Italian language, *ciao* and *arrivederci* and *a domani* rolling off her tongue like wine. She wears the culture the way she would a familiar dress. It appears as if Italy has given birth to her, and she's no longer an orphan. Her inheritance has freed Sibyl from her Canadian self. Tillie never thought she'd envy Sibyl, but she does. Tillie would give anything to own a pad in Venice—or anywhere else, for that matter. She would like to feel the pride and confidence that ownership can give.

Even Daddy is shedding her real-estate-broker self, loosening up. She's stopped compulsively calling her office and her broker several times a day.

"Forget time," Daddy said before they went touring that morning. "Live in the present. Go with the flow. Out with Chronos!"

Everyone agreed, tossing their watches and cell phones into their suitcases. Tillie would have joined them if she owned either piece of technology. Venice seems a perfect city for going with the flow. The old Daddy is reappearing, though there are so many, it's hard to keep track—the laidback radical eager to reject convention, the saleswoman, the proactive feminist, the sticky-fingered opportunist.

Tillie feels Venice altering her as well. It isn't so much her clothes. Today she's wearing red Mary Janes, ankle socks, a flowered skirt, white peasant blouse, and a shawl. But when she talks, she throws up her arms and waves them around, getting into the Italian body language. It's good for the circulation. It also reminds her that—unlike the torso she's been seeing—she does have limbs. And she plans to use them as long as she can.

Santa Maria Della Salute

The next day, while they're out exploring, Daddy points to the massive twin domes of Santa Maria della Salute that define the Venice skyline. "Wow," she says. "Mary has made her mark here."

"Yeah, but Mark beat her to it," Tillie says, thinking of the Basilica di San Marco and St. Mark's Square.

"Let's go! I could use a little church action," Moll says.

All canals lead to the Salute's domes, but Tillie's more interested in her immediate surroundings—the play of light and its reflection on water, the rich palate of colors hugging the liver-colored tones. A somber city on the surface. Middle Eastern in flavor. Splashes of vibrant color bursting from the interiors.

"Hey," Tillie says. "I don't feel so bad about my own aging body now. Venice puts it into perspective." She points at the ancient structures and artful decay, bare bones showing through in places, bricks crumbling, concrete and wooden pilings gnawed by the water's constant flow.

The others nod.

"Maybe humans are works of art, too. Or maybe our spirits live on in art," Tillie says wistfully, thinking about all the pieces she's done over the years. How much of her do they contain? When she dies, she wants to be cremated and interred inside one of her installations. She stole the idea from Canada's West Coast Indians: they once placed their dead inside totem poles they carved. The idea of hanging around in her art after death

101

pleases her. Jesus wasn't an artist, but it paid off for him to end up in a cave and rise from the dead. Who knows what might happen to Tillie? The rising-from-the-dead shtick has already been done, so maybe she can come up with something fresh.

It's no wonder she's thinking of death and its aftermath. Each time Tillie roams Venice's labyrinthine passages, she's taken back in time. Or into some timeless space. The city has avoided most of modern life's traps—no cars polluting the air or providing a constant background roar. No skyscrapers of steel and glass dominating the skyline. Just chimneys and tiled rooftops and a few spires, the Salute's amazing domes the first thing a visitor sees when approaching the city by water. She's read somewhere that the church was built in the 1600s. Venetians thought the Virgin Mary had cured them of the plague everyone was dying from, so they built a place of worship in her honor to protect them from future disease.

While the Muskrateers are roaming the streets and canals, Tillie watches for a spot where she can put her installation. She doesn't have long to assemble it. The work has been forming in her mind since she first got the idea. But it won't come together until she actually starts construction. Lots of surprises always appear in the final product. It's taught her just how much control humans have over their surroundings. Very little, if any. That knowledge has made her more tolerant of her own mistakes. She's tried to embrace them as art rather than getting down on herself.

Sibyl stops in the middle of a street and lights up. "That church is a mirage."

Daddy nods. "We've been walking for an hour. We're back where we started, St. Mark's Square."

Moll is studying a map of the area. She says, "The church is on a peninsula across the Grand Canal. We need to take a ferry."

The midday light on the water is startling, the sun turning it into a dazzling, impenetrable surface. To Tillie it feels like a voyage of no return, the light otherworldly in the way it interacts with the water. It isn't a dance of water and light, but more a symphony, choppy waves catching the rays and playing them, sometimes in jerky rhythms, sometimes legato, the boat bouncing around on the sea but still moving forward. No one speaks, wrapped in the light's ethereal quality. *They've* become art.

And then the spell is broken. The ferry pulls up to the dock and everyone gets off. Tillie stares at the massive Baroque church. It's supported by more than a million wooden piles, a breast atop each octagonal tower, a little lopsided, one larger than the other, announcing Mary's presence.

"My god," Tillie says, "those breasts are enormous, enough to feed a whole city!"

"The whole country," Daddy says.

Sibyl agrees. "Whoppers."

Tillie follows her friends up the stairs leading to the main entrance, flanked by columns. She studies the Byzantine exterior, time frozen in that structure. When she steps inside, it's like entering a large, dank cave, the main light coming from a few windows and some flickering candles. Splotches of red here and there a welcome relief from so much gray. Silence consumes the Muskrateers. The soaring ceilings, the sun captured in a few vividly colored windows. Only Moll kneels, crossing herself. The others stand there, looking around, overwhelmed by the formality.

"Think Mary would've liked this place?" Tillie asks.

Daddy rolls her eyes.

Sibyl says, "I don't see any mangers."

Tillie looks down at the intricately tiled floor. The design and subtle movement of white on black on coral fascinate her, geometric patterns shifting and undulating, the floor moving, rolling like waves. It reminds her of Kazimir Malevich's paintings, how they pulled her inside, throwing her off balance, as if she'd entered the canvas itself. The black segments in the floor tile pattern suck her in, black holes where not even light can escape the powerful grasp of gravity.

Wobbling, she reaches out for a pew to steady herself. Living in San Francisco, she's used to earth tremors and quakes. But Venice? Maybe it's hormones. Jet lag. Or low blood sugar. They haven't had lunch yet.

As long as she doesn't look at the floor, she's okay. The minute she does, things start moving again, and she feels unsteady, as if she's on a boat tossed by huge swells. Hanging out with her dizzy mother has made Tillie feel this way at times, out of control, on a roller coaster. But her mother's nowhere near Venice. It's better for Tillie's health to stay away from her. Whenever they're together, Tillie fogs up and has trouble breathing. Asthma attacks. The only time she has them. Her mother is oblivious to all this. Enclosed in a protective bubble of denial, she's shielded not only from aging—she looks like she could last another ninety-plus years—but also from life itself. At times, Tillie envies the way she just plows ahead, ignoring anything that doesn't fit her world and perceptions, an artist in her own right.

Sinking into a pew, Tillie sits immobile, though her feet feel as if they're still in motion, on a treadmill, the earth speeding up underneath her. She has the unpleasant sensation of entering the last third of her life. A swift descent. Over the edge. Next stop? Don't answer.

Daddy intrudes on her reverie, calling out, "Hey, a Black Madonna!"

Tillie glances at the painting of a mother and child, lit up in a recessed area, their skin a dark chocolate color.

Eyes avoiding the tiles, Tillie carefully stands and feels her way along the pews till she reaches the painting, ignoring someone in black who hovers nearby. She squints at the writing on a plaque under the image: "La Madonna della Salute, 12 C."

"Think she's related to Othello?" Daddy whispers. "She looks Moorish."

"Or a man in drag," Tillie says. "See how thick her neck is? No wonder she seems depressed."

"Is that a baby she's holding in her arm or a wizened old man?"

Tillie says, "Or even an old woman."

"Jesus," Daddy says. "A woman! Mary's a man. And her son's a woman. Cross-dressing? Christ."

Sibyl has joined them. "We're wasting our time here," she says. "I could use a glass of wine and a smoke."

Tillie also could use something to steady herself. A glass of wine and some food sound good. Glancing over her shoulder, she's unable to shake the feeling that someone is watching them, and she still can't look at the floor without getting vertigo. Maybe she's having a past life experience. Could she have lived in Venice in another century?

It makes sense. This city feels more like home than anywhere else. Nearly everything about Venice appeals to her—the ambiance, the history, the beauty, the color, the art, the architecture. The blending of so many periods and styles. Her favorite art gallery is the Accademia. All the Northern Italian painters speak to her—Titian, Giorgione, Veronese, Tintoretto, Tiepolo, Bellini. Their use of color and emotion. The dramatic contrasts and tension. Yes, she should be a Venetian. If art and architecture can survive through the centuries, why not humans? The Madonna of the Salute was created in the twelfth century, but she lives on. It gives Tillie hope.

Except Tillie herself is starting to feel headless, haunted. Something is shaking up her foundations. The earth is stirring under her feet. She needs to find her sea legs.

"I'm ready to move on," Tillie says. "What about you guys?"

"Yeah, I'm ready," Moll says. "It's too much like a museum here."

Sibyl's at the back of the cathedral, muffling a cough.

Again Tillie sees some movement out of the corner of her eye. Someone is watching them, lurking in the church's shadows, listening to their conversation. A flurry of black that sounds like the swish of wings. A giant bat? She freezes. Someone is darting from row to row, playing hide and seek with them. In a black robe and clerical collar. Bald head, a fringe of gray hair above his ears, a beard. Rimless glasses. Candlelight bouncing off the lenses. He's peering over the top of a pew.

Their eyes meet, and Cupid's arrows pierce them.

Father Lazarus Rises

No wonder Tillie's been getting dizzy. Her world has just been turned upside down.

Sibyl strolls over and shakes her arm. "What's up? You sick?"

Tillie stands there, pointing. Sibyl glances at the priest.

"I think I've found my father," Tillie says.

"Your father?" Sibyl hisses. "Jesus, Tillie, I didn't think you had one."

Tillie isn't listening, absorbed by the feeling charging her body like a battery long unused. A tingling sensation awakens her vulva. She's reminded of Inanna, the Sumerian goddess of heaven and earth, a myth she's consumed the way others might read the Bible. She's memorized Inanna's hymn to her consort Tammuz, and it gushes now from her mouth.

> He has sprouted; he has burgeoned;
> He is lettuce planted by the water.
> He is the one my womb loves best.

The Black Madonna in the painting trembles at the passion in Tillie's voice and lowers her eyelids. Moll runs up to Tillie, whispering, "Shhh! For god's sake. You'll get us thrown out, reciting all that sex stuff."

Tillie waves Moll away, her eyes, glazed over, still focused on the priest, the words—like the returning tide—refusing to be held back.

My well-stocked garden of the plain,
My barley growing high in its furrow . . .

She rubs her hands over her body, rotating her hips suggestively and thrusting out her pelvis. The other Muskrateers stare at her in disbelief.

My honey-man, my honey-man sweetens me always.
My lord, the honey-man of the gods,
He is the one my womb loves best.

Tillie flops onto a pew and lies there, writhing, her back arched.

He is the one my womb loves best,
He is lettuce planted by the water.

"Come on," Sibyl says, coughing. "Let's get some food, eh. All that talk of lettuce and barley and honey. You're just hungry, kid."

Drifting towards the door, Daddy says, "You guys ready to blow this place? I've seen enough."

A voice blurts out, "I'm Father Lazarus, and I've risen."

Tillie moves closer to him and laughs when he swipes at the bulge in his robe, clearly an erection, the top of his head no higher than her breasts. Her Berkeley friends would call him vertically challenged because he's shorter than Tillie, and she's no giant. But he has everything any man does—and more.

He also has Tillie's heart, as pure as when she was sixteen. Purer. The intensity takes her by surprise. Agape? No. She feels too much lust for that. Maybe some mix of agape and erotic and whatever else has been stirred between them. A potent brew.

He falls to his hands and knees at Tillie's feet.

The church bells ring, announcing midday mass. A flustered Father Lazarus scrambles to his feet, stepping on his robe and tripping himself, entangled in its confines. He finally breaks free and brushes the dust from his black habit. Church rituals reclaim him. For now.

TILLIE'S AWAKENING

A heavy melancholy settles on Tillie as she walks out of the church and into the sunlight. She feels as if she's been time traveling, time itself scrambled, not linear any longer but a palimpsest, creating the illusion of depth. Like the geometric patterns in the floor of the church. *Now* where is she? Almost the twenty-first century. What is a century? One hundred years that dissolve like sugar granules in liquid, leaving only the slippery slope of memory. No longer under the Salute's influence, she lands back on earth with a thud.

"I could use a drink," Sibyl says, hacking, fumbling around in her purse for a cigarette. "What in hell happened back there? You were pretty out of it, and that priest was loco."

"What was it with you and that priest?" Moll asks.

Tillie just flashes a Mona Lisa smile and climbs aboard a vaporetto, still feeling the impact of what happened in the church.

"See you later at Sibyl's," she calls out, wanting to be alone for a while, not ready to answer her friends' questions.

When the boat arrives at the St. Mark's Square stop, she follows the other passengers, dazed, part of her still on the water, bobbing and bouncing over waves. Her world has cracked open, and here she is crawling out, viewing her surroundings anew.

Sunlight does a dizzy dance on the water and climbs the walls. Venetian women sell masks, the holes for eyes haunting, unfathomable. Facades of crumbling red brick buildings shimmer, and a pigeon makes a nest in the fold of a canvas awning outside a café. Tillie loses herself in food smells drifting from each restaurant, simmering garlic and onion and tomatoes teasing passersby. A buzz of voices chattering in Italian/Spanish/Greek/Hungarian/English/German/Swedish/Japanese merges like the Tower of Babel. Children call out, gulls screech, and a sea breeze carries the fishy smell over the square. Iridescent soap bubbles cascade from an open second-story window and hover. They reflect the Square's bustle before popping and spreading a fine spray on Tillie's face and bare arms.

She eases into a chair at an outdoor cafe and orders a beer and *cicchetti*. While waiting for food and drink to arrive, Tillie plans her first confession, a great excuse to see the priest again. But reality is sinking in.

What a mess I'm in, falling for a fucking celibate. He can't marry me, and he lives in another country. I want to sin with him, but I can't seem to do things the easy way. I want to unbolt all my locks and let in something foreign. It's scary to be so open. Anything can slip in. Oh, and wouldn't I like something slippery? I shouldn't be thinking this way about a man of God. He'll just think I'm another sex-starved aging American, though I'm actually still Canadian at heart. It's nice to feel vital and juicy again, not parched like the Sahara Desert.

Later, while wandering around St. Mark's, Tillie replays what happened at the Santa Maria della Salute, trying to make sense of it all. But it doesn't make sense, no matter how many times she pushes forward and rewind.

Then it hits her. Father Lazarus strongly resembles Toulouse-Lautrec, her spiritual father. She discovered him in art school and read everything she could find about his life. His deformity attracted her as much as did his painting. Kinky things have always intrigued her. The dregs—others' discards—contain for her the essence of existence. Refuse can reveal more about a culture than the highest art because people often discard what they don't value in themselves.

Toulouse-Lautrec was drawn to the vitality he found among other misfits of his time: bohemians, prostitutes, circus performers, actresses, and dancers. He redeemed them in his drawings. His ability to transform them in his art was equivalent to a priest's ability to turn bread and wine into the flesh and blood of Christ. Toulouse-Lautrec not only lived for his art—he *was* his art.

He appealed to Tillie because she also has felt rejected, dumped by a father who never claimed her and raised by a mother who was out to lunch most of the time. If Toulouse-Lautrec could produce art that endures in spite of his affliction and circumstances, maybe there's hope for Tillie.

Father Lazarus also reminds her of Bif. He first introduced her to the world of art and artists. He made Tillie question conventional white culture, which she found terribly uptight, sexually and otherwise. Afraid of anything that deviated from the norm.

Toulouse-Lautrec and Bif make a potent combination.

Tillie hangs around St. Mark's all afternoon, still buzzing from the jolt that hit her earlier. Sipping beer and watching people, she lets the sights and sounds wash over her. The buildings creak and settle deeper into pilings. A stream of people passes in and out of St. Mark's Church, and she can't help thinking of Mark's bones, buried there, stolen from the infidels and given a home in Italian soil.

Later, she relaxes in Sibyl's living room after finishing an impromptu dinner they've all thrown together—pasta coated with olive oil and fresh Parmesan, served with a simple green salad. Still jet-lagged, both Moll and Daddy have gone to bed early. Tillie is thinking about her installation and the priest while watching Sibyl start a new puzzle. The pieces form a tiny mountain on the dining room table. Sibyl sits there in the mellow lamplight, patiently sorting through them, putting all the edges into a separate pile.

Her bond with these pieces of cardboard intrigues Tillie. Making connections that eventually reveal an underlying theme genuinely seems to please her, though it doesn't happen without some effort and concentration. It's as if by fitting together these parts, she's assembling her own broken self.

In the golden glow, bent over the puzzle and profiled against the wood-paneled wall, Sibyl resembles a woman caught in a Vermeer painting, intent on her project, depicted with lots of ochre and umber and rich, dark tones. One pearl earring glints on Sibyl's ear, a tiny world contained within it, the pearl's luminosity a contrast to the dark spot marking time in her lung.

Tillie's surprised to see Sibyl wearing pearls. They seem too conventional for her, not the kind of jewelry Tillie would expect her to choose. Yet just when Tillie thinks she's captured the other Muskrateers in her camcorder or has figured out who they are, they shift slightly, leaving a gap through which some other configuration shines.

Sibyl studies the puzzle, absently stroking the cat that's adopted them, a black one and a chip off the old block: like Sibyl, it looks as if it could use a few square meals. Still intent on her work, she lights a cigarette and blows smoke rings that break over Tillie's head.

TILLIE'S FIRST CONFESSION

Before the others are even up, Tillie leaves the apartment the next morning for the six thirty AM confession at the Santa Maria della Salute. Father Lazarus is listed as the confessor, and she has a lot to confess—a whole lifetime. Maybe more. The thought scares the hell out of her. Unzipping for a stranger. Exposing herself. Being vulnerable to the church's scrutiny. She almost turns back, but the priest, a strong magnet, draws her into his world.

Fog shrouds the city, so she makes her way to the vaporetto by sound and touch—water sloshing against the pilings, her footsteps echoing in the early morning streets. She stops for a few minutes at the water's edge to center and calm herself, knees bent, arms outstretched in front of her, communing with the water spirits and drawing in the earth's energy. Whenever she's by the water, Tillie performs this ritual, feeling a connection with Eastern practices, images of robed gurus floating past, seated with legs crossed in a lotus position. She does a few Tai Chi movements—white crane and sleeping dragon—to loosen herself up and prepare for her meeting.

The scent of coffee and freshly baked rolls drifts out of a café. Tillie's stomach growls, and she almost makes a detour. But Father Lazarus's image propels her forward and onto the boat. It glides confidently through the water, also following some inner radar.

As the boat approaches the Salute, the fog parts and the sun breaks through, flooding the church with its light, making the domes appear chalky. The bleached-out facade seems an odd contrast to the shadowy interior, the heart of the church a Black Madonna and a black priest, not the usual pasty-skinned cleric you expect to find in these places. She checks herself. She knows nothing of this Father Lazarus except he has a famous name. He might be as white on the inside as the church is on the outside.

When she enters the sanctuary this time, she doesn't look down at the floor. Eyes staring straight ahead, she marches to the confessional. It's as old as the church. Relieved to be the only confessor, she opens the door, sits down on the tiny wooden ledge, and waits, trying to ignore the claustrophobic feelings that threaten her. The booth reminds her of a coffin stood on end.

Not much to look at. A little light pokes through a rectangular opening covered with wire mesh and located high in the door. Several initials are carved into the wood. The space smells like stale sweat and dust and the stench of many sinners. Tillie is working up a sweat herself, staring at the little sliding panel that opens into the other side of the confessional where her confessor sits. The two of them are so close that—except for the wall between them—it's like being in bed together. No wonder the Catholic church has survived this long. The confessional offers more than release from sin.

Clearing her throat, she wonders if she should start with "Father, I have sinned." Born in sin, has her whole life been illegitimate? Just one orgy of transgression? She's never been baptized, though she was raised a Christian. Nothing formal. Dropping into churches sometimes at Easter or Christmas to sop up a little grape juice and tiny squares of stale white bread. Not long enough to do any real damage. No real wine in the churches her mother attended sporadically.

For years she thought Santa was Jesus in disguise; he brought gifts to everyone on his own birthday. But after seeing her mum's lover dressed as Santa when she was ten, Tillie became even more confused. God was sleeping with her mother?

A baritone voice rattles the confessional's walls, so deep and resonant it seems to come from God himself. No female gods in this church. Tillie hangs onto her seat, afraid she'll start vibrating from the reverberations and levitate out of the booth.

At first she's so startled that she doesn't hear what the priest is saying. A flurry of language surrounds her, spoken with an English accent. The rich, rounded tones have as much impact on her as the eye contact did the day before. The words enter her fragmented soul, piecing together its parts and patching them onto the priest's own tattered spirit. The opus has begun. Their words slip through the grate separating them, popping open, interpenetrating and piercing the two confessors.

I've lived in words all my life and now I find myself almost speechless in front of you my lady my wild mushroom my splendid rainbow your presence brings balm I would recognize you anywhere the mother I never knew died giving birth to me I've never forgiven myself my father was an Italian soldier in Ethiopia fighting for Mussolini spilling his seed on African soil and then disappearing I would still be there begging in the streets if someone hadn't left me at a church I was raised in an orphanage run by English nuns an Italian priest later took me with him to Rome to study the doctrine so the church has become my mother and father for better or worse I've never found my own father though I've followed in his foot-steps producing others who'll never know their father and will surely haunt me in heaven

I've lived a pretty rough life you know had a kid and the rest of it existing from hand to mouth half the time never knowing where the next dollar's coming from and look I neglected my son when he was younger I mean what can you expect from a teenage mother who didn't have a clue but I love him and wasn't a bad mother on purpose I've tried to make up for it I'm better than my own mother who was always off in her own world my biological father a mystery to me I've always wondered what it would be like to meet him someday so I've traveled around thinking I might run into him but I never have and I still wonder if I ever will of course how will we know each other besides the guy's probably dead by now so what's the use chasing a lost cause I'd sooner make art and let it be my father in heaven

For an hour they ignore the line-up of people outside the booth waiting to confess. They rap discreetly on the door, grumbling. Tillie and Father Lazarus end up blessing each other, and then they fall out of the confessional, Father Lazarus wrapping his arms around Tillie's waist and burying his face in her breasts. Tillie wraps her arms around his head. A relationship is starting, made on earth if not in heaven. The smattering of shocked onlookers cross themselves, their mouths hanging open.

Tillie hasn't seriously considered that the man she's fallen for is, in effect, married. It's the whole bloody Catholic and apostolic church she's competing with. Her priest is essentially married to another man: Jesus— the Christ story mainly a father/son event. Not much room for women except as handmaidens.

It occurs to Tillie that even Mary, the mother, is depicted as a servant who didn't have any say in the matter. But she did. Images of the saintly, passive mother mask the truth: Mary was ruthless and ambitious, wanting her son on the throne. He was going to be the son of God, and by God she got her wish. She's the one who breathed into Jesus his aspirations, brooding on them even before she got pregnant and especially when she was in labor that long night in the stable. Jesus might have been born just another animal, but he wasn't going to remain one. He became God.

But at the moment, here on earth, the church bells are ringing again, signaling mass or some other ritual that excludes Tillie. Before he leaves her, Father Lazarus whispers urgently in her ear: "Meet me tonight in the garden at the Palazzo Cavalli-Franchetti. Eight PM." And then he rushes off, looking a little like the Mad Hatter, his robe billowing out behind him, almost giving him wings.

THE KAT'S PAW

Tillie's afraid if she talks to anyone about her recent meeting with the priest, the whole thing could turn out to be a dream and dissolve. She also refuses to dwell on their mutual confessions, not wanting to think about it too much. The intensity might frighten her off. So she decides not to return to Sibyl's until later. Much later. The others would only pester her with questions, and she has no answers. She'll wait until her meeting that night with the priest before thinking of him again. Maybe.

Floating out of the church, she resembles Little Miss Muffett *and* the spider in the lacy, white, ruffled, ankle-length bloomers she's wearing under a black miniskirt. Lana Turner would have died for the body-hugging red top. Tillie's costume looks almost normal in Venice with *Carnevale*, celebrated every February. Except it isn't February. It's September, and for her, with or without a watch, there's no time to waste. Due to return home in less than three weeks, time's running out on her. A new man has shaken her foundations. And a new installation has its claws in her, pushing for completion, dependent on her for its existence. The feeling reminds her of the last month of her pregnancy when Valentine had dropped. Insistent on getting her attention.

He has her attention again now. So far, he's been the most important male in her life, a kind of father *and* son since she didn't really have a father. This encounter with the priest is bound to stir memories of Valentine, if only because of the guilt she feels for falling for someone else. She wanders through the maze of streets, thinking of him, feeling some affinity for Mary and her relationship with Jesus. No one talks about how Jesus must have affected Mary, not just in the sacrifice she made, but also in the impact he personally had on her, opening her up in new ways. Forcing her to see the world through his eyes and not just her own. Taking up permanent residence in her heart.

Valentine would think this new man was a blast. He'd say, "You're sure you didn't conjure him up for an installation?"

She would smile sweetly, discretely, not ready yet to reveal how deeply Eros's arrows have pierced her.

Her mind is reeling. She thinks, mothers and sons. Such a vexed relationship. So intimate *and* so separate. Sons slide down the birth canal, the site of both procreation and sex. What primal, incestuous guilt they must feel for having passed through this sacred place in their mother's bodies, their entry into the world a kind of orgasmic spasm. Most men can't avoid a kind of incest with their mother. It's a given.

Like the priest, Valentine had also shaken Tillie's foundations, changing the direction her life was to take. Nothing was the same after his birth, and it wasn't just the financial challenge of earning enough to support the two of them, or finding people to care for him while she worked, forcing her to grow up. Fast.

She had been innocent before giving birth, unaware that mothering would deepen her emotionally. Being a mother also gave her dominance over another person—absolute control and authority. It was heady and scary—this responsibility for another life, this ability to influence it forever.

But she had to acknowledge that Valentine had power, too. After he was born, she couldn't claim to be unconscious any longer. She knew too much. She also felt her vision enlarge. She saw the world not only through her eyes but also through his—the male other. She loved the idea that if you take "ale" out of the word "male" and combine the remaining "m" with "other," you get "mother." She wonders why she hasn't noticed that before—mother embraces the idea of maleness and other. Being a mother really is all about opening up in that way. Taking on something unfamiliar. Being enlarged. It's not unlike what happens when people fall in love.

It seemed that as Valentine grew, Tillie became increasingly aware of her impulses to defy convention—her behavior paralleling his. She copied his crazy clothes combos. Valentine had ridden the first wave of punk, dying his hair orange and spiking it, painting his fingernails green, wearing earrings, using her black eyeliner and mascara—experimenting. Crossing borders. At times, it wasn't clear if mother or son was the biggest influence. He imitated her by dropping out of school before graduating, just as she had.

A guitar player and singer, caught up in the music scene, Valentine could get away with his crazy costumes. Performing. Part of a new age. Experimenting with LSD, mescaline, cocaine—the works. Boundaries not so rigidly defined. For him, being outrageous was normal. The rest of the world was out of step, even Tillie, try as she did to keep up.

Tillie spends the day wandering the streets in a daze, unable to concentrate on anything for more than thirty seconds, dropping into several galleries and shops. Seeking inspiration and ideas she can steal for her own work, Tillie also visits some of the Biennale venues. Nothing much registers, but that doesn't prevent her from looking. It's good to be on the move, drifting in and out of the crowded parts of the city, passing over and under the Rialto Bridge, strolling along streets she's never traveled before. Scraps of conversation in other languages provide a comforting background padding she doesn't have to listen to. She stops now and then at a café for a beer and a snack.

Eventually, she drifts into a side street and steps inside a gallery, letting her feet take over. They guide her to a wall of photographs and then stop. Tillie stands in front of them, staring at images that seem oddly familiar, clearing away the haze that's been protecting her like a cocoon since she left the church. She's looking at herself.

That bastard Frank has beaten her to Venice, getting his art out there first. All of the photos he took of her body parts, shot in minute detail, are hung separately. Individually, none of the parts are recognizable as hers. That's some consolation. Nor do they resemble what they actually are.

The crease in her left elbow looks like a child's hairless pubic area. Erotic. Her nostrils, photographed from below and up-close (everything is up-close), appear to be twin train tunnels or the openings to mysterious caves. The sweep of her back, dunes in the desert. The profile of an erect nipple, a sacred temple.

Frank has a way with photos, all right. Deception's the name of his game. After living with him, she can never again believe anything she sees. He can photograph totally unrelated things, convincing the viewer they're actually the same. It makes Tillie doubt her own constitution.

Now she knows how a captured butterfly feels, pinned to a board, wings resembling a kind of a cross. Unable to escape the church's metaphors, she feels like she's been pinned to a cross. A new-age pinup girl.

Before leaving the gallery, she reads the write-up on Frank:

> It is difficult to describe Frank Gallo only as a photographer. His latest experimental works are totally ambiguous and original. He's more of a performance artist in the way each photograph seems part of a larger production, suggesting something happening just offstage.

Ambiguous? Original? Is the curator describing Frank's work or Tillie's body?

Running into Frank in this way, via his art, shakes her up. She stumbles out of the gallery, expecting to see him at any minute, certain he's lurking somewhere in Venice, aiming his camera at her. Enough. She doesn't want to get tangled up with that dude again. She spent enough hours listening to the egomaniac go on and on about his theories of art and the big plans he had for one-man shows, ignoring her and her work except when he wanted something. Frank had seemed unable to talk about anything but himself. She refuses to be his captive audience any longer.

Except he controls her now in a way she doesn't quite understand. These pictures keep her attached to him, as if she's his creation. He's transformed her into art but left her incomplete, fragmented, having taken her apart and abandoned her. A kind of female Humpty Dumpty. Who'll put her back together again? Sibyl? Father Lazarus? Herself?

She notes the gallery's name and its location, the Kat's Paw, Calle del Mondo Nuovo, hoping she can find it again. In the days ahead, she'll feel compelled to visit the place. To be in contact with herself. Resurrected.

Tillie Stakes Out the Palazzo Cavalli—Franchetti

Tillie reaches the Palazzo Cavalli-Franchetti a little early, needing to center herself after the shock of seeing Frank's photos. She gets lost only twice trying to find the place, not counting the numerous times she went astray earlier in the day, washing ashore like flotsam at La Giudecca and then at the Lido. While there, she spent some time haunting the shore, poking around in the debris, looking for objects she could use in her piece. Tillie had filled her net shopping bag with a star fish, its one eye staring up at her blankly; a doll's plastic arm, the tiny fingernails painted scarlet; an old hardcover book, written in Italian, the pages waterlogged; a kaleidoscope, the lens broken; a piece of driftwood that resembles a Canadian beaver—or was it a muskrat? Found art.

Now she stares at the Palazzo's ornate facade. A Greek cross is carved into the white lacey trim that frames the floor-to-ceiling windows. More found art. The early evening light softens the building's angular corners, the place reminding her of an elderly beauty, a bit overdressed and trying to keep up appearances. She knows the feeling.

Tillie half expects her suitor to step out on the second-floor balcony and burst into song. Or maybe she's the one who should be serenading him, a reverse Romeo and Juliet scene. She can feel the "Indian Love Call" welling up in her throat.

"I'll be loving youououououou, with a love that's trueueueueueueue."

A passing gondolier drowns her out with his rendition of "Cara Mia." His boat glides by, a pair of embracing lovers sprawled in its belly.

After passing through the gate into the garden, Tillie strolls the labyrinthine path, stopping and centering herself periodically. Knees bent, arms outstretched, eyes partly closed, she feels the earth's energy surge up through her feet and into her body. She chants "Om" so the sound can vibrate her third eye, but it rattles her chest instead, making her cough.

On the move again, she rounds a corner, and there he is, standing in the path, appearing to materialize out of the garden. She shrieks and swoons, lurching forward, and so does the priest. Each falls into the other's arms, rolling off into the bushes together.

Titillated by his bushy beard grazing her neck, Tillie inhales the distinctive male body odor, a mixture of sweat and testosterone. Both of them would still be savoring the tender sprouts of love but for an intrusion. The torso image appears again to Tillie, distracting her. She groans and disentangles herself from her new lover's embrace, straightening her bloomers.

"I'm haunted," she says, staring at him, relieved he isn't wearing his robes. She runs her fingers through her spiked hair. "This is crazy! What do I call you? Father? Dad?"

"Bud."

"Bud?" She wonders if the location has inspired him, with so many flowers sprouting, but he tells her that the orphanage gave him the name.

His hands folded in his lap, he stares at them, avoiding her eyes. "I chose Lazarus—my favorite Biblical character—when I became a priest." He brushes leaves and twigs off his black turtleneck and trousers. "I use it as a last name now since I don't know my father's."

"Call me Tillie. I changed my surname to Bloom after reading *Ulysses*. I thought the name might bring me luck. Make me bloom, you know?"

He nods. "I'm sure Leopold Bloom would be proud of his daughter."

She can't help but notice that "bud" and "bloom" have a semantic relationship. She hopes it's a good omen. If they should marry and he chooses not to keep his church name, Lazarus, he could become Bud Bloom. She wonders why men and women don't just exchange surnames when they marry—the man taking on the woman's, the woman taking on the man's—so they each have an opportunity to enlarge their identities. In the midst of her musings, she glimpses the torso from her peripheral vision.

"Oh Christ, not again."

He frowns. "I hurt your feelings?"

"No, nothing like that. I've been having visions since I arrived in Venice. I think I need to be exorcised."

He bows slightly. "The church's chief exorcist at your service, Madame. What's possessing you?"

"A pregnant black woman's torso. Reminds me of the *Venus de Milo*. Or the *Black Madonna*."

"No wonder. The Black Madonna appeared to people during the plague—and still does. The mother of Venice. The city might not exist without her."

Tillie shrugs. "I'm not a Catholic. Why me?"

"She's ecumenical."

"But I'm not even a Christian."

"She isn't either."

"The Black Madonna?"

"She wasn't baptized. She doesn't take communion."

"Got it. I guess Christ wouldn't be Christian either."

Tillie watches a snail chomp away at a flower. It reminds her of how priests transform bread and wine into body and blood. She almost gags at the cannibalistic quality of the Eucharist, the communicant's symbolic swallowing of Christ's body. Yet it isn't much different from the cannibalistic nature of art, the artist devouring everything in her path that helps express her vision—and art devouring the artist. Consuming each other.

Relieved to have a sympathetic ear, Tillie asks, "Why am I just seeing her torso?"

He waves his hands, as if conducting a choir or giving a blessing. "Maybe that's the essential part of her."

"Her heart and reproductive organs? I'd be weeping too if I were her."

"But you aren't her, my dear. You have lovely hands and arms and legs."

"I have a head too!"

"Indeed. And a good one." He leans over and brushes her lips with his, making them tingle, and flicks a leaf from her shoulder.

"How should the exorcism proceed?" she asks, touching his cheeks and beard with her fingertips, as if reading Braille.

"I don't know," Bud says. "Each case is different. I'll need to study yours more closely." He nibbles on her neck and she moans with delight, surrendering to the darkness that's descending on the garden *and* to his embrace.

Hidden by shrubs, they nestle in each other's arms, talking and nuzzling. He tells her that in college he majored in theater arts. Acting gave him a new life, tools to tolerate the one he was born into. He discovered how the imagination can turn grotesque circumstances into high art. It's why he chose the name Lazarus when he became a priest. Like his namesake, Bud also had risen from a kind of death and into a new life. He knew the roles he might get on stage would be limited. How many half-Black, stunted Laurence Oliviers are there?

It's dark now, and only his sonorous voice fills the night. Tillie listens, eager to learn more about this man, feeling like a priest herself in the way she listens to his confession.

"Priests are already oddities," he says. "We denounce normal relationships with women. Take vows of poverty. Refuse to procreate. I've blended in, become part of God's family. In secular life, I was invisible to women except to be pitied. As a priest, I've had to fight them off, sometimes successfully, other times not."

She squirms while listening to this latest revelation. She hasn't expected him to be celibate. In fact, she prefers that he not be. But she doesn't fancy the idea of him fighting off hordes of women or sharing him with anyone else.

"You're very quiet," Bud says. "Do you want to hear more?"

She says, "Ma si," but she's really thinking "Ma no." Yet she doesn't want to offend him by saying so. She feels he's trying to open himself to her, and she doesn't want to close him down.

He continues: "Often I wear what's essentially a long dress. I think it makes me seem safe to women. My more cloistered world is similar to women's when they were sheltered exclusively in the household. Some women recognize a bit of themselves in me. Something denied and deformed but wanting expression."

Tillie wonders if she fits into this description of the women he's known. Then she brushes away the idea, wishing the headless Black Madonna would appear again to distract her.

"The priestly garb I wear suggests I have a direct line to God. That could be intimidating for some women. But my size makes me less threatening— I'm both son and father. I've managed to manipulate the structure and the hierarchy, finding the acceptance and love that has transformed me from an oddity into God's messenger."

"Whew! Heavy-duty stuff."

"I know. Until now, my early sixties by the way, I've led a satisfactory, cultured life. But I've never deeply fallen for a woman before. Many times I've spoken of love from the pulpit, but I've never fully understood its power, except theoretically. I've assumed the novels I've read and the movies I've seen have overstated Eros's arrows. Fantasies. Fluff. Real people don't fall in love, their lives forever changed from the encounter. Now look at me!"

Her head is bursting from so much of Bud packed into a few minutes, but it's understandable given her fast-approaching departure date. They don't have time for a leisurely courtship.

He suddenly jumps to his feet and announces, "I have to leave before midnight or I turn into a pumpkin."

"Wait! Can you have dinner with me and my friends tomorrow night at our place?"

"Not tomorrow—I'm already committed—but the following evening."

She yells the address to him, and then he melts into the night.

Tillie lingers, digesting these discoveries about Bud. Somehow, in this setting, everything he said seems reasonable, even justifiable. Of course he would have sexual relations with women. Vows of celibacy needn't extend to the body. It's enough to be spiritually pure. He fits her ideal of a true priest, someone who inhabits multiple worlds and can lead others into them.

While savoring the past few hours *and* this place, Tillie realizes she's found a site for Death in Menace—DIM. The garden of the Palazzo Cavalli-Franchetti. A revisit to the Garden of Eden theme. Female body parts returning to that original garden in protest, poking out of bushes and from under benches. Taped voices rigged up so they seem to come from the flowers. Maybe she'll play them at a higher speed so the words aren't fully discernible and they resemble something unearthly.

She decides against her original vision of the walk-in meat locker effect, but she'll still spin replicas of the Four Muskrateers' legs pinwheel fashion from stakes driven into the ground so they resemble surreal giant flower petals. She'll paint them vivid pinks and oranges and reds. The stakes could evoke the witchy stuff associated with women, a complaint against all those burned at the stake in previous centuries.

She'll also include torsos as part of the presentation, a symbol of how women have been dismembered culturally, unable to function fully. She's known lots of women who run around as if they've misplaced their heads, her mother being one of them.

It reminds Tillie of chickens whose heads her mother had chopped off on the farm. They tore around the yard for at least five minutes afterward, not realizing they'd lost something essential. It was gruesome and amazing, blood splattering everywhere, the chickens thoroughly out of control. Tillie was sure at those times she could still hear the hen squawking, but of course that couldn't have happened. It must have been the other chickens screeching in protest.

She never knew where one of these beheaded chickens would end up, darting everywhere. Sometimes, Tillie and her friends would play dodge the chicken. She feels she's playing that game now with the headless body that's pursuing her in visions.

Bird

At breakfast, the Muskrateers sit on the balcony in their nightclothes, sipping strong Italian coffee and munching on sweet rolls. Moll is the first to speak, addressing Tillie.

"Did you fall into a black hole yesterday?"

Tillie brushes some crumbs from her lap. "You could call it that. Ran into Bud."

Actually, parts of Tillie's life feel like one big black hole. She fell into it once for a year. Severe depression. Married to a jock—a womanizer, her second husband. Another loser. She was working at a dead-end office job. Fucking up her kid. Her life had seemed like one big dead end.

"Bud?" the others cry out.

"He's the priest we met at Santa Maria della Salute. Real name is Bud."

"Wild," Daddy says. "So did you guys hang out together?"

"Sort of," Tillie says.

"And?" Sibyl asks.

"Frank's photographs of me are hanging in a gallery here."

"Frank? I thought we were talking about Bud," Moll says.

"It was a real shock."

"Bud?"

"No, the photos. There I am, for all of Venice to see."

"So what's the deal with Bud?" Sibyl asks.

Tillie pulls her hand across her mouth, as if closing a zipper. "He's coming for dinner tomorrow night if that's okay with everyone."

"Cool," Sibyl says. "We'll have a party."

Tillie wants to avoid any more questions about Bud, afraid they might stimulate her own concerns, and excuses herself. She heads for St. Mark's Square, planting herself at an outdoor table. Watching tourists, she's carried along on the river of languages being spoken there, not following any particular conversation. Lounging in a chair, sipping on a German dark beer, she lets her mind drift, halfheartedly aiming her camcorder now and then if she sees an arresting image.

Some passersby glance in her direction, laughing and pointing. Tillie thinks a street performer has set up near her, and she looks to her right and left. Nothing. The performer must be behind her. Tillie slowly rotates in her chair. Nothing. Maybe the person has gone.

She returns to dozing in the midday sun, soaking up the ambiance of this historic square and fantasizing about Bud, dimly aware that her head feels heavier than usual. Tillie opens her eyes. Several people are clustered in front of her, smiling, gesticulating. Something flutters near her left ear. She notices a dark shape in her peripheral vision and some flapping. Then she hears a cooing sound and feels a faint breath on her neck. What seems to be a fingernail pokes her.

A kid shouts out, "Mummy, Mummy, the lady has a pigeon on her head!"

Tillie feels claws digging into her scalp and a beak pecking at her hair. The sensation is almost erotic, like a head massage with lots of different pressures. Has Bud turned into a bird?

Bird flaps its wings and drops to the table, tilting its head from side to side, looking at her first from one eye, a sea-green color, and then the other, a lifeless gray. It dips its beak into her beer, pecking at the pizza crust she's left uneaten. Temporarily sated, it jumps onto her right shoulder and nuzzles her ear.

Someone passes the table and drops a few foreign coins onto it. More and more people gather. Tillie realizes they think she has trained the bird to do tricks. Since she can use the money, she pushes the situation for what it's worth. Maybe her feathered friend can talk or even sing. This could be a *real* moneymaker.

Tillie has always liked an audience, so she puts out her hand, and Bird hops from her shoulder onto her middle finger, its claws gripping it. That gets a round of applause. Bird and Tillie bow, and she hears the clink of more coins hitting the table. One falls on the ground. Bird hops down and grabs it in its beak, returns the coin to the tabletop, and takes another sip of beer. Another round of applause. More coins. Even a little paper money. And no taxes.

They keep it up until Tillie has enough cash to buy wine and some groceries for the dinner party the next night. Sibyl, really into her new domestic self, has offered to cook the meal; Tillie has eagerly accepted. Her dinner parties usually consist of canned tuna and canned veggies, a kind of salad niçoise without the French touch. She doesn't think she needs to prove her culinary skills to Bud, but she'd just as soon not take a chance. Still, Tillie's a little leery of Sibyl's motives, given her taste for Tillie's men.

Ready to move on, Tillie grabs her backpack and heads for one of the streets that run off the square. Bird hitches a ride on her shoulder, cooing in her ear and nibbling her ear lobe. She lowers it to the ground and starts running, trying to lose the pigeon in one of the side streets, but it waddles after her, managing to keep up, tail bobbing up and down and flying a bit. Tillie takes a hunk of bread from a table in a sidewalk café and scatters some breadcrumbs near a fountain in a tiny square. While Bird's distracted, she runs away, diving inside a nearby Internet café and stopping at the counter. A young guy is standing there, and she tells him she wants to check her email. He answers her in English.

"You want to-a rent a machine-a? Sixty thousand lira for an hour-a."

She figures that's about six dollars. It shouldn't take her more than twenty minutes to do her business, so she nods and follows him to one of the empty computers.

Young men are sitting in front of the machines, eyes fixed on the monitors, worshiping at the electronic altar. Most are playing an interactive game with one another, shouting and cursing raucously when a character on the screen makes a key move.

Tillie sits down and boots up, connecting with Mailstart.com, soon buried under an avalanche of spam. She quickly sorts through about five hundred messages, dumping them into the trash, contributing in her own small way to cleaning up the electronic airways and making the Internet a kinder, gentler place for all. She's humming along, skimming the subject lines, when the words "Frank's Memorial" stop her.

Dead.

Tanya, a friend since art school days, has sent Tillie the message. She opens it and starts reading:

> Hey, Tillie.
>
> I know you're away, but I hope you're checking your messages. Thought you'd want to know that Frank passed suddenly a week ago. He had emergency surgery for cancer of the trachea. They say the chemicals he used over the years for processing film caused it. The tumor was too far along, and he had to have radiation and chemo, the works, really weakening him. He got pneumonia. That's what did him in.
>
> We just had a memorial at Bodega Bay. His kids turned up for the service (Did you know he had four of them, all by different mothers? None were made legal by marriage so they can't claim his estate) and they got into a fight over who should get his ashes. It seemed sanest to divide them up equally. I didn't think you'd want any, so Frank will be scattered to the four winds, literally. Maybe he'll even turn up in Venice! You know Frank. He always loved to travel.
>
> Anyway, you'll flip when you hear that he left you all his artwork and supplies. Isn't that wild? He actually made out a will before he croaked. His kids get the rest. The attorney for his estate wants to talk to you ASAP so they can sign off his photographs and camera equipment to you! Here's his name and phone number: Michael Love, (415) 554-2583.

P.S. The weirdest thing happened at his wake. This pigeon turned up out of nowhere (Can you imagine a pigeon at the beach?) and wouldn't leave us alone. When people were making their tributes to Frank, the bird had to be in the center of everything. It jumped on the women's heads, their shoulders (though it seemed to only do this with women). Followed us everywhere. Dove into the food, the drinks. I was ready to wring its neck until someone suggested it might be Frank's spirit trying to get our attention.

That really got to me. The bird must have sensed I was weakening because the damn thing even got into the car with me, refusing to be left behind. (Or maybe it needed to hitch a ride back to the city!) Its connection to Frank seemed so strong that I took it home with me, forgetting what a mess pigeons can make. (Of course, Frank made a few messes in his life, too!) Every time I tried to get rid of it, I'd find it on our doorstep again. I mean, I'd drop it in a park blocks away with some food. One day I even took it to Union Square in San Francisco so it would have some buddies to hang out with. But it was always there when I got home. This went on for several days, I forget how many now, and then it disappeared as mysteriously as it arrived. What a trip! You think it was Frank?

Frank dead? His work now hers? Holy shit. She hadn't even loved the guy. A relationship of convenience for both of them, it cut living expenses in half and provided a warm body to sleep with. He must've gone soft in his last days. Or was putting her in his will just another way to control her from the grave?

She sits there in shock, trying to take in this news. She's had uncles die—her mum's brothers. And her mother could go any minute. When Tillie was in her teens, she had friends die or commit suicide, but she never identified with them then. Their deaths seemed very distant; it could never happen to her. But at this age, her friend's departure makes death seem up-close and personal, not an abstract idea. And it has happened so fast. The last time she saw Frank, about four or five months earlier, he was his usual garrulous self.

An image of Sibyl, bent over, hacking, gets mixed up with images of Frank bent over his negatives, resembling an alchemist with his long white hair in a ponytail. Was Frank's death preparing her for Sibyl's? Of course, you're never prepared for someone's death. Besides, there's no defini- tive evidence that Sibyl's in immediate danger. Still, a spot on the lung combined with her chain-smoking and constant coughing doesn't look promising. It's one thing to know in some oblique way that everyone will die—that we're all given a death sentence at birth. But it's something else to face it straight on without any analgesics, as Tillie is now. She wonders who would attend *her* funeral. She needs to put a notice in the personal ads for mourners when she returns to San Francisco.

For some time she feels sealed off inside the Internet, unaware of any- thing around her. Gradually, she becomes conscious again of the sounds in the room. Moaning and groaning punctuated with ecstatic shouts of joy. These computer freaks are all having orgasmic responses to their games, group masturbation through the mouse. To hear of Frank's death in this surreal environment makes sense somehow. Shouts of joy mixed with her own mounting sorrow. These two responses are never far apart, the pain and joy of birth and death. Tragedy and comedy.

Tillie holds back the threatening tears, though she's not sure if they're for Frank or for herself. His death stirs a vision of her own death. She takes inventory of her body, wondering what secrets it's hiding, picturing all of the places where a tumor could be lurking, sites that Frank didn't photo- graph. How might her art be killing *her*? Luckily, installation pieces don't require chemicals. Usually. The genre is pretty benign, except for what it awakens inside the artist in the process of creating it.

She's read that if you get through your sixties intact, you have a better chance of living a long time. But the waiting to safely get through that decade is hell, like looking down a gun barrel that could go off at any moment. She stares at the computer monitor. Its screensaver has taken over, and a bear comes loping towards her out of a dark woods.

Tillie has come to Venice to celebrate life, not to brood on death, though being in a city that's gradually submerging should have tipped her off. Death is always nearby here, palpable in the decomposing structures. The person who said Death is the mother of Beauty had it wrong. Beauty is the mother of Death. Venice certainly is beautiful. But is Death? Her aesthetic side recognizes that a body reduced to mainly bones has a kind of majestic quality, like a sculpture. Reduced to its essence. Is Bird Frank's essence?

Tillie can't say she'll miss her former lover. It was always a relief to see him go to sleep, the only time he didn't talk about himself and his work. The Fates must have black humor, giving him a tumor on the trachea. Anyway, Tillie has always seen Frank as partly dead. He spent most of his life in the dark.

No matter, he was a big part of her life for a period of time and left an imprint, so Tillie can't help but mourn. And she's sorry she didn't get a chance to say goodbye to him. They have unfinished business. They didn't exactly part on good terms as friends or lovers. She already has a big enough guilt complex. Not only does she regret there being no closure between them, but she also has an extra burden. She must carry around the guilt of inheriting his art.

She remembers Tanya's message and, in a daze, jots down Michael Love's name and number, planning to call him later. It's time for her to claim the photos of herself she saw at the Kat's Paw.

She's sitting there, sorting through her complex feelings about Frank, when a consistent tapping sound irritates her. Tillie looks around, ready to tell the culprit to knock it off, but the noise isn't coming from inside the room. Bird is standing outside the plate glass window, tapping against it with its beak. Frank's image flashes in front of her. He had an irritating habit of drumming his fingernails against hard surfaces and would just laugh when she asked him to stop. Has his spirit taken over that poor pigeon and somehow ended up in Venice? Tillie has heard of birds migrating thousands of miles. And pigeons are trained to carry messages over long distances.

She tries to ignore Bird, checking the rest of her email, pushing Frank's death to the farther recesses of her mind. She's never understood how messages can be transmitted electronically. It's enough to make her believe in ghosts, except science and technology are supposed to do the opposite, negate such superstitions. But email messages don't really exist any more than Frank does now; she can erase them with a flick of the mouse. Yet they have a lot of impact, and so does her former lover. He was always the kind of guy who might not want her himself, but he also didn't want anyone else to have her. Selfish and possessive. One reason they separated, other than Tillie being tired of living in the dark with an egomaniac.

Suddenly it *really* dawns on her. She now owns all of the photos he took of her. She can put herself back together again; she doesn't have to depend on Frank or anyone else to do it. That's a great consolation, a reason to celebrate his death. She's been feeling at his mercy, even though they've parted. Now she's really free to hook up with Bud—if he wants her. If she wants him.

Bird's insistent tapping cuts into her thoughts again, and she thinks of her mother's skill at chopping off chickens' heads. If she could kill chickens, what's to stop Tillie from doing it? What does roast pigeon à la mode taste like? When in Rome, do what the Romans do. Don't they eat pigeons? It would be one less thing to buy for their dinner party.

The thought that Bird actually might be Frank reincarnated is the only thing that stops Tillie. Who knows? Maybe reincarnation is an interim state, a kind of holding pattern or decompression stage. Like being in a pupa. Maybe people reincarnate temporarily, moving on eventually to whatever happens after death. If this is what's happening with Frank, she doesn't want to interfere with the process.

Still, though artists are cannibalistic by nature, having Frank for dinner might be going a little too far. So would serving him to her new lover. Even so, she has never believed in transmigration of souls, at least not as the final step. She hopes that, if there is a creator, S/He is more inventive than just recycling souls. Reincarnation doesn't seem very original to her. Ecological, yes, but even a human could think of that idea. Surely if there is a God, S/He can come up with something more imaginative.

A bird is a bird is a bird. Tillie mustn't get sentimental and anthropomorphize a pigeon. Some imprinting must be going on. It mistakes her for its mother. But so did Frank at times. Surely this couldn't be the same bird that turned up at his wake. It would be too bizarre, though she's almost ready to believe anything. She can't help but wonder what Frank would want with her now. Unless he's trying to use her so he can control his estate. She wouldn't put it past him.

After dumping most of her messages, she notices one she's missed. The subject jumps out at her, all in caps: BLACK MADONNA. How could she have overlooked it?

She's about to open the email when Bird hops onto her shoulder—it had slipped through the door when no one was looking—and digs in its claws, hard. Tillie yelps. It jumps onto the keyboard, staring at the computer screen, and does a little dance, unloading a whopper on the control key. The Internet guy with dreadlocks rushes over, holding his nose.

"Hey-a, you're-a ruining my computer! No-a animals allowed. You-a and the bird-a must-a leave." He dabs at Bird's glob with some paper he's snatched off the desk, smearing it around, making it even worse.

Tillie's determined to finish reading her email, but the keyboard is so messed up she can't use it, and she's afraid the guy will charge her to replace the bloody thing. Fucking Bird has hopped onto her head, refusing to come down. She decides she had better get out of there before the polizia show up and accuse her of disturbing the peace—or worse. She drops some lire on the counter by the cash register, Bird's and her earnings from earlier in the day, and slips out the door, losing herself in the streets.

AMBOS MUNDOS

Still in a daze, Tillie wends her way back to Sibyl's place in the Cannaregio section. She's given up trying to dump Bird. It rides on her shoulder, cooing in her ear and nibbling on her neck, sending shivers down her spine. Frank's a much better lover as a bird, but she longs for a real relationship, a complete one, not just the hit-or-miss affairs she's fallen into over the years. She can't help but feel a certain melancholy that she and Frank didn't make it as a couple. She also feels sad that Frank will never experience again the wonders of this world—the play of light on water, the sound of waves slapping pilings, the distinctive fishy smell of the ocean.

Letting her feet lead her, she ends up in an unfamiliar square, facing a handsome old church. The gothic brick facade is welcoming, and the church's white baroque trim resembles lace in places, graced with several turrets containing religious sculptures. She approaches the entrance, recognizing the structure from guidebooks she's read. She's sure it's the Madonna dell'Orto, famous for its Tintorettos—one of her favorite painters. In spite of her aversion to churches, she's been planning to stop there to view his work.

She also has another motive: she needs the solace of a formal sanctuary where she can say a prayer for Frank's soul and light a candle for him. She does believe that humans have souls and that they somehow survive death of the physical body. But she hasn't a clue what happens to them then. Do they go through a washing cycle and then are hung up to dry? All she can do is speculate.

Tillie follows the scent of incense inside, passing through the Renaissance doorway, and pays the entrance fee. Then she walks down the center aisle to the chancel, straining in the dim light to read a brochure the attendant has given her. Built first in the fourteenth century and then reconstructed in the sixteenth century, the church captures layers of history in its walls.

And then Tintoretto takes over, his rendering of *The Last Judgment* dominating the interior. She slides into a wooden pew, her bottom fitting into one of the hollows made by other pilgrims down through the centuries. Ignoring the painting's subject matter, she falls into the rhythms and colors that make the wall come alive. It's like watching a movie projected there of the artist's soul.

Rivers of light tumble through the darker hues, illuminating a basin of bones at the bottom of the picture. Forms seem to topple out of the painting, garments of bright blue, red, orange, and gold reminding Tillie of the structures she just passed in the streets, many of them painted these same colors. The painting reflects life outside the church, seizing the chaos underlying the surface order, much as Venice itself seems to barely hold back the surrounding ocean that threatens to swallow it.

Never has Tillie felt so insignificant and naked, stripped by this artist of any illusions she's had of control and human power in the light of the unknown. She came here for solace, but instead she's been shown humanity in its most vulnerable state, at the mercy of its own blindness. She glances at Bird, wondering if the pigeon is an art aficionado, but it's no longer on her shoulder. Caught up in her musings, she hasn't noticed its departure. It must have taken off before she entered the church. If Bird really is an incarnation of Frank, she can see why he'd take a powder. He was even more allergic to churches than she is.

The pigeon's disappearance triggers a flood of weeping in her. The state of shock she was in after hearing about Frank's death has worn off. Her feelings and fears are surfacing, matching the overwhelming emotions evoked by Tintoretto's work. She thinks of the email message from Tanya, who makes sculptures out of wire and fabric. It's hard to believe Frank really has died, his ashes carried by the wind to who knows where. Tillie has just seen his photos of her in the Kat's Paw gallery. How can he be dead when his art is so alive?

Tillie gets caught up again in the swirl of emotion *The Last Judgment* evokes, crying now not just for Frank but also for Sibyl and herself and everyone else who will eventually have to depart this world. The idea of saying goodbye to all that she loves and holds dear in this life seems overwhelming.

All this weeping reminds Tillie of the torso that's visited her since she arrived in Venice. Maybe this headless Black Madonna is lamenting the human condition, sorrow dominating everything else.

Yes, there is hope, Tillie thinks. Yes, there are periods of sublime happiness. But the reality is, humans live for a short time, sometimes suffering greatly, and then die, leaving hardly a ripple in their wake.

Some of this grimness comes through in *The Last Judgment*. It's almost enough to make a believer out of her just to have the reassurance of resurrection. Isn't this church itself a reflection of that possibility, having reconstituted itself? But to suddenly embrace Christianity would be too easy. She knows it isn't her path, though she does feel some affinity for the Gnostics—pre-Christian but also early followers of Christ. They didn't buy into the church's orthodoxies. Nor does she.

Her tears spent, for now at least, Tillie grabs some Kleenexes from her pack and blows her nose. Then she leaves the pew and moves forward till she reaches the candles. She lights one for Frank and watches the wick flicker and flare, mesmerized by the light. Seeing his face in the candle's glow unleashes another torrent of tears. Sniffling, she bows her head and closes her eyes, thinking of their better times together, sitting across from each other in their favorite Italian restaurant in North Beach, eating gnocchi and drinking cheap Chianti, a candle flame wavering between them. At least she ate well with Frank. He was always generous when it came to food, and he was a much better cook than Tillie.

She remembers the first time they met. It was July 1996 in San Miguel de Allende. He was feeding peanuts to Pedro, the hotel parrot, in the lobby of the Ambos Mundos, a flophouse for expatriates and artists. The parrot bit his hand, obviously preferring flesh to legumes, leaving a nasty gash that was gushing blood.

Tillie happened to be passing through just then, on her way to breakfast. "Need a hand?" she'd said.

He rolled his eyes, and she wrapped the hem of her peasant skirt around his wound. The action left them connected, a little like Siamese twins.

"You'll need to come to my room so I can change."

"Florence Nightingale?" he asked.

"Wrong bird. Tillie Bloom to your rescue."

"Frank Gallo, your slave."

Before this meeting, she'd noticed him at the Instituto where they both were teaching—Tillie had landed a temporary summer gig—but she didn't realize they also were staying at the same pad. His white hair was especially striking against his tanned skin, the color of walnut. He looked almost Indian, his hair hanging down his back, his weather-beaten face a map of all the gullies and crevices he'd traversed in his life. And he had heavenly blue eyes. But his biceps were what really attracted her, bulging out of the sleeveless white t-shirt he wore. He looked like he'd been carved out of the earth, a cross between a Norse god and a Hell's Angel. It was lust at first sight.

Since she had wanted to meet him, Tillie didn't mind having her skirt drenched in his blood. After all, it *was* Mexico. The Aztecs believed blood was the way to appease the gods well before the blood of Christ became such a big thing for Mexicans.

Tillie was renting a studio dirt-cheap for the summer from the Ambos Mundos. Frank followed her back there. It had red tile floors, a brick ceiling, and a tiny kitchenette where she stored her art supplies.

"I guess I owe you a skirt. Blood doesn't wash out easily."

"Buy me dinner instead."

That marked the beginning of their relationship. Ambos Mundos means "both worlds," and the place lived up to its name, though multiple worlds would have been a more accurate description of the action there. Americans, Europeans, Canadians, Latin Americans—even a few Asians—all called Ambos Mundos home. A San Miguel regular, Frank knew everyone. He showed Tillie around, introducing her to his many friends and acquaintances.

Claiming to like her little-girl-lost look, he wanted to protect her. She went along with him in spite of her feminist leanings. Not long after they returned to the States, they moved in together and the fun began.

Tillie reminds herself that those times together are past, and in the present she is sitting on a pew in the Madonna dell'Orto, grieving Frank's death. Something brushes up against her ankles. She looks down and bursts out laughing. Bird's standing there, clutching a communion wafer in its beak. She thinks the pigeon is offering it to her. But when she reaches for it, Bird swallows the thin disc and leaves one of its deposits on the church floor.

Bird has brought Tillie back to reality. She realizes she mustn't sentimentalize Frank and her relationship with him. If it had been so wonderful, she'd still be with the image-soul-stealing son-of-a-bitch. But their lives did touch, however briefly, and he has immortalized her in his photographs, no matter how much she may resent it. And now she owns his art.

When Tillie leaves the church, the candle flame is still fluttering.

BIRD FLIES THE COOP

No one is at the flat when Tillie arrives. She's relieved to have the place to herself, except for Jet, the cat. Jet puts Bird in its place, claiming her territory immediately, hissing and arching her back before pouncing at the pigeon. For the first time, Tillie sees Bird on the defensive, chased around the flat until it wises up and lands on Jet's back, temporarily immobilizing the cat.

They finally separate, and there's a shaky truce. Perched on a sideboard in the dining room, Jet follows Bird's every movement. Bird makes a wide berth of the cat, waddling from room to room, settling finally on top of Sibyl's new puzzle.

Tillie leaves her things in the bedroom, grabs her bathrobe, and heads for the shower, washing off the day's residue and humming "I'm gonna wash that man right outa my hair."

Then Sibyl arrives home from shopping. She walks in the door and lets out a shriek. "Who let this fucking bird in here? It shit all over my puzzle."

Tillie jumps out of the shower, wraps herself in a towel, and runs into the living room. Cleaver in hand, Sibyl chases the pigeon around the apartment, cornering it in the bathroom. Tillie grabs her arm before Sibyl can cut off Bird's head.

"Stop, Sib! I think it's Frank."

Sibyl stands there, cleaver dangling from her hand, and gapes at Tillie. "Frank? Frank who? It's a fucking pigeon. You losing it?"

"Trust me. I can explain. Frank my ex-whatever has died and come back as a pigeon."

"You nuts?"

"I know it sounds weird." She tries to explain, telling Sibyl about her run-in with Bird and the email message.

"This pigeon could be the king of England for all I care. It goes!" Sibyl grabs a bath towel, throws it over the squawking bird, and carries it outside.

Tillie dries herself quickly and dresses, actually relieved that Sibyl has gotten rid of Bird, releasing her from feeling guilt over abandoning it. Besides, she doesn't need any complications with Bud; he might not like having a bird for competition. Yet she's grown attached to the wacky creature and its bizarre behavior.

It has occurred to Tillie—even before Bird showed up—that animals could be intermediaries between the living and the dead. Maybe it isn't even the dead exactly that animals mediate. But they seem tuned into something she can't quite identify. Some special knowledge. Connected to another reality. Experiencing things humans aren't aware of. She doesn't think that spirits take over animals exactly, and she doesn't even know what she means by "spirits," yet she believes they can influence creatures.

Tillie doesn't think that once the body's gone, some disembodied entity floats around, looking for a new form. But here she thinks she's a little Platonic. Maybe once a person has died and is free of the body, whatever makes up consciousness—the soul perhaps—can tap into an animal's brain more easily than when it was contained in human shape. So she doesn't think that Bird = Frank. Too literal. Though Frank could be communicating with her via the pigeon.

Too bad. If he has something to say to her, he'll have to find another medium. Bird's gone.

The least she can do is clean up its mess before Sibyl returns. Tillie grabs some paper towels from the kitchen and dampens them. Back in the dining room, she carefully lifts the droppings from the puzzle, curious to see what images are lurking there this time, amazed to find a scene with pigeons frolicking in St. Mark's Square.

Sibyl returns, dropping the towel next to the puzzle.

"Where'd you leave Bird?"

"In the garbage can. Put the lid on. Tight." Sibyl smiles her taut little smile and lights a cigarette, her wandering gray eye focusing on something Tillie can't see.

Tillie feels a little queasy at the thought of Bird being trapped in a container. Buried alive. Sibyl's a tough cookie.

"Look at the image you've been putting together."

Sibyl leans over the table, laughs, and puffs away, her face disappearing behind a cloud of smoke.

Tillie says, "Have you ever wondered if images can become three dimensional? I mean, everything came out of someone's imagination once: trees, rivers, oceans, animals. Call it God or whatever. The ability to talk about these things came later. Words followed. Not the other way around. 'In the beginning was the image.'"

Caught up in her maze of ideas, Tillie trips over a leg sticking out from under the dining room table. Forgetting for a moment it's one of her casts of the Muskrateers' legs, she shrieks, afraid she's stumbled onto someone's body part, breaking her fall by grabbing Sibyl's arm, the two of them almost going down together. Tillie had stored the casts at the Venice train station when she first arrived. Sibyl, curious to see how an artist works, has let her keep them in the apartment. They're crammed into any available corner. Afraid to wear out her welcome, Tillie has promised to move everything out—soon. But Sibyl seems to like being part of this production. Tillie calls her a patron of the arts; Sibyl says she likes the way that sounds.

Embarrassed, Tillie says, "I guess I'd better find another place for my stuff."

Sibyl nods, dragging deeply on her cigarette and exhaling smoke signals that hover for a minute between them before dissolving.

For once Tillie doesn't mind Sibyl's endless smoking. It gives her time to think. She's been wondering about the power of images and the way theories and other ideas control human perception, dictating how things should be. If you believe the world is flat, the world is flat. People thought that for a long time. Some still do. Your beliefs box you in, limit you.

These are themes she's tried to explore in her installations. Like a scientist, she carries on her investigations, using sound, film/video, computers, artifacts, humans, and odds and ends, trying to create other realities and to probe the existing one. Attempting to slip behind the looking glass. Moving away from mere reflection to something else.

Being around Frank helped Tillie to see how complex the relationship is between an artist and his/her subject, especially a photographer, how incestuous the process is. No wonder some tribal people have trouble being photographed. They sense something more is going on when their picture is taken—the camera seizing something vital from them, stealing their image, their soul. Something mysterious does happen with a picture. It's more than just surface. A whole other world lurks there. Disembodied. Another reason why Frank's photos of her are so upsetting. His camera probed her, revealing too much. Stole her soul.

Frank seemed to understand what he was doing; he realized his power as a photographer. They frequently talked about this esoteric stuff—when he shut up long enough to let her speak. That's the other thing she misses about their relationship: shoptalk. A chance to express her far-out ideas without being laughed at. He was further out than she was.

TILLIE ENTERS THE LOOKING GLASS

Emotionally drained, Tillie feels ready for a nap and drifts off to the bedroom. Then she remembers Tanya's instructions to call Michael Love and checks the time. He should be at his law office now. So she phones before falling asleep. He agrees to send her a letter via express mail, giving her the rights to Frank's photos. She can't wait to get the ones of herself out of that gallery. Maybe she'll use them in her next installation.

The minute Tillie drops off, she falls into a dream where she's outside at night in an unfamiliar city, surrounded by bears. She's not sure why so many are roaming around, but they're everywhere. One of them stalks her, and if Valentine hadn't showed up to help her escape, she would have been a goner. Then she's in bed somewhere and Frank's trying to climb in, too. She pushes him away, repulsed. Meanwhile, the bears are right outside the bedroom door, waiting to get inside.

Voices from the living room nudge Tillie into wakefulness. She lies there a minute, at first unable to remember where she is, heart still jumping around from her encounter with the wild animals. Time for inventory: she's in Venice, sprawled out on a twin bed, staring at the mirror over the bureau.

Tillie has the strongest urge to enter that mirror, to see where it would lead her, to escape. But of course, that's nuts. Though the mirror gives the illusion of depth, of something inside it, she knows better. The surface just parrots, mimicking whatever is in front of it. She's never liked parrots much—except for their splendid colors—or mirrors for that matter. They're as limited as parrots in what they can project. In what they reveal. Maybe images also are only flat surfaces, giving the illusion of depth. What you see is what you get. Nothing more.

She doesn't believe it. She knows better.

Why is she dreaming of bears? There aren't any in Venice. They're too wild for this civilized city. Unless she's picking up on something under the calm surface: Serenissima Res Publica, the Most Serene Republic. She's read that somewhere. Maybe the kind of wildness bears represent has been ignored here, and she's compensating for it in her dream. They also could symbolize death, Venice's disease, the city sinking daily, though Tillie refuses to believe it, just as she refuses to believe that she will ever disappear.

Her stomach starts to growl, a pretty wimpy imitation of the sound a bear makes. The dream might be calling her attention to her own hunger, all these instinctual desires and appetites flooding her now, so close to her seventh decade, wanting to be recognized, to be embraced, just as death wants to be taken in. Acknowledged. It's a tall order.

Tillie makes out Moll's voice in the living room. She and Daddy have just returned from the Lido. Tillie hears Moll say, "Hey, there are lots of trees there! Real trees."

Sibyl says something about Bird that Tillie can't quite make out. She must be telling the others how it hitched a ride with Tillie.

"Need any help with dinner?" That's Daddy speaking.

Tillie remembers then: Bud's coming over the next night at eight thirty PM to eat with them. She's falling through the looking glass, tumbling down a dark hole, sixteen again and waiting for her beau to arrive. It's been years since she's had butterflies in her stomach. She thought she'd outgrown such things.

Then she remembers that Frank is dead and feels guilty for feeling so excited about Bud. She stretches, trying to ignore the chronic ache in the lower part of her back, aggravated when she lies flat. She turns onto her side to take the pressure off her disc and reviews the day's happenings. She can't fully assimilate the fact that Frank is dead, that she'll never see

145

him again, and wonders if she's dreamed it too. She tries to push away the memory.

Then she recalls her email messages. Tillie has to return to the café—if they'll let her back in—and read the message that has "Black Madonna" in the subject. What in hell could it be about? Bloody emails. So intrusive. They follow you all over. Like Bird. Impose themselves on you. Take over your life.

But who in hell has sent Tillie a message about the Black Madonna? She hadn't the time previously to look at who the sender was, and she can't think of anyone except Frank. He's the one who first made her aware of Black Madonnas and the only one she's discussed them with. One of his former lovers had been into goddesses and the like. She got Frank interested. Had he sent Tillie a message before he died? After he died? Or had Tillie told Tanya about the torso Sibyl had assembled in Whistler before leaving for Venice, which had inspired the molds Tillie had made of her own body and the other Muskrateers? Might Tanya have mentioned this to Frank before he died?

Well, the message from Tanya wasn't a dream. Nor was Bird. Shit! Death does remind her of shit. It stinks up everything. You want to push it away, get rid of it quickly, not think about it too much, though feces make good fertilizer. Death's a kind of fertilizer. Promotes growth. Death and birth are always linked. No wonder. Everything returning to the earth. Nature consuming it all. Mother Nature? Bears as the Great Mother? Is this the connection in her dream between bears and death and Frank?

Why visit Venice if you don't want to think about death? Life there seems so precarious—fragile. Even in this romantic city, a lovers' paradise, death permeates everything, never far away. The Romantics understood this dynamic, equating Love and Death, especially the Germans.

Tillie feels herself overheating, her whole body suddenly inflamed. Bloody hormones. They still intrude. She kicks off the light throw she's been using, wondering if she could die of heat stroke from hot flashes.

Through the open window she can hear people's voices from the street below *and* from the canal, accompanied by the slap slap of water, moored boats rubbing against wooden piers. She swings her legs over the side of the bed and sits up, slipping into black tights and a black miniskirt to express mourning and a scoop-necked, short-sleeved, rainbow-striped top to convey life. Her body is still trim after all these years. Just a little potbelly to give away her age.

She's sitting on the bed, pulling on her cowboy boots, when Daddy strolls in and plops down on the other bed, kicking off her shoes and sprawling out.

"Sorry to hear about Frank. What a downer."

"Yeah, well, thanks. Death's always a downer. I just can't believe he left me his art."

"He left you his art?"

"Yeah, and all of his photographic equipment. Go figure."

"Must have thought you were pretty special."

"I modeled for so many of the photos, he probably thought they were mine anyway."

"Can you believe Sibyl out there, cooking up a storm?"

"I know," Tillie says. "Venice has really gone to her head. Maybe she'll put on some weight."

"You think she's okay?"

"Sibyl? Her smoking and hacking scare the hell out of me," Tillie says.

"Me, too. She tell you about the spot on her lung?"

"Yeah. She refuses to see a doctor."

"Guess she has a right to go out that way if she wants."

The Gypsies become Muskrateers

The next day, before returning to the flat late in the afternoon, Tillie picks up wine, bread, and cheese for their dinner and pays for it out of her earnings with Bird. She finds Sibyl in the kitchen—cigarette clenched between her teeth, chopping onions, eyes watering. Jet brushes against Sibyl's legs, winding her tail around one of them and meowing softly.

"That cat's really hot for you." Tillie grabs the garlic and starts separating the cloves. "How many?"

"Six for the sauce and three for the salad."

"Who's coming besides Bud?"

"My neighbors. Flamenco dancers."

"Wow! Flamenco. What a trip. Husband and wife?"

"Not sure. Thought they'd liven things up. Could get pretty dead with just a priest."

"Don't prejudge Bud," Tillie says. "He's not your usual cleric."

"Hope not. I don't want to be converted."

"Me neither!"

Sibyl jabs the cigarette into an ashtray and dumps the onions into a big frying pan with some olive oil. "Garlic ready?"

"Yes. Want me to do something with these mushrooms?"

"Wash and slice them."

Tillie moves to the sink, dumps the bag of mushrooms into the strainer, and runs some water over them, drying each one with a paper towel, inhaling their pungent odor.

Sibyl grabs the cleaver and hacks away at some sausages. The cat jumps up on the windowsill overlooking the canal and watches Tillie and Sibyl, waiting for something edible to drop onto the floor.

"Guess I should move my puzzle so we'll have a place to eat. Not enough room here in the kitchen." She heads into the dining room, Jet following.

"I'll help."

Sibyl snaps a puzzle piece into place and lets out a whoop of pleasure.

Tillie takes a look. "Hey, it's Bird! Bird's ended up in your puzzle. At least it looks like Bird."

Sibyl looks more closely. "Oh, shit! That fucking pigeon is everywhere!"

At eight thirty sharp, the doorbell buzzes. Moll and Sibyl are in the kitchen, cooking. Sibyl hollers, amidst the clanging of pots, "Can somebody get that?"

"No problem," Tillie says and opens the door, not sure whether to genuflect or just curtsy.

Bud's standing there, staring up at her, a bouquet of flowers in one hand, a bottle of red wine in the other. But before she can greet him, Bird lands on Tillie's shoulder and coos softly in her ear.

"Oh fuck," she blurts out.

Bud's smile changes to a look of puzzlement.

"Sorry. I wasn't referring to you. This pigeon's latched onto me. I can't get rid of it."

"I understand why," he says, staring hungrily at Tillie's breasts.

His voice turns Tillie weak in the knees, and she finds herself giggling, something she hasn't done in years. She bows and takes the flowers and wine from him.

He says, "I'll take the pigeon if you want."

"Please do! It's driving me crazy."

He reaches up and clasps the bird with both of his hands, holding it at arm's length in front of him. "A nice plump one. They eat well in Venice."

Bird makes a guttural sound and looks at Tillie, but she ignores it, retreating into the flat. She remembers reading somewhere that pigeons mate for life. Maybe Bird mistakes her for its mate.

Leaving the door ajar, Tillie grabs a vase and stuffs the flowers into it, setting them on the table with the wine.

Sibyl calls out, "I'm outta matches and Moll has her hands full. Will someone get them from my shoulder bag? I think it's on the sideboard."

"I'll do it." Tillie grabs the bag, opens it, and looks inside. A coiled snake stares back at her, ready to spring. Tillie screams.

Sibyl comes running. "Oh shit, I forgot. Xena's still in my bag. Poor thing must be hungry."

"Why are you carrying a snake around? I could've had a heart attack!"

If there's one creature Tillie thinks Noah should not have taken on his ark, it's snakes. She loathes them. "I almost touched it! Jesus."

"Jesus can't help you," Sibyl says. "Where's your priest?"

"Getting rid of Bird."

"That wretch again? I should let Xena take care of him."

"Bud?"

"Only if he tries to convert me. But I meant Bird."

Sibyl takes her bag and wraps her arms around it, strolling into her bedroom, patting the wriggling mass inside and crooning, "It's okay, baby. No one's going to convert you."

Tillie shakes her head in disbelief. What kind of craziness has she gotten into? How will she sleep, knowing there's a snake under the same roof?

She hears Bud yelp and the outside door bang. He strolls in, wrapping a white handkerchief around his left hand.

"Oh no! Bird bit you. I hope it doesn't have rabies."

"Italian pigeons drink too much wine to get rabies. It's nothing. Just a nip."

He sweeps into the living room, wearing a black turtleneck and slacks. Except for the cross hanging from his neck, no one would think he was a priest. He may not be wearing his clerical robes, but he walks as if he is, filling up the place with his presence, a giant in stature and spirit if not in height. Tillie ogles his well-defined biceps, triceps, and pecs.

The other Muskrateers appear, and Tillie introduces them.

"I didn't know you were involved with the military," Bud says.

"The military?"

"You mentioned Musketeers."

Tillie roars. "Muskrateers. A name we gave ourselves in our wild and crazy youth."

"That's a relief. I've no fondness for the military."

Carmine and Emil arrive a half hour late. At least twenty years younger than the others, they're a striking couple. White teeth flashing against naturally tanned skin. Carmine's eyes accented with kohl, her Middle-Eastern beauty compelling. An ankle-length sarong accentuates her hips and buttocks, and a simple, sleeveless, black silk top shows off her firm breasts. There follows a flurry of hellos and pleased to meet yous and awkward handshakes. They all have a little Cinzano and Punt e Mes, along with an antipasto Moll and Daddy have put together. Soon Carmine and Emil seem like old friends, honorary members of the Muskrateers, the Muskrateers and Bud honorary Gypsies.

"Roma," Carmine says, rolling the rrrrr and snapping her fingers. "We don't call ourselves 'Gypsies.'" The words rise and fall as if she's singing. Her long black hair is caught in a single braid that hangs down her back like a gleaming rope, wispy tendrils falling onto her face.

Tillie looks greedily at Carmine's mane and self-consciously pats her own short spikes. Sibyl had told Tillie the night before that her hair resembled the Statue of Liberty. Tillie had laughed, loving the comparison.

Tillie once had hair like Carmine's. It reminds her of youth and abundance and a luxurious femininity that she seems to have lost. Not that a woman has to have long hair to be feminine, or a man short hair to be masculine. Look at Samson! But there's power in long hair, whether it's on a man or a woman. And why not? It's long been rumored that hair continues to grow after death, a veritable river into the underworld.

Tillie isn't the only one who stares at Carmine. Daddy and Moll watch the younger woman, their thoughts hard to read from the blank expressions on their faces. Is she stirring in them some primitive memory?

Carmine could be invisible for all Sibyl seems to notice her, but Sibyl hungrily ogles Emil, his curly dark hair a cap that tapers into a ringlet at the nape of his neck. He wears a green silk shirt, a coral scarf tied at his throat. His eyes are riveting, drawing everyone into their dark centers. Tillie has never seen eyes like that. They seem to penetrate her depths and more. Unnerving. It reminds her of the photographic study Frank made of her body.

But Bud is the group's focal point. Not because of his beauty or even his dusky skin color. Everyone seems to feel comfortable around him. He's been listening to confessions for years and has a receptive, boyish quality that draws out people. His own naturalness and willingness to talk freely about himself puts others at ease.

Recalling his earlier comment about the military, Tillie asks why he dislikes it. He tells the others of his birth and how he became a priest.

"Every time I see an Italian soldier, I think of my father who abandoned me. It makes me sad and angry at the same time. I'm like a bull caught in the bullring. I see red."

They all nod, not wanting that powerful force to be snuffed out by the matador and his tricks.

"Aren't you supposed to teach forgiveness?" Moll says, pouring more wine into everyone's glasses and turning on a couple of the lamps. Light spills out from under the shades. Moll looks smashing in a top and skirt she picked up at one of the markets. A simple peasant skirt and blouse of soft, flowing material. Not her usual wardrobe of jeans and shorts. She actually resembles a sexual being again, her hips and buttocks accentuated as she moves.

"Yes, but how many doctors practice what they preach?" Bud says. "I know lots of unhealthy doctors. It isn't always easy to forgive and forget."

"I know," Tillie says. "It reminds me of all those twelve-step programs that insist on it. Maybe it's healthier to hate and not forgive, especially if someone's ruined your life."

Sibyl nods. "I'm all for a good hate."

"I'll drink to that," Daddy says.

Everyone raises a glass and drinks.

"I don't get why you've stayed in the church," Tillie says.

"I love theatre, and I like the drama and ritual of the liturgy. It's the closest I can get to acting. Anyway, it's the form that intrigues me. I don't think much about the content of what I'm saying, even when I'm giving the homily." He shrugs his shoulders. "I'm afraid I'm not a very good advocate of the church. You'll have to forgive me." He sips his wine and swings his legs, feet not touching the floor. "But then again, it's free will. Maybe you won't forgive me."

"Or can't," Daddy says, passing around the antipasto.

"Yes! Or can't." He laughs and pops an olive into his mouth, chewing around the pit and spitting it into his napkin.

"I'm surprised they didn't kick you out," Moll says, filling up the empty glasses.

Tillie wants to kick her for being so moralistic and putting Bud on the spot.

"Me?" He gives a mock scowl. "What a scandal that would be, defrocking an orphaned priest. Half Black. No. That wouldn't be prudent. The church can't afford bad publicity. As long as I don't get too outrageous, they put up with me and I with them. It's convenient for all parties. I think they believe I'm less trouble in the church than I would be outside of it."

"Why?" Carmine asks, leaning towards him, her dark eyes limpid and bottomless.

He winks. "They know I'm somewhat of a rebel. I don't like hierarchies, and I don't think priests are necessary to mediate between them and God. So the church structure puts some restraints on me that there otherwise wouldn't be. I might be more of a threat to ecclesiastical authority if I weren't under its wing. My ideas don't exactly gibe with theirs."

"Strange," Sibyl says, her wandering eye focused on Emil.

"No stranger than you carrying that snake around," Tillie says. "What God are you worshipping?"

Daddy stiffens. "Who has a snake?"

"You didn't hear the ruckus earlier? Check out Sibyl's purse."

"Snakes bring good luck," Carmine says, nodding sagely. "What kind is it?"

"Damned if I know," Sibyl says. "A snake's a snake. It was at the market, slithering down an aisle. I popped it into my shopping bag. Always wanted a pet snake."

"Maybe it came on a boat from another country," Moll says. "It could be poisonous!"

"It's just a baby," Sibyl protests. "Wouldn't harm anyone."

"I'm amazed," Tillie says. "Here you're terrified of basements and spiders and other crawly things. But you like snakes."

Sibyl shrugs, lighting a cigarette. "Wonders never cease."

"I like that attitude," Bud says. "Wonders are what make the church such a fascinating place to work. It's like a large retort. Mix in a few angels, the Holy Spirit, the saints, some sinners, red wine, bread, a magic chant or two, and you never know what will happen." A magician conjuring up spirits, he sets his glass down on the coffee table, waves his hands over it, raises his arms above his head, and snaps his fingers a few times like a flamenco dancer—"Ole!"

Tillie hasn't thought of priests as artists, but Bud's description sounds like her own process. A little of this. A little of that. Presto. Art! Only he's working more with the invisible, the spirit. Her material tends to be tangible, the combination adding up to something invisible. But both are voyeurs. And both lost their father. Is she drawn to him because he represents God the Father and fills up a hole for her?

"Something similar happens when we dance flamenco," Carmine says. Castanets mysteriously appear in her hands, and she clicks them together expertly, setting up a counter rhythm with her tapping feet. "We never know where a dance will lead us. Each time it's different. New. It can be very spiritual. Not in the church's sense of course. Flamenco's too sensual. It puts us in a kind of trance."

"Oh, the church can be sensual, too," Bud says and laughs, looking at Tillie.

"I guess it depends on what you mean by sensual," Daddy says, passing the antipasto to Carmine, her fingers grazing the other woman's hand in the process. Carmine gives a Mona Lisa smile and returns the plate. Daddy takes a slice of salami and says, "I suppose the Eucharist could pass for food."

Sibyl pipes up, "And there's all that incense." She smiles at Emil.

"And music. Not my taste, though," Tillie says. "No offense, Bud, but give me flamenco any day." She looks at him over the top of her wine glass, savoring the full-bodied flavor of Chianti. His bald head gleams.

Carmine is still talking about flamenco, her eyes glazed over, fingers working the castanets, lost in the memory of a performance.

"You ever watch flamenco dancers? Everything's in motion—feet, fingers, eyes, body. Faster and faster. The audience gets caught up in the music and rhythms, too. In a good performance, everyone gets involved. We *all* lose ourselves in the song."

Jet stands in the kitchen doorway, rubbing against the doorjamb and meowing.

"Oh, there's the maid," Sibyl says, standing up. "Time to serve dinner. Come on, everyone."

The others follow, and she places them around the table, one man on each side between two women, Sibyl at the head. The center overflows with food and drink: bowls of pasta and salad and bread and more antipasto and wine. Moll lights the candles that Daddy lifted from Santa Maria della Salute. Tillie hopes Bud doesn't recognize them. Sibyl plays a CD that Carmine and Emil recorded. The music blends Turkish with Hungarian and Spanish sounds.

They all dig in, even Sibyl, who usually just pokes at her food. She digs into Emil too, giving him her best come hither look.

At least she isn't after Bud, Tillie thinks, stroking his thigh under the table. He returns her touch. Emil's so busy attending to Moll that he doesn't notice Sibyl's attentions. And Daddy is having an intense conversation with Carmine.

Soon the talk turns more personal and confessional. Though Bud may not see himself as a priest exactly, he can't shake the aura he gives off. After listening for so many years to strangers pour out their hearts and reveal their secrets, he unconsciously seems to draw out disclosures from others.

So in the midst of chewing a mushroom—perhaps mistaking it for those perception-shattering ones she devoured in her younger, wilder days—and tongue loosened by wine, Daddy blurts out, "My mother's a Gypsy."

Daddy's confession appears to surprise her. She glances warily around the table, but no one seems to have heard her. She takes another swig of wine and repeats her announcement, louder this time. "I'm a Gypsy."

Moll stops talking, mid-sentence, and turns to her friend. "What's the big deal?"

"I just remembered Mum's shame about her family's immigration to Canada. Let's face it—if you weren't Scots-Irish—at least when I was growing up—you were considered weird."

"Oh, it isn't just Canada," Carmine says.

Emil nods in agreement.

Tillie says to Daddy, "Ironic that your mother married a Scot."

"Yeah. And he never let her forget it. His superiority."

Tillie remembers how Daddy had looked before she bleached her hair and had her nose bobbed. Her nose had once resembled Carmine's, slightly hooked. Now Tillie understands why Daddy has changed herself so drastically. She was trying to separate from her Roma ancestry, but she can't deny it completely. Her dark roots seep into the blonde hair, threatening to take over.

Had the Gypsie's light-fingered ways taken over Daddy? Tillie realizes she's stereotyping the Gypsies, as if theft is in their genes, yet it is a cultural component. Some seem proud of it, excelling in the art of pilfering.

Tillie suddenly remembers her long-ago dream of Daddy wearing a magician's outfit. Magic requires sleight of hand. Isn't stealing a kind of magic, making something disappear and reappear somewhere else? Maybe the impulse to steal comes from a deeper one, like an artist's involvement in creating illusion. Gypsies don't share the Ten Commandment's values. Could share be the key word? If they don't believe in private property, it's okay to take what isn't theirs because it's sharing. It belongs to them anyway.

Situational ethics.

Being in Venice reminds Tillie again that there are more things in heaven and earth than Horatio would have dreamt of in his philosophy. But it's his philosophy that dominates her thinking—and most people she knows. Still, she longs to break free of it. She has always felt out of step and out of place, rarely taking the usual or expected path. In Canada she doesn't feel Canadian; in the U.S. she doesn't feel American. In Venice, she fits in.

She tunes in on the table talk. Carmine and Emil are involved in an intense discussion with Daddy about Roma, the pros and cons of Gypsy life and the intense discrimination they've experienced. Carmine reminds Daddy that Gypsy women are extremely oppressed. They're expected to marry young and have children. They can't have a life outside the family. Away from Gypsy culture, the two dancers disguise themselves as Spaniards so they can find work and places to live.

"We're worse off than your American Blacks. Our language has been outlawed in some countries. No one wants a Gypsy for a neighbor or a friend. We're everyone's scapegoat."

Carmine's singing coils around them from the CD player, a controlled wail that pierces Tillie.

It's paradoxical that while Daddy was struggling to free women and Blacks from oppression and discrimination, she was denying half of her own heritage, oppressing herself. How much of this woman has Daddy discarded over the years, literally cutting off her nose to spite her face? No wonder she needs to steal. It's one way to get back what she's lost or given up. To feel powerful.

The words "Weathermen" and "underground" drift over to Tillie's end of the table. Daddy's telling Emil and Carmine that ". . . the SDS wasn't going anywhere, and the Weathermen took control of it—I either went along with them or I was out in the cold—I was in too deep at that point to just walk away, so I got in even deeper."

"The Weathermen?" Tillie says. "Holy shit. They were really rad! Bombs. Kidnappings. Robberies. I can't believe you were doing all that." She stares at her old friend. *How much more is she hiding?*

Daddy shrugs. "I had a Joan of Arc complex, I guess. Thought we could create a just society. But first we had to get more revolutionary, make real changes in how Blacks and others were treated—shake up the whole system—destroy it." Daddy smiles ruefully. "All we ended up destroying was the SDS. It was like killing an important part of myself—I cut my teeth on that organization. I think we did make a difference, though. At least we made people more aware of the problems."

Amazed at what she's hearing, Tillie realizes Daddy had put her life on the line for her beliefs. And she isn't even an American. Tillie doesn't think the end justifies the means, but she respects people who fight for a cause, misguided or not. She has her own causes—art for one. Yet she's not sure how well she's fought for it. Maybe she should get more political.

Tillie asks Daddy, "When did you go underground?"

"After some housemates were arrested for setting off a bomb at a local government office—no one was killed or anything!"

"Wow! Why didn't they arrest you?"

"I took off for Canada—hid out—used an alias—worked at menial jobs—identified with the 'workers of the world.' I even tried to write a novel about the movement." She shrugs. "It was a way of continuing my protest and it gave me an identity—I was a writer—I also hooked up with others who were underground."

Sibyl lets out a whoop. "Hell, I've been underground all my life!"

Tillie looks around the table. Aren't they all underground in some way, masquerading as something they're not? Using aliases?

The only one whose identity seems secure is Moll, and at the moment she's talking animatedly with Sibyl. Tillie can't hear what they're saying and wonders if she really knows these women. Daddy's revelations have shaken Tillie's perceptions of the Muskrateers. Who are they? Who is she? At almost sixty, she shouldn't be having an identity crisis.

Bud pokes Tillie with his elbow. "Penny for your thoughts."

"Same old stuff. People are so different than what they seem on the surface. I mean, I'm not naïve. I knew that before. But—"

"I know. I see it all the time in the confessional. The most interesting part of my job. Like reading fiction. Multiple themes. Multiple selves. The pious housewife who pilfers. The upright businessman who can't keep his hands off young boys. The thief who secretly writes religious poetry. Terrorists who can't fall asleep without their teddy."

Tillie has the impulse to rub Bud's shiny bald spot. Maybe it's a talisman, a font of wisdom.

"Yeah," she says. "Everything seems to be a metaphor. Multilayered. It's what I try to get into my installations. Complexity and ambiguity."

"I'd like to see your work."

So would I, Tillie thinks. She hasn't done much since she arrived in Venice, distracted by the city and all that's happened. And now more distractions. She can hear scratching and a kind of tapping inside the dining room wall. Bird? An invasion of mice? Ants using Morse code? Or is she losing it? No one else seems to notice the sounds, so she ignores them. It's her overactive imagination again.

Sibyl jumps up and puts on a CD of flamenco music. On her way back to the table, she sways her hips. The swirly, flowered peasant skirt she's wearing hides her bones, making her almost voluptuous looking. Sibyl could pass for a woman, not a dying girl.

Emil jumps up and begins to stamp his feet to the beat, snapping his fingers overhead, circling Sibyl. He holds her in his gaze and she stands there, barely moving, mesmerized. He arches his back, turning his head from side to side and looking over his shoulder. The others tap their feet and clap their hands and shout "Olé!"

Sibyl looks self-conscious, not sure what to do, overwhelmed by Emil's skill as a dancer and his magnetic presence. She snaps her fingers a few times, trying to appear with it, but she's had a few too many glasses of wine, and her lopsided smile meanders across her face. The piece ends and she breaks for the kitchen, stepping out of her shoes on the way, and calls out "Dessert, anyone?"

Moll takes Sibyl's place and starts to dance with Emil, drawn into the rhythms, her eyes locked on his. Carmine and Daddy break the tension by joining the other dancers too, the four of them interweaving.

Tillie leans over and says to Bud, "You said the church wants to keep you under wraps. Why?"

"They suspect I don't share all their doctrine. I'm more of a follower of the old school."

"The Catholic church is pretty old."

"I'm talking about pre-Christian. The same heritage as the Black Madonna."

Carmine stops dancing, her braid slithering over one bare shoulder. "The Black Madonna? You mean Sara, don't you? The Gypsies love her."

"The same. An Egyptian serving-maid. Some people think she's an incarnation of Isis, the Egyptian goddess, one of the Black Madonna's precursors. You know, Egypt means black."

"Whatever she is, she's mother to us outcasts," Carmine says.

"Who's a mother to outcasts?" Daddy asks.

"The Black Madonna," Tillie says.

"And to many other outcasts too," Bud says, "including moi! She came to me in a vision. I was just a boy, around six years of age. I've never forgotten it. Her image is burned in my memory. Milk dripped from her breasts, and I drank it. I couldn't get enough!"

"Wow! Chocolate milk." Tillie blurts out the words without thinking. When she realizes what she's said, she covers her mouth with one hand. "Jesus, I'm sorry. I didn't mean to say that."

Bud pats her arm. "The milk actually had a chocolate flavor. Or maybe it was wishful thinking."

Mollified, Tillie asks, "So what's the church's problem with the Black Madonna?"

"The real Black Madonna—not the one the Church has adopted and sanitized—doesn't insist on rigid, authoritarian rules. Sin's a very different thing with her. She blesses the flesh and sexuality. From her perspective, it's sinful to consider such pleasures a sin!"

"How heretical!"

"Exactly. She overturns all of our usual ideas—especially church dogma. Makes us reconsider what we're doing and why. She's very powerful. A great force in the world. Personally, I think she represents the true Christianity. It started out as a very radical movement, you know. To be Christian really means rejecting the status quo and finding your own path to God."

"She sounds more radical than the Weathermen," Daddy says. "That's really revolutionary."

"She's my kind of woman," Tillie says. "I can see why the church fathers would want to keep a close eye on you." She looks at Bud with increased interest and respect. "You're like a bomb in their midst, waiting to go off. If your ideas took hold, it would cost them their jobs."

Bud shrugs. "It's really the Black Madonna they want to keep a close eye on. She's the bomb that could go off. I'm just her advocate. Darkness and death are the source of life, not just the end. The womb isn't filled with light. Nor is the earth. She's the real church, embracing death *and* life, good *and* evil, love *and* hate, virgin *and* whore, good mother *and* witch, yin *and* yang—all of the opposites. She doesn't identify with one side or the other. She contains the world! Everything the church split in two."

Daddy shrieks, "What power!"

Gesturing excitedly with his arms, Bud says, "Yes, but the church downplays it by making her just a symbol of the downtrodden, the poor, the earthy peasants. She can't be squeezed into that mold. Robert Graves knew this. He says,

'How shall he watch at the stroke of midnight
Dove become phoenix, plumed with green and gold?
Or be caught up by jeweled talons
And haled away to a fastness of the hills
Where an unveiled woman, black as Mother Night,
Teaches him a new degree of love
And the tongues and song of birds?'"

Bud finishes his glass of wine and wipes his mouth with the back of his hand.

Tillie swoons at those words coming to her via Bud's sonorous vocal cords. She pulls herself together and squeaks out, "Amazing images. The peaceful dove the church has appropriated turns into something fierce and beautiful. The night unveiled. I wonder what 'new degree of love' she teaches."

In the dim candlelight, Bud reminds her of Bird, of some quality they share that she can't quite put her finger on. Persistence, perhaps. Determination. Passion. Intensity.

161

He hasn't stopped talking. "Ironically, the Black Madonna is the spirit of light in darkness. She wants to free those who are prisoners of orthodoxies. This dark feminine principle won't remain in the shadows much longer. She's on the move and will sweep us all up in her arms, her breasts dripping with milk, enough to nourish the world."

By now everyone is riveted by Bud's words. The seven of them are sitting around the table, drinking Bellinis and Campari, nibbling on biscotti, the candlelight sharpening the shadows in the room and highlighting their faces, flushed from wine, food, flamenco, and conversation. Gypsy music pulses in the background.

A lassitude overtakes them, a dreamlike stasis, as if they are under a spell or caught in a painting or photograph. While they're suspended in this mood, a portion of the dining room wall nearest the table starts to crumble, slowly at first, a kind of mushy substance giving way to bits of plaster carried by a colony of ambitious and hungry Formosan termites. They storm the place, creating a hole the size of a small dog—maybe a terrier.

The diners all sit there in stunned silence, watching these miniscule warriors bombard the place. It takes a few minutes for the magnitude of what's happened to penetrate.

"The snake," Sibyl hisses. "Where's the snake? She'll finish them off."

Bird Meets the Black Madonna

A ruckus in the living room wakes Tillie the next morning. She opens her eyes and looks around the room, wondering if she dreamed the dinner party, the termite invasion (bloody little terrorists!), the hole in the wall, Bird, the works. Maybe she even dreamed she's in Venice. But when she hears Daddy's snoring, she knows it isn't a dream.

"Holy shit!" Sibyl shouts from the living room.

Tillie jumps out of bed. So does Daddy. They leap through the door, colliding with a sleepy Moll, prepared to defend their hostess, but it isn't Sibyl who's in danger. The hole in the wall has doubled in size overnight. And Bird is back, feasting on termites, so engrossed he doesn't even notice Tillie. Jet has the snake cornered, and the two are spitting at each other.

Tillie feels oddly elated to see this dizzy pigeon again. It reminds her of May, who may be difficult in lots of ways, yet there's still something about her that keeps Tillie going back to her mother for more. Bird is similar.

Seeing Bird reminds her of the email she hasn't read with the Black Madonna as its subject. She feels some urgency to access the Internet again and finish going through her messages. After Bud's revelations, the Black Madonna communication seems more important than it did the day before.

She's also concerned because a week has gone by and she still hasn't done much to her installation. She's determined not to be sidetracked any longer—by Frank, by Bud, by Bird. She must get it constructed, though she'll have to do it mainly at night, when no one can see her and the garden isn't being used. She can hide her work there, in the bushes, until it's ready to be shown. Since Sibyl wants Tillie's stuff out of the flat, pronto, she'll kill two stones with one bird.

But first there's this crisis in the living room that needs to be resolved. Daddy's terrified of the snake—Tillie's not keen on it either, but it doesn't send her off her rocker—and is standing on a chair, babbling. Sibyl is sputtering about Bird shitting all over the place—the more it eats, the more of a mess it leaves—and is threatening again to behead it. And Moll is mooning around, not at all her usual *sportif* self, listening to Emile and Carmine's CD.

They all look at Tillie. She can't do much about the snake. Sibyl will have to take care of *that* problem. Maybe Moll can help her. Or perhaps Moll can hang out at the Lido and climb some trees. But if Tillie gets Bird out of the flat, it might ease the situation.

So she ducks into the bedroom and throws on some clothes, not paying much attention to what she's grabbed. When she appears in the living room again, Daddy says, "Hey, I wish you'd ask first before wearing my stuff."

Tillie realizes she's slipped into Daddy's tights and tank top. No time now to change, so she grabs her red poncho and says, "Sorry, mate, next time." She scoops up Bird, swishing out of the place, leaving them to deal with the mess, thankful she's not a property owner and doesn't have to find workmen to fix the wall. At least she's taking care of one problem.

It's one of those magical Venetian mornings. The sun has partially broken through, and wisps of morning fog hang suspended on red-tiled rooftops, appearing to hold the city aloft. A rosy light plays on all the reflective surfaces. Tillie thinks she's found the solution to Venice sinking. Hook up thousands—millions—of pigeons to the buildings and let the birds keep the city afloat. The pull in the opposite direction, skyward, could offset the effects of gravity and the drag from the depths. That should thwart Hades and whatever plans he has for Venice.

She ignores the bemused stares of passersby at Bird. It's perched on her right shoulder, acting as her navigator, when she runs into Bud. Absorbed in her thoughts, she almost knocks him over. He's wearing a wide-brimmed black hat and reminds her of the Mad Hatter. The hat topples off his head and wobbles down the street. He chases after it muttering, "I'm late, I'm late," the cloak he's wearing billowing out behind him. He doesn't look back.

Tillie feels disoriented, wondering why Bud's speaking the rabbit's lines from *Alice in Wonderland*. If he's the rabbit or Mad Hatter, then she's Alice, lost in the wonderland of Venice's many mirrors, all the art in the Biennale adding to the multiple reflections. She wouldn't mind being lost there permanently.

She and Bud had parted in haste the previous night, after the termite invasion. In the uproar, they didn't make another date. Still, that doesn't explain him taking off just now as if the Mafia were hot on his heels. Does he have secrets, too? This city feels brimming with them, submerged depths, nothing what it appears on the surface, everything a reflection of something else.

Bird pecks at Tillie's ear, reminding her of her mission to check her email. She swerves right, heading in the general direction of the Internet café she'd found the previous day, hoping the manager won't recognize her. She's glad she brought her backpack. She'll smuggle Bird inside, under wraps. Everything else is under wraps. Why not Bird? The pigeon seems to have a double life too. Tillie thought this divided-self stuff was a thing of the Victorian past, nineteenth-century craziness. But it's still lurking, threatening to bubble over.

She walks and walks, going in circles again, thoroughly adrift, tempted to drop into all the shops and bakeries, sights and smells so tantalizing she feels like Odysseus being tempted by the Sirens. The thought of Sirens reminds her of Carmine and Emil, their compelling music firmly planted in her memory. She clicks her heels on the sidewalk and pretends she has a red cape, swooping it to the side to let an imaginary bull pass by. She can hear the infectious rhythm of castanets echo in her footsteps. Carmine and

Emile are not only extremely handsome but the two of them also live fully in their bodies, instruments for their art.

She keeps moving, playing the music over and over in her mind, crossing and crisscrossing canals. Venice is the only city in the world where it's not only okay to be lost, but preferred. Lost most of her life, no wonder Tillie feels at home here.

Out of the corner of her eye, she notices a sign: "Internet Café." She veers left. It isn't the one she visited before, but maybe that's just as well. Even so, she opens her backpack and shoves Bird inside. It coos a few times and eyes Tillie skeptically before settling down in the dark, warm cave. If Bird really is Frank in disguise, he's used to dark places. She fastens the straps and hangs the pack from one shoulder.

The scene in this café isn't much different from the other one. A similar group of young guys engage in covert mutual masturbation, all playing the same game. Tillie asks to check her email, and a teenager in baggy pants dangling tentatively from his hips ushers her past the maze of machines, daring his trousers to stay up. It's a gravity-defying phenomenon she's never understood. How do they walk in those things, their range of motion so severely limited? Of course, he's also wearing a Yankees baseball hat backwards.

Her guide points to a machine and boots it up. Tillie never has understood where these computer terms come from and always feels a little self-conscious about using them. Someone's sure to discover she doesn't know what in hell she's talking about. It's like wandering into a secret society and using their code words without permission. Her literal imagination always takes over, and she pictures a Tom Thumb type, wearing combat boots, secreted inside the computer, giving its inner workings a hell of a kick. A boot is a boot is a boot. How dare the computer industry boost a perfectly good noun and turn it into a verb.

Booted up, she drops her backpack onto the floor next to the chair. Bird protests, squawking sharply. Tillie's guide looks at her quizzically and at the bag. She gives a little coo herself to divert him and sits down. He rolls his eyes, shrugs, and walks away.

While she's waiting for Mailstart.com to fetch her email messages, she goes to Google and types in Black Madonna. Tillie doesn't know what she expects to find. She clicks on the first URL that comes up. It reads, *The Black Madonna: Primordial Ancestress,* by Deborah Rose. The words "primordial ancestress" give her goosebumps. She's never thought of herself as having an ancestress, far less a primordial one. She starts reading, pulled into Deborah's Rose's narrative of when she visited the great Chartres cathedral, amazed to learn that a Black mother with an equally Black child seemed to provide the spiritual foundation for this community, an image even older than the Christian Mary.

To Tillie, it's ironic that the Catholic faithful revere this dark mother. They intuit something, willing to accept this simple figure, free of orthodoxy and dogma. It's what she has been seeking for years, a religion with a female base, something pre- or post-Christian. The Black Madonna seems like a real goddess and one that Tillie can respect.

She reads on, discovering that the natives of this area had worshipped statues of black and brown women giving birth for some time. When the Christian missionaries first arrived there and discovered what these people were doing, they concluded the images were a foreshadowing of the Virgin Mary. Believing that the people were already Christian, the priests built their chapels around these mother statues. That response continued into the twentieth century. Tillie cringes when she reads the part about the missionaries—Christian imperialism at its worst. The church fathers stole the people's goddess and claimed her for themselves.

Tillie is eager to tell Bud about her discovery. That's assuming she ever sees him again. He had seemed so preoccupied earlier. But first she needs to check out her email. Trolling through the swamp of spam, she finds the subject "Black Madonna" and clicks on it. Instead of words, she sees what looks like a target from a shooting gallery, concentric circles of black and white chasing each other, a bullseye in the center. At first she thinks her eyesight is going and the black letters she expected to see have turned fluid, congealing and coiling around themselves on the screen.

She reaches into the outer pocket of her pack and takes out her reading glasses, necessity overcoming vanity. They only confirm her initial take. She's beginning to understand what tunnel vision means. The more she stares at the screen, the more it seems three-dimensional, as if she's looking through a tunnel with no light at the end. Then she gets the weird feeling that she's at the other end of the tunnel—in the target—and someone is looking at her from behind the screen.

Frank? Could this be his way of contacting her from the other side? Or maybe he's playing a deathbed joke, sending her a farewell message in code. Does the bullseye symbolize the void at the center of the universe? Is he saying there's no Black Madonna/Earth Mother waiting to take us to her bosom at death, only a black hole (figuratively and literally)—empty, meaningless? He used to say that life is a black hole and everyone is in freefall, though most people don't recognize it. Or else they deny it. That's the *real* divine comedy. The bullseye would appeal to Frank's sense of irony. She can hear him laughing in hell, or maybe it's Bird gasping inside her backpack. Tillie loosens the straps a little to let in some air.

Or could the image on the screen be a mandala, representing the entire universe, an abstracted Black Madonna at the center, the one who gave birth to it? Tillie is getting into the swing of it now. Maybe she could get a job as a steganographer, decoding messages submitted in pictures. But that seems to be what art is all about—manipulating images that contain a deeper message, layers and layers of meaning leading everyone into the unknown, like the spiraling circles on the screen in front of her.

Frank was such a sadist. It must have given him intense pleasure to send this message before he died, knowing he was on his way out, knowing, too, how frightened Tillie is of total darkness and of falling into an abyss she can't escape from. The grave.

Just staring at the concentric circles makes her feel dizzy, off balance, as if she's being sucked into a vortex. They begin to ripple when she stares at them for a while, like waves, white predominating, then black. Frank—who loved seeing her on the edge, under his control—probably knew it would have this effect on her. She struggles to regain her equilibrium, refusing to let him have so much power over her. She owns his photographs now. He's dead. *Her* finger is on the trigger. She can hit the bullseye.

She thinks.

She hopes.

She feels a sharp pain in her ankle and looks down. Bird has managed to work its head out of the pack and is nipping at her skin. Reflexively, she almost kicks the pigeon but catches herself in time, afraid of being hauled in for animal abuse, delighted to think she might have Frank groveling at her feet. She wonders how Frankie boy likes hanging out in a darkroom— her backpack—though it occurs to her that the "other side" is the ultimate darkroom.

Bird tilts its head sideways and stares at her from one eye, then the other. She stares back, trying to penetrate its disguise. Does she recognize the probing intensity of Frank's camera lens in those eyes?

She pulls the flap over its head again and skips through her other email messages, wondering if Frank left any more deathbed communications, but they all seem pretty standard. Lots of porn sites offering their wares, Viagra manufacturers in hot pursuit.

She logs off and congratulates herself on getting the jargon right, though she can't shake the image of logs tumbling out of the screen, chasing her down a Venice street. In her fantasy, the guy from the Internet café is in pursuit, waving the bill at her, hobbling along, his low-slung trousers tripping him.

But he's waiting for Tillie at the cash register, eyes glued to the pack slung over her right shoulder. She follows his gaze. Bird has wriggled its head free again and is staring back at the guy. Tillie bursts out singing, "Oh, sweet mystery of life, at last you've found me," and drops some coins on the counter, ones that she and Bird had earned at St. Mark's. She tries to give the song a kind of hip-hop beat, doing a little soft-shoe as she zips out of the door.

Tillie rescues Bird

Tillie sets her course for Santa Maria della Salute, needing to talk to Bud about the Black Madonna email message and Bird. Maybe he has some answers. She may as well take advantage of his direct pipeline to God.

Frank would have a good laugh if he knew she was involved with a priest. He never had much use for the church or its officials, though Bud isn't exactly an official. But he does work for the church, and he's limited somewhat by his involvement there.

Then Tillie remembers her run-in with Bud earlier in the day and wonders how she can track him down. Where do priests live? *Bud, where are you? I need to talk to you!*

She decides to head for the Palazzo Cavalli-Franchetti since that's where they met their first time together. Even if he isn't there, she needs to begin assembling her installation. But first she must stop at Sibyl's and pick up some supplies so she can start working.

It suddenly occurs to her that the things she's been storing at the apartment could be in danger. Those bloody termites! She lets out a shriek and starts running, dodging tourists, ignoring Bird's protesting coos, amazed at her speed, arriving at Sibyl's pad out of breath. Flamenco music pours from the open door, a CD that Carmine and Emil gave to Sibyl.

Tillie slips inside, hair covered by her poncho's red hood, hoping to arrive and leave incognito. Instead, she walks into a flurry of pesticide people gesturing wildly and talking to Sibyl in Italian. Though she envies

Sibyl's ability to slither into another identity, Tillie for once is glad she doesn't speak the language. Sometimes it's better to be less aware. She can pretend she's deaf and ignore the chaos surrounding her. Become invisible. That's her M.O. anyway. She's spent most of her life overlooking disorder, pretending it doesn't exist, disappearing one way or another.

Tillie's boxes and casts have been dumped in the center of the living room along with other things that have been in storage, the place torn apart. It's discombobulating to see the Muskrateers' torsos resting against the sofa and chairs, a leg here and there poking out from under cushions and rugs.

At least the termites haven't devoured everything. If they had, she'd need to enlist them in her production, advertise them as another stage in her conception of it—post-installation artifact perhaps, giving the whole thing a post-postmodern flare. Or maybe she should add some termites anyway to represent the passage of time and how death chomps away at us like some invisible pest. She remembers reading somewhere that death enters the world with the body and remains its constant companion throughout life.

But how will she store the termites? They'll eat through whatever she puts them in. Not metal, though, or glass. An aquarium will do nicely. She can toss in bits of rotten wood and whatever else she can find to keep them happy. Even Bird if the pigeon gets out of line. Tillie scoops up a few termites in an empty jam jar and screws on the lid. Maybe she'll turn them loose on the whole installation after it's been viewed, demonstrating an important phase in the creation process—destruction.

She feels like God, constructing a work of art that self-destructs. People can watch this happen in the Edenic garden of the Palazzo Cavalli-Franchetti. Brilliant! Even God couldn't have thought that up. Adam and Eve were banished from the Garden before they self-destructed. Of course, they made up for it later. Tillie hopes S/He doesn't steal her idea. For posterity, she'll record the whole process on her trusty camcorder.

While Tillie is wondering how to cart everything to the Palazzo Cavalli-Franchetti, Bud shows up, his appearance so unexpected that she almost thinks he is a magician with magical powers to appear and disappear at will. Or maybe he got her telepathic message after all. Who needs cell phones when you can use ESP? If she could package this ability, she'd make a fortune and drive the cell phone industry out of business. Transmitting messages via brain waves sounds far superior to the current clunky method. And you don't have to stand there like an idiot, talking into a machine as if it could answer back, blathering to yourself. She feels she's missed her calling. In another life, she might have been a successful businesswoman like Daddy, a super saleswoman promoting her wares.

And then it dawns on her. Standing in the middle of Sibyl's living room, Tillie realizes why Daddy has been jailed in so many of her dreams. Tillie has locked up this latent ability to advance herself and her art. She also has put on hold her strong social consciousness. In a moment of startling clarity, her whole failed life passes before her eyes. No wonder she's been having visions of a weeping, headless black torso. Blacks have been denigrated and scapegoated over the centuries, denied their rightful place in the world. Tillie identifies with them. And just as Blacks are pregnant with potential, so is she.

Of course, if this pregnant torso is connected to the Black Madonna, she also could be crying because she's still a virgin *and* pregnant. What a paradox! Maybe something in the Madonna and Tillie has not been fully penetrated. For all her worldly experience, at times Tillie feels virginal. Her inability to establish herself fully in the world or to view herself as a capable person has its roots in being fatherless herself. It will take some time to absorb all of this, but thank god for Bud. This insight somehow seems connected to him.

At the moment, he's standing in the open doorway, looking puzzled. Tillie hurries over to greet him, throwing off her hood. Something hisses at her. Two distinct hisses. Jet and Xena pop out from behind some boxes, appearing ready to attack, their eyes fixed on Tillie's backpack. The cat she can handle, but not the snake. She screams and falls into Bud's arms, knocking him off balance, dropping her pack. He struggles to hold her up, in danger of going over himself, and grabs a railing on the landing for support.

Bird has escaped from the bag and is half running, half flying around the room, cat and snake in hot pursuit, weaving in and out of the workers and debris.

Tillie cries out, "You've got to stop them, Bud. They're going to kill Frank!"

"Your former lover?" Bud asks suspiciously, eyeing the workers. "Let me at him!" He tackles one of the men around the knees and holds on, pummeling the guy with his fists, shouting "Lay off my woman!" Both go over, and the cat, snake, and bird run in circles around the men struggling on the floor. Tillie hasn't had anyone fight over her since teenage days, and she likes the attention, flattering at her age. But there's something ludicrous about an older man, wearing a priest's collar, rolling around on the floor with a younger guy, each pummeling the other, flamenco rhythms punctuating their punches.

"Stop!" Tillie cries, trying to separate them. "He isn't Frank. There's Frank!"

Bud sits up, startled. Tillie is pointing at Bird. It peers over the top of a box it's hiding in.

"The pigeon?"

"Exactly."

Bud disentangles himself from the young worker, brushing off his clothes and straightening his priest collar, offering the guy his hand in apology and helping him up. The worker shakes the priest's hand and crosses himself, muttering something in Italian, and returns to work.

Sibyl has been standing there, watching. And then she notices Bird. But before she can grab her cleaver, Tillie stuffs the pigeon into one of her boxes, ignoring its muffled coos, and hands the carton to Bud.

"I need help moving these things to the garden at the Palazzo Cavalli-Franchetti. And you've got to do an exorcism! The pigeon thinks it's human."

Bud steadies himself and heads down the creaky wooden stairs to his boat. Tillie follows, carrying one of her boxes. While Bud loads up the rest of her art supplies, Tillie changes into her own clothes. She slips into a sage-colored '40's dress with cap sleeves, blousy top, and swinging skirt, grabs her poncho, throws a kiss to Sibyl, calls out "ciao," hisses at the cat and snake, clatters down the stairs, steps into the boat with Bud, and plops down.

The water reminds Tillie of where she is and just how tantalizing Venice can be.

Shimmering surfaces draw her in, tugging at some deep, shared, collective memory, casting alluring reflections that materialize and then dissolve like fog. She wants to move towards them, hoping to enter, but at the last moment, she's thrown back onto herself. A tease, Venice has more than seven veils that she flaunts, mistress of illusion and seduction. The dance goes on.

Tillie leans over the side of the boat and stares at her indistinct image. Sibyl's right. With her hair spiked, she does resemble the Statue of Liberty, and she's proud of it. Proud that a woman stands at the entrance to the New York Harbor. Proud to be connected to her. Sisterhood is powerful, and liberty might be the most powerful condition of all. Tillie—a new immigrant herself during her first visit to New York—had identified with all the others who had landed on America's shores, seeking freedom and an enlarged life. Even though Canada offered much to its sons and daughters, it lacked America's abundance and power.

A few words of the Russian immigrant Emma Lazarus, inscribed on the base of the statue, have stayed with Tillie. She holds one hand aloft, as if clutching a torch, and spouts: "Give me your tired, your poor, your huddled masses yearning to breathe free . . . Send these, the homeless, tempest-tost to me, I lift my lamp beside the golden door!"

That had described Tillie. Tired. Homeless. Tempest tossed. Yearning to be free. Not much has changed over the years. America hasn't exactly rescued her or made life easier. But she's learned that if she wants more, she has to put out extra. Being in America has placed bigger demands on her, forcing her to become more conscious. She wouldn't be in Venice now if it hadn't been for her sojourn in the States and the awakening that came with it.

Tillie's words get sucked into the motor's roar. Bud, who is standing at the wheel, feet planted firmly, revs the motor, weaving through the other vessels. They ride waves kicked up by other boats, traveling faster than the legal five-mile-per-hour speed limit, a wake rippling behind them. He smiles and waves at her.

Tillie feels like Cleopatra, traveling on her barge down the Nile, attendants waiting on her. The fantasy absorbs her until one of the boxes starts to shake and a hole appears in its side. Bird's beak emerges. Soon its whole head is freed. The pigeon looks around, fixing its gaze on Bud. Tillie is sure she detects a jealous gleam in its eyes. She dips her hand into her pocket and grabs a couple of peanuts that she offers Bird, hoping to distract it till they reach their destination and Bud can rid it of Frank's spirit. Liberty begins at home.

She leans over and trails one hand in the water, enjoying the velvety sensation between her fingers, letting herself drift and dream, not worrying about a destination, understanding Huck's attachment to his raft, the Mississippi carrying him along. Bird has finished the nuts and has shifted its focus to Tillie now, watching her from one eye, then the other. They stare at each other. She wonders if the pigeon can read her mind.

She's starting to feel the usual intense anxiety that fills her before she begins working on an installation, never knowing in advance how it will turn out or whether she'll be able to bring it off. Tillie begins with only a vague idea of where to start, forced to find and follow the work's inner core, the story it wants to tell. These aren't just butterflies frolicking in her stomach. They're bloody termites, gnawing at her gut, not giving her any peace until she's finally found the installation's focus.

It's fucking awful to be an artist, like having your liver eaten out every day. Or maybe Sisyphus is a better comparison. She's always at the bottom of some mountain she has to climb while pushing a huge rock in front of her. For the moment, it's seductive to just let herself float on the canal with Bud steering the boat, forgetting what's ahead of her.

Or behind. The headless one appears briefly in the boat's wake. Tillie tries to ignore her, not wanting to be distracted from the work she has to do. That's when it dawns on her: she can create a head for the torso. Maybe even some arms and legs. Actually, she already has casts she can use. Tillie doesn't know why she hasn't thought of this solution before. Maybe then she'll be free of the vision and Bud won't have to exorcise her, too.

The Palazzo Cavalli-Franchetti dock is fast approaching. Too fast. Bud slows down, creeping along, the boat settling more into the water. Nearing the Palazzo, he barely scrapes the dock as he brings the boat safely to rest next to it, jumps out, and ties up to the pier. He offers Tillie his hand, saying "My Lady," and helps her ashore. Then he helps her unload everything, and they hide the boxes behind a wall of bushes and shrubs.

Bird wriggles out of the box and perches on Tillie's shoulder, chewing on one ear and cooing. Bud and the pigeon eye each other warily.

Church bells chime, and Bud says, "Got to run. Evening mass and confession." But he plans to come by later and take Tillie out to dinner. He also agrees to perform an exorcism on Bird, though Tillie has mixed feelings about the whole thing. She's not sure she wants the pigeon cured if it will just become an ordinary bird, melting into the throng at St. Mark's. Yet something has to be done. She feels too much like Frank's puppet that he's controlling from the grave.

DEATH IN MENACE

Tillie works in the garden throughout the evening under a shroud of fog, fingers flying, ideas flowing, inspired by the creatures around her, visible and invisible: ground squirrels, birds, butterflies, ants, snails, bees, worms, spiders, snakes. Even a cat or two. The way they pursue their lives, focusing intently on the present moment, reinforces her approach to art. She loses herself in each piece she creates. She's grateful to have found this perfect spot where no one will stumble on her work until its ready to be revealed.

Humming a tune she recalls Carmine and Emil playing, she dresses the Muskrateers' torsos in outfits she made before leaving the States, identical tunics layered with Marin's famous peacock feathers. Turquoise becomes an island of color amidst black and various shades of brown, giving the effect of hundreds of aqua eyes peering out at the world. Bird mistakes the torsos for his own species and tries to mate with them, perching on their shoulders and poking around in the feathers with his beak, appearing puzzled when it doesn't find what it's looking for. It tilts its head, eyeing Tillie quizzically.

She laughs and steps back, studying the forms. Holy Christ, she can't believe it. They all resemble clones of the *Venus de Milo*. It hadn't dawned on her that she was unconsciously creating her own headless females. The idea must have been developing in her unconscious for a while, simultaneously showing up in Sibyl's puzzle. But aren't ideas themselves headless, seeming to form out of nothing?

Without heads, the torsos appear to lack direction or guidance. But Tillie wants to show that even without heads women are a compelling force in the world. They may have a long way to go before they can flesh themselves out fully, but they *are* rising, claiming bit by bit what's rightly theirs. Not unlike Joan of Arc, the *Venus de Milo*, without limbs or a head, could get an army to follow her, so potent are her wiles.

Satisfied with the way her vision is taking shape, Tillie has chosen things for her installation that will deconstruct over time, return to the earth. Life's ephemeral. So is much art. Creating a work that resembles her own existence appeals to her. Not getting bogged down in one place or with one person for any length of time parallels her art. It's why installations attract her. They don't hold up well, speaking more to the moment. Most curators won't buy them for their museum's permanent collections. Like humans, installations have only one life, surviving as long as the artist can find venues for them.

By the time Bud returns for her later that evening, Tillie has transformed the garden, incorporating it into her piece, melding the two, the torsos seeming to emerge from the earth. A few finishing touches remain. She needs to pick up a small aquarium for the Formosan termites. She likes the idea of them using their unique talents to help her piece decompose after the Biennale is over. It's also ecologically sound.

Tillie hopes Bud can help her hook up electrical wiring so she can show videos and play the sounds she's collected on tape. She wants to create the effect of women's voices speaking from within the flowers along the pathways. And she still needs to make a head for the headless Black Madonna. She's decided that wood is the most appropriate material, something she can chip away at. It doesn't require any special processing like clay does, and it's also biodegradable.

Essentially, though, her installation is complete. The various parts came together more quickly than she expected. Now she needs an audience for it. Here's where Bird could be a big help. It could fly over the city, floating a banner behind it that invites people to the Palazzo Cavalli-Franchetti for an opening extravaganza. A combination sixtieth birthday celebration and Carnivale for the Muskrateers, a breakout installation for Tillie, and a welcoming of the twenty-first century.

Just thinking of entering another century, as well as her sixtieth year, makes Tillie's heart palpitate and her mouth go dry. Until now, she's managed to push away the full reality of aging and the passing of time. But entering her sixties as well as a new millennium forces her to acknowledge the sad truth: death is chipping away at her, leaving its mark. It's turning her into a work of art, death the ultimate artist, giving shape to the visible and invisible. She's realizing she can't stop this process. Yet accepting it doesn't seem a very viable option. Accepting the unacceptable. She needs some distractions.

She looks around for Bird, already imagining a filmy, feminine-looking banner announcing the extravaganza that wouldn't be too heavy for the pigeon to carry. But the pigeon must have gotten wind of her plans. It's flown the coop.

Tillie and Bud Dally

Tillie feels totally energized after her efforts in the garden and is eager to have some time alone with Bud. He intrigues her more than any man she's met. Worldly. Erudite. A "man of God" who also seems non-conformist— or maybe a true man of God *is* non-conformist. And there's still so much more to discover about him. He's an unexplored continent and completely foreign.

At six PM, Bud picks Tillie up in his boat and takes her to the Trattoria Poste Vecie near the Grand Canal. She asks if he's concerned about parishioners seeing him with her, but he shakes his head.

"I often dine with potential church supporters or troubled church members. There's a lot of public relations involved in my job. Money raising."

The host leads them to their seats and a waiter brings complimentary glasses of Prosecco. They order an antipasto of grilled mollusks to be followed by *orata* for Bud and *fritto misto* for Tillie with some grilled vegetables to be shared. When the waiter leaves, they look shyly at each other, struggling to make conversation.

"A crazy day, eh," Tillie says.

"*Molto pazzesco!*" Bud says, making a circle with one hand in the air. "Eh?"

"Very crazy. Termites taking over your friend's flat. The pigeon taking you over. What happened to that bird?"

"Vamoosed. Decided it didn't want to be exorcised, I guess."

"I don't blame it for not wanting to lose its distinctiveness. Or to lose you."

Tillie can feel herself blush. She's grateful for the candlelight and for the food's arrival. With nothing to eat since morning, she digs in, famished. Aware of Bud studying her, she looks up, but his glasses hide his eyes, her own image reflected in the lenses. It's strange to see herself in that way, slightly distorted. Her spikes have wilted, and her hair resembles newly mown hay, falling every which way on her head.

"A penny for your thoughts," he says.

His question disappoints her. So mundane. But it breaks the silence.

"If you want the truth . . ."

"Always!"

"Always? Okay." She gulps some wine. "I'm thinking how weird it is to be sitting in a restaurant in Venice, having dinner with a priest and thinking lustful things about him. I've never dated a clergyman before."

"Neither have I!"

They both laugh, and he raises his glass in a toast.

"To our communion."

"Except I'm not clergy," Tillie says.

"Some artists are priests, too."

Tillie takes a piece of bread and dips it into some sauce left on the antipasto plate. Then she offers it to Bud, placing it on his tongue, watching him swallow it. He puts his glass to her lips so she can sip his drink, and they stare at each other across the table, eyes locked, though for Tillie it's her own eyes she's staring into, reflected in his glasses.

After dinner, they climb into Bud's outboard. The three-quarter moon makes a zig-zaggy silvery path for them. Lights bounce off the canal's surface, and Tillie feels soothed by the sound of water lapping against pilings.

The boat passes under a bridge, and they pull up to a dock. She stands up and staggers a little, the boat's motion throwing her off balance. Bud bows and takes her hand, helping her ashore. She titters and follows him into the dimly lighted vestibule of the *pensione*, owned by a discreet friend of his, Bud's home away from home. She's grateful to avoid Sibyl's flat and all the chaos there, though she feels a little guilty about leaving the others to deal with it.

After following Bud up the stairs, she waits while he unlocks a door on the second floor. He bows, ushering her into the room. Then he turns on a table lamp. Long lavender fringes dangle from the shade. A bottle of Veuve Clicquot sits in a small bucket of ice on the table next to the bed along with two champagne glasses and some truffles.

She claps her hands. "Wow. What's the occasion?"

He looks at her and says, "To celebrate our meeting." His voice sounds as if it comes from the bottom of a rain barrel, its resonance turning her inside out and making her heart scurry around in her chest.

He switches on the radio and finds a station that's playing flamenco. She snaps her fingers, and her feet, refusing to keep still, flit around the room. Bud gets a towel from the bathroom and wraps it around the champagne bottle's top, gently loosening the cork until it pops. Then he fills the glasses, raises his, and says, "To us and the night."

The bubbles burst on Tillie's lips. She avoids his eyes, enjoying the smell and taste of the champagne. She says, "Let's sit on the balcony and watch the boats go by." Her mind starts racing, and she wonders if she's worn her diaphragm. Then she remembers she doesn't need one anymore.

It's dawning on Tillie that she doesn't even know this man, and she's thrown back into the anxiety she used to feel as a young woman when she first started sleeping around. How awkward it all felt, the groping and clenching and being afraid to tell the men they weren't doing it right. Tillie ended up frustrated more times than not, needing to go home and masturbate, using whatever was handy—a cucumber, a banana, a carrot. It's a wonder she hasn't turned vegetarian.

Bud leads her out to the tiny balcony, and they sit there on a wooden love seat, holding hands, sipping champagne, and feeding each other truffles. He isn't wearing his clerical collar but is dressed in the black turtleneck that shows off his pecs.

She suddenly gets an overwhelming yearning for her mother. Something about Bud reminds her of May, though she can't identify just what it is. Maybe she's longing for the nourishment her mother didn't give her.

Tillie visited May in Calgary right after leaving Whistler and helped her move into the Little Bo Peep rest home. Tillie called her before leaving for Venice, and her mother said she'd met some old-timer named Sam in the new place. He'd been a rodeo star in his youth. Tillie could tell May had her spurs into him already and was giving the other men a run for their money as well. At her mother's age, she needs to move fast, though Tillie realizes it's true at her age, too. She had given her mother Sibyl's number in Venice and said, "Invite me to the wedding."

These thoughts are running through her mind when she turns to Bud and calls him "Mother" by mistake. They both look at each other, startled.

"Oops! A Freudian slip," Tillie says. She really meant to say Father, she says, as a way of teasing him and loosening things up a bit. The situation has made her tense, and she wishes she did have a father *and* a mother to turn to.

She almost wishes Bird would show up and rescue her, but the only birds in sight are some seagulls making their haunting sound.

Once again Bud says, "A penny for your thoughts," only this time she's grateful to tell him what she's thinking. He says, "You must be feeling homesick," which makes Tillie laugh because she really doesn't have a home to speak of. She tells him that, and he says, "I'll shelter you."

His response makes her think of mother birds and the nests they make for their young and Bird's disappearance. That then makes her think of Frank's death, and it occurs to her that May can't live forever either, even if she gives every indication of doing so. Tillie starts feeling weepy, though she tries to hide it, not wanting to spoil the evening. But Bud has heard lots of women crying in that cage he hangs out in and seems to sense what's going on inside her. He pats her arm affectionately, setting off a flood of tears.

The ephemeral relationship with Bud contributes to her sorrow. Tillie will be leaving Venice soon, and there's no way she can budge him from the church. She's a little girl again, her life out of control and on the verge of something she doesn't understand. Worse, Bud triggers all sorts of realizations in her she hasn't thought about much, including the makeshift life she lives, flitting from one place to the next, as transient as her art. He's so grounded, part of an institution that isn't going anywhere. He might not believe much in the church, but he still has something concrete to hold onto that has deep roots. He also knows where his next meal is coming from. Tillie made the mistake of depending on art, the most fickle thing to rely on.

These concerns pour out of her mouth. Bud sets down his glass and hers, embracing her. She blubbers, "I feel like a bloody cliché, the starving artist, living from day to day. I'm tired of the insecurity and not having a place to call my own, rattling around the world like one of those dandelion puffs I watched as a kid. I loved the magical white fluffy seed head floating on air and the wind carrying it all over the place before its parts fell to the earth and sometimes germinated."

She blurts out all of her fears of aging and not succeeding as an artist and growing old alone. Her words are interspersed with wails, tears filling the place, their night of love turning into a squall instead.

Bud tries to convince Tillie that she's creating her own testament in each installation she makes, but Tillie doesn't quite buy it.

"No one's really interested in my crazy compositions. I do them to keep sane. They give my life some meaning and purpose. Otherwise, I'd just be another pitiful bourgeois."

This flood of tears builds a bridge between them, and she realizes how intimate it can be to cry with someone, more intimate than sex in its way. She wonders out loud if women's tears have kept Venice partly under water over the years, especially with Venus, the goddess of love, being the city's patroness, all that beauty pulling at everyone's heartstrings.

Tillie's storm subsides to a few sniffles and hiccups. They finish the champagne, and she feels emotionally spent, wanting to sink into the velvety Venetian night and Bud's arms. By now he feels like someone she's known all her life. She rests her head on his shoulder and stares at the lights streaking the canal, feeling as if she has just been burped after a big emotional spewing. They sit that way for a long while, suspended in time and space.

And then Bud tells her to close her eyes. "I have a surprise for you." He gets up and goes inside.

She waits, listening to the late-night revelers passing below. They're singing an unfamiliar song in Italian. A cat howls in response.

Then Bud says, "Open your eyes."

He's standing there, silhouetted in the doorway, wearing a Mountie outfit and singing the song Nelson Eddy and Jeanette MacDonald had made famous, the "Indian Love Call." She can't believe what she's seeing and hearing.

After, he says, "I've always dreamed of meeting a real Mountie, so this is the next best thing. I also want you to feel at home."

Tillie's says, "I wonder if 'Mounted,' as in Royal Canadian Mounted Police, has sexual connotations."

Bud laughs. "If it doesn't, it should."

He leaps towards her in a blur of red and black, the spurs on his boots clicking, and they melt into each other's arms, walking as one into the bedroom and falling onto the bed. She undoes the cross-strap and belt before unbuttoning the gold tabs on his scarlet tunic, giving her access to his breeches and all they contain—a pair of white boxer shorts with images of Popeye in various poses flexing his muscles. But nothing pops out of the shorts.

Tillie strokes Bud's thighs and his stomach, working her way slowly towards the prize. Yet when she reaches it, she finds that Bud's bud won't be budged. It sleeps in the thick nest of his pubic hair, refusing to be roused. The scene reminds her of fairy tales where the princess is under a spell and won't awaken until the prince appears and breaks it. In this case, it isn't the princess who's under a spell. It's Bud's cock.

This isn't the first time she's been with a man who couldn't get it up, but it's never easy, and she's hesitant to disturb his nub. A man's cock is so intimately tied in with his identity and manhood. A woman doesn't have the same pressure to perform. Still, his impotence makes her feel undesirable, but he quickly reassures her.

"You've had such an impact on me, I've become too concerned about pleasing you."

So they shift their focus from genitals to playfully exploring each other's bodies more fully. Tillie tries on the Mountie garb because she wants to see if Mounties really do always get their man. But being buttoned up to her chin and belted in tightly makes her feel claustrophobic. She has trouble breathing, and the boots fit too snugly. She can't change fast enough. Would a serious relationship give her a similar feeling?

That's when Bud shows her the closet full of costumes he keeps there. He throws open the door and says, "Voila! I still haven't given up my interest in acting. You can take an actor out of the theatre, but you can't take the theatre out of the actor."

Tillie also is a ham, wanting to get more physically involved in her installations and do performance pieces as well. She dives into the closet, fingering a nun's habit; a sea captain's outfit; a cowboy's chaps, shirt, and hat; an American Indian chief's headdress and ceremonial dress; a sailor suit; a sheik's robes; costumes for a hobo, gangster, jockey, Saint Nicolas, clown, elf, gnome, animal trainer, ballerina, Buddhist monk, horse, bear, tuba, Martian, Indian maid, robot, undertaker, doorman, witch, belly dancer, Superman, spider, and kangaroo.

They spend the next couple of hours turning the room into a stage and performing for each other, mixing and matching genders and types, pairing the Buddhist monk with a witch, Tillie the monk and Bud the witch.

By the time he becomes an Indian Chief and she a nun, Bud asserts himself, his erect cock having a noble tilt. She wraps prayer beads around it and says a few Hail Marys, intent on the eye staring at her, weeping a little. She licks the tip. The prayer beads fall away, as does the nun's habit, and she rubs her firm nipples against his swollen penis.

Unlike some of her friends, Tillie hasn't lost her taste for sex, though she may have to work at it more now. She shares her sexual fantasies with Bud, and they both dissolve into the heat of lovemaking, holding off the little death as long as they can.

It's close to dawn when their age catches up with them and they prepare for sleep. When Tillie sees Bud wearing the Mountie's hat to bed, as well as a black leather glove on his left hand, she thinks he's still playacting. But he says he always sleeps wearing this hat. Tillie thinks that wearing a hat to bed fits if he's the Mad Hatter. She asks about the glove, and he says he's been waking up with bloody welts on his hand every morning.

"I thought it was stigmata. Then I realized I was biting my own hand. I've been wearing the glove to protect myself from my impulses."

Just before they fall asleep, she remembers their earlier encounter that day when he avoided her.

"Where were you going in such a rush?"

He laughs and pulls the covers up to his chin. "The Mad Hatter's tea party."

Tillie's unveiling

Though she slept only a couple of hours, Tillie feels renewed the next day, refreshed by the morning mist and amorous memories. Love itself can be an aphrodisiac, eroticizing everything. Floating along the Calle della Madonna, she plans to finish her installation that day and inhales the mold and decay smell that permeates these old structures. Today it seems more evident and appealing, helping her to appreciate her own decomposing body. She also feels love for the Muskrateers and anticipates seeing them. She hopes the other women will help publicize her artwork and organize their celebration. Daddy, especially, should have some ideas.

Bursting with plans, invigorated by Bud's stimulating imagination and other attributes, she meanders through the streets and canals until she reaches Sibyl's place. There's a little spring in her step as she climbs the stairs, echoes of her younger self still lingering.

Inside the apartment, she finds the women sitting around the dining room table in their nightclothes, listening to Carmine and Emil's CDs.

"Jesus Christ, I knew it, he's converted you," Sibyl screeches, throwing up her hands.

The others burst out laughing and point at Tillie. She had put on the first thing she grabbed when she woke up that morning—the nun's wimple, the spider's black tights, and the Indian maid's leather tunic, not bothering to check herself out in a mirror. No wonder she got some strange looks on her way to Sibyl's.

"Thought you'd drowned," Daddy says, snapping her fingers in time to the music but looking ghoulish, her face coated in some green goop.

"Or gotten arrested for copulating in the Palazzo Cavalli-Franchetti's garden," Moll adds.

"We were about to start dredging the canals," Sibyl says. "After breakfast, of course. Hey, you've got mail, kid." She points at a Global Express envelope on the sideboard.

Tillie grabs it, plops onto a chair, and rips open the wrapper. "Look! It confirms I've inherited Frank's art. Let's celebrate!" Tillie explains everything to the Muskrateers. "Those photos are mine now. I can't believe it."

"I'd like to see them," Daddy says.

Tillie doesn't mind strangers looking at the photos. And she has no problem with the Muskrateers seeing her naked. But she's surprised at how much she resists the idea of being viewed through Frank's lenses in the intimate close-ups he did. The images themselves are anonymous. It isn't likely anyone would say "Hey, that's Tillie's breast." The anonymity made it okay for her to model for him. But she hadn't anticipated the pictures hanging in public view, even though she knew Frank was an artist and would want to display them.

There's not much she can do now. She's exposed herself already by telling the women the gallery's name. Let the cat out of the bag, so to speak. On cue, Jet rubs against her leg and winds her tail around Tillie's calf, meowing. Tillie starts to sneeze, her allergies acting up for the first time in a while.

She said, "I need to publicize my installation first. And fast. Time's running out."

Sibyl suggests an ad in the paper. Full page.

"That's costly," Daddy says, "and there's no hook for people. What's going to draw them in? She's not a famous artist, and there's plenty of art to see around here."

"I was thinking of a Carnivale and welcoming of the twenty-first century combined with our sixtieth birthday celebration," Tillie says. "A happening."

"I'm for turning this birthday into a happening," Daddy says. "Maybe menopause isn't the end of our productive years after all."

"It can be a resurgence. Another chance," Tillie says. "Maybe we're coming to age instead of coming of age. Coming into our own."

"That's a mouthful," Sibyl says, muffling a cough. Her lungs sound like they're filled with gravel. "You really believe that stuff?"

Tillie nods. "We need to push beyond our mothers' limits and fully claim our own lives. Maybe we can even claim their lost lives. Rescue them from oblivion. Give them a voice."

No longer ensnared by the social and biological expectations to procreate, Tillie feels the Muskrateers *are* entering a new age, personally and collectively. Everything's up for grabs. New identities are surfacing. It's heady stuff.

"Hey, we could carry banners naked through St. Mark's Square announcing the happening," Sibyl says.

"We want to attract people, not scare them away," Moll says.

"I know Carmine and Emil will announce it where they're performing," Sibyl says.

"I'd like them to come to the celebration," Tillie says. "But we've got to get on it, now!"

"Why not run a full-page ad inviting the whole city to a party in the Palazzo Cavalli-Franchetti garden," Daddy says. "People love free booze and the works—food, music. That should draw a crowd."

Tillie takes off the wimple. "Yeah, but who's going to pay for it?"

"I still like the idea of running naked through St. Mark's Square with banners," Sibyl says, slithering off to the bedroom.

Reluctantly, Tillie takes the Muskrateers to the Kat's Paw Gallery, managing to get them lost a few times in the maze of streets and canals, anything to delay the inevitable. They accidentally run into the place on one of the side streets, and she has no choice but to enter with her entourage. Her stomach's doing loop the loops. She's nervous about seeing these pictures now that she knows Frank is dead. What will they reveal about her? About him?

Nothing has prepared her for the crowd gathered in front of the photos.

"What's going on here?" Sibyl hisses. "It's only art. You'd think someone has died."

"Someone has died," Tillie says.

"Hey, Tillie, look," Daddy says. "These photos have won some big prize from the Biennale judges—they've put your guy on the map."

Tillie is standing eyeball to nipple with an image of her left breast. In black and white, it resembles the center of a bullseye. The price tag attached to it reads three million lira. Fragmented, she has more value than she ever did in one piece.

"Holy cow, you guys. I'm rich! I'm fucking rich! I don't have to stow away in the baggage compartment going home."

The other Muskrateers stand there, gaping, looking puzzled.

Sibyl says, "Where's the Marilyn Monroe shot?"

"Yeah," Moll says. "This just looks like abstract art."

Daddy is studying the images. She says, "Pretty skilled stuff. He's blown up each body part and superimposed each one with other parts. A palimpsest."

Presented like this, Tillie comprises more in her fragmented sections than she could hope to in a full-body nude. The images each have their own meaning, and when they're all placed together, as they are in the gallery, they make a statement greater than the parts. By probing her biology, they comment on humanity in general. Nothing personal. Just art. It wasn't Frank so much as his camera that did the work, giving concrete form to his vision, pulling something forth from him *and* Tillie that has transcended both of them.

Now that she owns these images, Tillie feels reconstructed—resurrected. They used to say that life begins at forty, but for Tillie it seems to be sixty. Her life is starting to feel as if it has meaning and substance. She isn't just a surface hanging on a wall. She has depth and integrity.

And the photos are also making some money. A lot.

Tillie stands there in shock, staring at the images, her mouth hanging open. She says, "I didn't think art was a money-making thing. I thought only business people made money. Jesus, am I going to be corrupted?"

"Don't worry, kid," Sibyl says. "If it's a problem, I'll take it off your hands."

Always alert for a good marketing opportunity, Daddy says, "You know, if you just put one of these photos in your installation, you'll have instant publicity—hell, why not take advantage of Frank's new celebrity?"

"Geez, Daddy," Moll says, "I'm surprised at you. Always preaching about women making it on their own, not depending on men."

"Yeah," Daddy says, "but I'm not a fool. Some of my best friends are men."

Sibyl's staring out the window, watching an elderly Italian matron dressed in black bite into a pastry. "I'd like to take my money and run before Raleigh loses it all. Maybe I'll go underground. Become an outlaw. Just disappear. Let him face the music. He got us into this mess."

Tillie blanches at Sibyl's choice of words: "underground" and "disappear." That might be happening sooner for Sibyl than she thinks.

"I know what you mean," Tillie says. "I don't have any problem using Frank's work for business purposes. He owes me. All those hours of posing for nothing."

When they had lived together, she and Frank had talked of collaborating on something. This isn't exactly a collaboration, unless you can count Bird's input. But she doesn't mind having a picture of herself included in her installation. For now, she decides to take the one that reminds her of a bullseye since Frank had apparently emailed her that image before he died and called it Black Madonna. She'll officially give it that title. If it resembles a black hole, she'll just have to live with it. Perhaps some things are absolute. Except black holes seem to be evolving. Just as humans are.

It isn't easy convincing the gallery owner that Tillie now owns the photos. The letter from Michael Love and a phone call to his law office clinches it. Amidst a good deal of emotional Italian verbiage that Sibyl helps interpret, and the owner's flailing hands and arms, Tillie finally leaves the place, the Muskrateers escorting her, carting off some of Frank's pictures so she has a way to pay for the ad.

After safely depositing everything at Sibyl's (she reassures Tillie that the Formosan termites have been completely wiped out), they're just in time to put a full-page ad in the next day's *Venice Gondolier Sun*. It announces a millennium celebration that Saturday, a mini-Carnivale, featuring an award-winning photographer's work. Not exactly a lie. Art's a fiction anyway, and at least the notice will get Tillie the audience she seeks for her work.

The Mad Hatter meets Mary Magdalene

That night, at Bud's request, Tillie returns to the *pensione*. Feeling like old familiars, they explore each other's minds and bodies. He seems genuinely interested in all of her parts, but not in the way that Frank had been, through a camera lens. For a man who's never been married, to a woman at least, Bud has a great appreciation for—and curiosity about—her anatomy.

On his knees, as if in prayer, he first inspects her feet. "This little piggy went to market. This little piggy stayed home. This little piggy went . . ." He squeals, chewing on one of her big toes, bouncing around the bed like a puppy. He nibbles on her ear lobes, sending shivers down her spine, reminding her of a black lab she had as a girl whose erect red penis always aroused her. He intersperses licks and kisses with playful love bites all over her, inserting his tongue between her fingers and toes, finding crevices in Tillie's body that even she didn't know existed.

When he does finally reach her genitals, he's worshipful, effusively describing her garden of delights, reeling off a lot of "Mamma Mias" and "poesías" and "dolcis." He seems sincere in his praise of the many pink petals he finds there—her rose garden. She responds to his tongue and fingers that search for the hidden pearl and whatever else remains out of sight.

Odors from her genitals that she finds offensive he thinks are redolent, evocative, and he buries his nose in them. He fondles her breasts, buzzing around her, dipping from time to time into her honey pot, but equally as interested in the rest of her body, each part awakening gradually under his touch. She surrenders to his attentions, reshaped by his caresses, her whole being singing in response. The words from Inanna's hymn spout forth again from her lips:

> My honey-man, my honey-man sweetens me always.
> My lord, the honey-man of the gods,
> He is the one my womb loves best.
> His hand is honey, his foot is honey,
> He sweetens me always.

These Italian men. Tillie has heard about their lovemaking abilities, and it seems to be true. She's never been with a man so sincere in his appreciation of her as a woman.

Later, propped up on the pillows, they idly stroke each other's skin, chatting. They're about to have another go at it, but Bud's tulip doesn't open, remaining limp, vulnerable—a sprout. He pokes at it, disconsolately, but it's unresponsive. He shrugs.

"It's getting harder to get hard. The truth is, I'm not as potent as I once was. I never know when it'll stiffen."

Tillie brushes it with her lips. "I like it even more when it's limp. Like a finger pointing downward. A stiffened penis can be impersonal and demanding. An independent force asserting its will on the world. The uncivilizable side of Pan." She's grateful Bud isn't just this remote energy.

She circles her neck with his clerical collar and drapes his robe over her shoulders, turning her head from side to side. "Geez, this feels like a dog collar. How can you wear it all the time?"

He barks. She laughs and runs her fingers through his beard.

"Got it, sweetie. I really don't get it, though. You're such a free spirit. How can you—a lover!—stay with an institution that's done so much damage in the name of love? I hate imperialism, especially religious imperialism."

Bud gets out of bed and slips into his boxer shorts—tonight they're covered with images of Superman—and starts to do charades, acting out his response.

"You mean you've been carrying on a charade all these years?"

He nods, sprinting over to the closet and slipping into a tan trench coat, collar raised, planting a fedora on his head.

"You've been spying? Doing undercover work?"

"Madam, you have just won a weekend in Venice with yours truly."

She sits up straight, wrapping herself in his clerical robe. "Look at all the damage Christians have done in the name of love."

"They've had the wrong kind of love in mind." He does a pirouette. "They left out Eros!"

"You're not kidding. Except the arrows of Eros don't always bring happiness and union." She tosses his robe onto the floor, pulls the sheet around her, and, frowning, takes a sip of wine. "I think all institutions get ossified, not just the church. They're more interested in perpetuating themselves than evolving and changing. That's where the devil gets a foothold. I think it's evil to stop growth, to kill off new life."

Bud flops down next to her on the bed, pretending to shoot a rifle at some invisible foe in the ceiling. "I agree. The church has done a lot of damage, driving out other religions. Except not everything associated with the church is evil. The structure might be rotten, but I think ritual's important—transforming. It's the most important thing we do. That and confession. Soul cleansing. Being part of a community of believers. I have faith in these things. It allows me to tolerate the organization. Besides, the church has been my only parent. I might rebel against it, but if I destroy what gave me life, then I destroy myself. That doesn't mean I like everything about it. Do you like everything about your parents? Your mother, that is?"

"No. I have to work at finding things to like. It's just that I hate how the Catholic Church treats women. It might have made Mary equal with the Holy Spirit, but, hey, women don't have much say in the ruling structure. I haven't seen any female popes or cardinals or bishops."

"I know. I prefer more diversity myself."

"Come to North America!" she says.

"Is that an invitation?"

"If you need one. Choice. Multiple expressions of the divinity and ways to reach God. It's all there."

She rolls onto her stomach and rests her cheek on Bud's hairy chest, listening to his heartbeat, amazed at its regularity, stunned that something so tiny could be so powerful. Frightening to think it could stop and her life would stop, too. Already she's that attached to him. She wonders how much damage Bud will do to her in the name of love.

Pushing aside her fear, she plows on. "I want to return to pre-Christian times. Start again. Uncover what we've lost or concealed with church doctrine. We can't experience ecstasy if we're squashed under all that dogma."

She remembers the pill Daddy had given them and how it—temporarily—loosened their restraints, opening them to a fuller experience of their surroundings and their emotions, letting them out of prison. It seemed like pure communion with the known and unknown, the only kind of religion she can tolerate.

"I still don't understand how you've stayed in the church all this time."

He turns towards her, lying on his side, and leans on one elbow, lightly fingering her nipples with his gloved hand.

"Simple. I don't think you change anything by attacking from outside. You have to infiltrate. Become one of the oppressors. Undermine their authority. Offer an alternative."

"So what's your alternative?"

He licks his lips. "Sex."

"The goddess of love instead of the god of love?"

"I'd prefer to have both. The two of them copulating. That would produce something interesting. Create a new religion."

"Yeah. I'm for that. Poor Mary and Joséph. Their son's immaculate conception. No wonder Jesus turned out the way he did. It's time for him to grow up and get married."

Tillie tries to picture Venus and Jesus doing it. She's sure Jesus was dark skinned considering where he was born. And she's always imagined Venus the way Botticelli did, light-skinned, on the half shell. She never could eat shellfish again after viewing that painting. It would be like eating the goddess.

"If that happened," Tillie says, "we could stop polarizing black and white. We'd all be people of color."

"Aren't we anyway? I wouldn't call you white, exactly. Sort of a creamy beige." He holds up her arm and stares at it. Then he licks it and smacks his lips. "Definitely not white."

She pulls away. "Compared to you I am."

"You've got your own Black genes. All of us originated over fifty thousand years ago in Africa. Maybe more. We all began there." He lies back again and stares at the ceiling, waving his arms as if he's conducting an orchestra. "I think the flesh is sacred and should be worshipped and enjoyed. Fully. Not just some abstract spirit." He pounds his chest. "Me Tarzan; you Jane! Let's go off into the jungle together."

"You're saying no spirit except in the flesh. You *are* radical!"

He tilts his hat. "*Grazie, Signora.* You are so perceptive. Except the Jews have a similar idea."

Tillie shivers. "I just thought of a grizzly I saw recently in Canada. I can see why people have formed bear cults. Bears seem so human—awakening something basic in us, something we've lost touch with, an untamed feminine spirit. It could be dangerous. Ripping things apart. Deadly, even."

Bud dips his fingers into the wine and sprinkles it on her forehead. "I now christen you in the name of the bear cult." He licks the wine off his fingers. "Anyone who offers a direction different from the status quo is a menace."

"That's the title of my latest installation: 'Death in Menace.'"

"Very appropriate. Death certainly can be a menace." Bud yawns and strokes his beard.

"So how do you promote your kind of spirituality?"

"I write scripts and make art films, Signora, under a pseudonym, of course. 'The Mad Hatter's Tea Party' is the name of my production company. You didn't think they were just having tea, did you?"

"*Art* films? A film's a film. Right?"

"Wrong."

"So what's so artful about the films you make?"

"They're tasteful, erotic productions."

"Porn?"

"Never! We produce well-crafted films that cater to one's prurient impulses."

"Was that where you were going the other morning?"

"We had a crisis. One of our actresses didn't show up for filming, but the show must go on. I'm in charge of recruiting, too, so I had to find a replacement—fast."

"You found one?"

"Of course. Many actors want to devote themselves to the god and goddess of love. We have a very high-quality production. Subtle. Suggestive. Nothing overt. A lot takes places under the covers. But the point gets across, if you get my meaning."

"Get it. You mean you don't show genitals on camera?"

"Never. That's vulgar. I admit that occasionally a sheep or horse can't control its erection and the camera captures it, but that's understandable."

"Bestiality?"

"Only hinted at. We do a lot of tricks with the camera, using computer editing. Provoke viewers' fantasies. Titillate. Nothing crass. We're trying to resexualize life. Awaken sexual energy. It binds us together and unites us with the Divine. In fact, the body's the only way to the Divine. Why else would we have it?"

"What's your pseudonym?"

For the first time, Bud appears embarrassed. He looks away, pretending to be studying the hand that he chews on in the night. "Mary Magdalene. My favorite Biblical character, next to Lazarus."

She stares at him, her mouth hanging open, wondering if she's fallen for a hermaphrodite. But he's all man. It's just unsettling to call her lover Mary. She understands, in principle at least, that everyone is bisexual. Maybe that orientation will be the wave of the twenty-first century. And she's noticed that as people age, they take on more characteristics of the opposite sex. It could be easier, then, to slip into bisexuality, to not be so rigidly separated by gender. Yet at the moment, she's still a '50's girl at heart, from the prairies, where a man is a man and a woman is a woman.

"What happens to all the money you're making? I thought priests took a vow of poverty."

"Not all of us. Most of what's left over after expenses goes back into the film company and our many projects. The rest supplements my retirement fund. I plan to travel—see the world. Interested in joining me?"

Tillie is still trying to digest this latest disclosure about Bud. She feels as if she's opened the Book of Revelation, only the content isn't what she's expected. She gets up and looks at herself in the mirror. Her spiked hair has lost its spikes again, falling into a shaggy cap on her head. Her face is beginning to deconstruct, puffy circles forming under her eyes, the skin loosening from the bones beneath.

She slips into one of Bud's undershirts, using it for a nightie. He turns off the light on his nightstand. His eyelids droop and his head falls back onto the pillow, giving the Mountie hat a rakish angle. The night claims him. Soon he's asleep, his snores sounding like a nest of angry bees.

Tillie glides out to the balcony to work on the head she's begun sculpting. A block of dark wood she found on the shore is the right size. She works on it only at night, in total darkness, after Bud's fallen asleep, letting her fingers and carving tools find in the wood's grain the features hidden there, wanting to surprise herself with the outcome. Only the starlight guides her, and she works on, ignoring the time. The voices of gondoliers drift through the darkness, the disembodied sounds floating in the fertile soil of her imagination.

Maybe darkness and death *are* the source of life and not just the end. The Black Madonna the death mother? Death like rich black earth that, when turned regularly, produces abundant growth? Death, an artist, a creator, not just the destroyer, shaping us, pushing us into a deeper awareness of all that existence offers? It's a view of mortality she's never considered before. Death, a rich underground spring that feeds everyone. Maybe black holes needn't be feared after all.

Now if she can just get used to having Mary Magdalene for her lover.

MAY'S EARTHQUAKE

On her way back to Sibyl's the next morning, Tillie runs into flyers plastered everywhere announcing the "Canadian Carnivale and Centennial Bash at the Palazzo Cavalli-Franchetti Gardens, featuring the work of world-renowned artist Tillie Bloom and award-winning photographer Frank Gallo. Food, Drinks, Ethnic Music, and Surprise Guests. Costume required for admittance. Saturday, 5 PM to ???"

She bursts out laughing. The Muskrateers have really come through, the best PR group she's ever had.

When she steps into Sibyl's flat, she almost doesn't recognize Daddy. Her hair's dyed black, its original color, reminding Tillie of when they first met.

"Hey, girl," Tillie says, "what's happened to you? Your roots are showing."

"All these Mediterranean types inspired me—time for a change anyway—been bleaching my hair longer than I can remember—it's falling out. Curious to see what I really look like."

"What's left looks groovy."

"I agree," Moll says.

"Thanks for all the flyers, guys," Tillie says. "You must've worked all night getting them out."

Between coughing fits, Sibyl shouts from her bedroom, "Hey, Tillie, your mum called. It's urgent. Wants you to call her."

Tillie heads for the bedroom and digs into her backpack, searching for her address book. "Anyone know what time it is? I need to figure out when to phone Mum."

"Ten o'clock here," Sibyl says.

"The middle of the night in Calgary. I'll have to wait till later to call."

The message has set off a major drama in the pit of Tillie's stomach. It's reacting as if the floor has suddenly opened up and there's a lion pit below. An urgent call from her mother could mean only one thing: there must be a medical emergency. May has limitations as a mother, but she's Tillie's only parent. It's hard to imagine her dying. She embodies the life force, filled with a real *joie de vivre*. Food, men, sex—she's never lost her appetite for any of them, her main reason for living.

When Tillie was just a girl, she'd watched her mother sitting at the kitchen table, head lost in clouds of smoke that drifted out of her mouth and nostrils. She never did learn to inhale. May tripped out for hours, sipping coffee, puffing away on a package of Players, living in a dream world.

Tillie did eventually figure out what her mother was thinking about, at least some of the time. She found a big deck of cards in one of May's dresser drawers. They were stuck under a fancy nightgown that Tillie never saw her wear, at least not with Harold. Some of the cards had pictures of naked women in all different positions—bent over, legs spread, standing on their heads almost. Some had naked men with big, erect cocks. When Tillie shuffled the deck, it looked like the men and women were having sex. Sometimes the cards got mixed up and women were doing it with women and men with other men.

That experience almost made Tillie give up snooping for good. All she could think of for days were those erotic images. She spent a lot of time in the bathroom, rubbing herself raw. Imagine what the pictures did to May. No wonder she brought in a string of male boarders to service her. Tillie didn't know where May found them, but she dragged them home, some of the time ending up in their beds in the basement room, right under Harold's nose.

May really got going with Maurice La Blanc, a Frenchie. Tillie didn't blame her for falling for him. If she'd been older, she would have too. He had Rock Hudson's good looks, only Maurice definitely wasn't gay.

The two of them really steamed up that basement. Tillie used to climb the pipes down there so she could peer over the rafters into the spare room.

The furnace rattled and wheezed, masking any noises she made. May and Maurice put on quite a show, huffing and puffing, slipping and sliding, arousing Tillie. She understood then why some women want to be house-wives. Her earliest sexual experience was with a water pipe.

She used water pipes in the first installation she ever did, a room full of them, all different shapes and sizes, caught up in a giant spider's web. Spiders were always attacking her in the basement. Of course, Tillie had to make the pipes leak a little to simulate dripping penises. But the really difficult part was getting friends to let her film them doing it so she could flash images of copulating couples on the walls. It was a big hit.

One Christmas Eve, Maurice dressed up as Santa. He looked like the real thing. He planned to pass out the gifts on Christmas morning, but he was giving May a preview. The tree was lit up, the colored red and blue and green blobs the only light in the room. It looked magical. While Tillie knew Santa didn't really exist, for a few minutes she believed he did, and she and her mother had an option on him.

May and Maurice must have thought everyone was sleeping, but Tillie was watching through the French doors from the hallway. May filled Tillie and her brothers' stockings with tangerines, nuts, and candies, a quarter in each toe. (She had two boys with Harold, four and six years younger than Tillie.) Then she and Maurice made out under the Xmas tree, and May sang, "Won't you guide my sleigh tonight?"

Tillie crept off to bed, but all night she dreamt of Santa coming down their chimney. She never saw Santa Claus or a chimney again without get-ting aroused.

The thought of her mother checking out makes the earth move under Tillie's feet, a sensation she's had many times during actual earthquakes, causing uncertainty, terror. Where will she be once the quaking stops?

She tries to calm herself down. The call needn't be something dire. Maybe her mum's getting married again. That's a possibility. She probably wants Tillie to stand up for her.

Tillie clings to that hope.

"Come on, Tillie, we need your ideas," Daddy says. "It'll get your mind off your mum."

Daddy and Moll have moved to the dining table. It's covered with bits of fabric, beads, colored tissue paper, ribbons, feathers, sea shells of all shapes and sizes, pasta, glitter, sequins, glue, scissors, a stapler, and plain white mask forms they're using as a base for their own creations. Jet watches from her perch on top of the china cabinet.

Tillie asks, "What happened to Sibyl's puzzle?"

Sibyl totters into the room, wearing her mules. "The bloody termites ate it."

"You mean you never got to see the final image?"

"It was just starting to make sense when they made a meal out of it. Hope they choked."

"Oh no! Bloody fiends. You're sure the little bastards have been destroyed?" Tillie looks around the place, worried about Frank's photos stored there. She has mixed feelings. Part of her would like to see them ruined. She doesn't like to be reminded of what a fool she was to make herself so vulnerable in those images, and she doesn't enjoy being frozen alive in them, locked in a time warp. But another part, her more practical side, recognizes that they're her meal ticket. She may take after her dizzy mother in many ways, but neither she nor May is a complete fool.

Then Tillie remembers the snake and asks, "Where's Xena?"

"Gone," Sibyl says. "Vamoosed."

Tillie shivers. "You mean it's somewhere in the flat?"

"Could be. Got away."

"Terrific." Tillie checks the floor.

"Don't worry," Daddy says. "I've looked everywhere—couldn't sleep in this bloody place if I thought that snake was around—it must've gotten out through the hole the termites made."

"Xena'll be okay," Sibyl says. "She's a survivor, eh."

"That's what I'm afraid of," Tillie says.

"Anyway, here's the scoop," Sibyl says between coughs. "Carmine and Emil have promised to sing and dance at the party. Gypsy music. They'll bring a friend who plays flamenco guitar."

"I haven't been able to get their music out of my head," Tillie says. "It keeps playing over and over."

"You're not the only one," Sibyl says. "Moll's ga-ga over Emil, and Daddy has the hots for Carmine."

"You should talk," Moll says. "You follow Emil around like a puppy."

"*I* do? You're the one who wouldn't leave their place last night. Carmine was pissed with the way you sucked up to him. Showing off your big boobs."

"Whoa," Moll says, "do I detect some jealousy?"

"I saw him first," Sibyl says.

"But he's married," Moll says.

"No, he isn't. They just live together. I've seen both of them make out with others. What's the difference anyway?"

"Well, he can put his shoes under my bed anytime," Moll says, stretching and yawning.

Sibyl scowls.

Tillie eyes the black phone. It reminds her of May's call, and she wishes it would vanish so her life could return to normal. She says, "It's great that you've worked out the music. What about food and drinks?"

"We've arranged with a restaurant to set up a booth and sell tapas and wine," Moll says.

"Yeah," Daddy says, "they're giving us a good deal because of all the publicity they're getting."

"Wow. You guys have thought of everything."

"Turning sixty is a big deal," Moll says.

"So is the millennium," Daddy says.

No one mentions Tillie's installation, for her the most important thing. They don't seem to get it. This could be her last chance as an artist to become more visible, to gain the same international recognition as Frank. They don't take her art seriously. Of course, neither does her mother.

"Maybe your mum called to wish you happy birthday," Sibyl says.

"It's a bit early."

"At her age she might not remember the exact date."

Moll holds her mask in front of her face, only her eyes showing. It's beginning to resemble a bear.

"Yeah," Moll says, "but didn't she know you were going to celebrate it in Venice?"

"How's your priest?" Sibyl asks, her words punctuated with coughs. "Made any converts recently? Resurrected anyone? Or is Father Lazarus too busy rising himself?" She laughs at her own joke and starts choking.

Tillie frowns. "You had your chest x-rayed lately? You're coughing nonstop."

"Lazarus doesn't believe in that life after death stuff, does he?" Sibyl says. "I mean, if you're cremated, that's it, a one-way ticket to never-never land. The end. Fini. Destined for an urn on someone's mantel."

"Unless your ashes are thrown to the winds and end up in the stomach of some other creature," Tillie says. "We gorge on the animals, swallowing the remains of all those dead people. The ashes live on like parasites in someone else's body. Just one person could contain multitudes."

Moll makes a face. "Gross! It's enough to turn me into a vegan."

Tillie laughs. "That won't save you. The ashes get absorbed into the soil too, showing up in the plants we eat."

"You can't seem to stop making installations," Daddy says, tugging at a snarl in her hair. "So now you've got whole communities inhabiting one body."

Tillie throws up her hands. "Just another way of thinking about resurrection."

"Hey," Sibyl says, "how do you get a round trip to never-never land? Ask the priest that for me. I'd like a round-trip ticket out of this life and back on a Concorde."

"How'd we get on this subject?" Daddy asks.

"My mum's call. Sibyl's hacking. Venice. Death's in the air."

"What a drag. How about a hit of Ecstasy? That'll put us in a better space."

"Save it for our bash," Sibyl says. "We'll put it in all the drinks. Give them their money's worth."

"Hey," Daddy says, "I was reading about this other drug that's just becoming known in the States."

"Oh no," Tillie says. "You're not going to use us again as guinea pigs."

"Wait! Indians in the mountains outside of Oaxaca have used this drug *Salvia divinorum*—or something like that—for ages. It causes altered states—out-of-body experiences—merging with inanimate objects—taking over another identity—hallucinations—time and space travel. Your everyday all-purpose drug!"

"I'm all for getting out of this body," Sibyl says, lighting up another cigarette. "Hell, we've just been talking about the ashes of dead people merging with the living. It would be neat to be a fire hydrant or lampshade for a change. I could use a rest."

"Hey," Tillie says, "you don't need a drug to merge with others. Just breathing the same air does that. Particles of our breath penetrate those around us. And our psyches are really porous. We're always camping out in someone's inner space. Amazing how interconnected we all are."

"You'd have made a great scientist," Daddy says. "Got any proof?" She picks up her mask again, putting the finishing touches on it—one half black, the other white, multi-colored sequins for eyebrows and circling the eye holes, a beak for the nose, feathers instead of hair. "We're definitely limited by what we agree on as reality. If we found out the drug-induced state is the natural one and not this other reality we've created, we'd flip—it would shake up all our assumptions—destroy our institutions—throw us into chaos—our nice orderly world would be in smithereens—telepathy— ESP—all that stuff. It scares people because it doesn't fit our conditioning."

Sibyl wanders into the kitchen, trying to muffle her coughs. "Anyone want coffee?"

The flip-flops have begun again in Tillie's stomach. Her orderly universe is being shaken. "What time is it?"

"Almost eleven thirty," Sibyl says.

"Still too early to call. I've got more work to do on my installation. See you guys later."

Tillie doesn't head immediately for the Palazzo Cavalli-Franchetti. She's realizing that the ethos of the '60s shadows every word the Muskrateers utter and every gesture they make, a ghostly presence that formed their identities and still does. A youth culture was born, flaunting its own music

207

and mores. Civil Rights broke new ground. Women woke up, insisting on sexual freedom and equality. Others found their voices as well. Mind-altering drugs exploded preconceived ideas about reality and the self as homogeneous and stable. Multiple selves. Multiple lives. Variousness. The standardized, one-dimensional nature of the previous era had collapsed.

Those years were essential and cataclysmic, more so than the women had realized at the time. They can't shake the influence, having come of age in the '60s, just as they're coming to age now *in* their sixties. At the same time, they're entering another new age, promising even more upheaval than the '60s, and they'll have participated in both eras. They're being pulled in both directions simultaneously, one foot in each world.

Tillie sucks in the fresh air, eager to experience the rich tapestry of life—the sights, sounds, smells, and various textures more precious to her now and more vivid. Everything still seems eroticized, pulsing with energy, from her time with Bud. It reminds her of descriptions she's heard of people on mushrooms or LSD, only her heightened perceptions don't require any help from drugs.

She heads for St. Mark's Square, wanting to merge with the crowds and pigeons. To forget herself and the future. She even hopes to bump into Bird. For old times' sake. Never mind Frank. He's dead. Maybe Bird's just a bird after all.

And Venice, for all of its dying—or maybe because of it—teems with life. The elegant throats of the gondolas resemble graceful black swans, gliding on the canal. The bright flash of red scarf the gondoliers wear. The straight backs of the boatmen staring straight head, eyes fixed on something Tillie can't see. The jumble of streets always offering up something unexpected, people disappearing into the maze as mysteriously as they appeared. The whole city a dreamscape. She can't quite believe she isn't dreaming it all or that Venice isn't a collective vision. Or maybe Venice is dreaming her.

At St. Mark's, she finds an empty bench and sits down, watching the vendors selling masks, brooches, flags, Venetian scenes, earrings, dolls, glassware—the sights and sounds washing over her. Pigeons waddle by, pecking at crumbs, scurrying from passing feet, their wings flapping anxiously and then settling down, reminding her of Frank and Bird. Was her relationship with Frank more important to her than she's been willing to admit? She may have disliked some things about his personality, especially his monologues, but they did have some good times together. And he did leave his soul in her care—his art.

She looks at one bird that stands out, not because of its size or color, but because of its darting eyes, on the alert—one sea green, the other gunmetal gray. Tillie calls out "Bird," and she's sure he hesitated a moment, looking over his shoulder, before following another, smaller pigeon through the forest of legs. She follows the birds to the café she stopped at during an earlier visit to the Square. Both pigeons fly onto the canvas awning, hovering over the nest she saw there previously. She can see the beaks of baby birds and hear their cries. No wonder Bird had disappeared so suddenly from the garden. Its mate and fatherhood had called.

The baby birds make Tillie aware of her own dependence on her mother, her mouth still open, waiting for food. Italy, where mothers reign supreme, the family the center of life. It reminds her of all she missed herself growing up and her inability to give Valentine the kind of family he needed. Still, mother and daughter count for something; so do mother and son. It might not be the ideal two-parent extended family, but Tillie has something at least. Some have less.

The church bells chime out two o'clock. She leaves Bird and his brood and searches for a public phone where she can make her call. She could return to Sibyl's and ring May from there, but she doesn't want to discuss her mother with anyone just now.

Wandering into a deserted square, Tillie spots a faded red phone booth standing at one end. She takes out her long-distance card, inserts it into the slot, and dials her mother's number. While she waits for her to answer, she studies the Italian graffiti inside the phone booth, unable to understand anything, but it gives her something to occupy her mind. Her eyes come to rest on the bullseye someone has sketched. The dark spot in the center draws her in. And then the ringing stops. May's voice fills the line, still resonant and strong. That's reassuring. But the words aren't.

"I've got bad news, Tillie. Cancer."

The bullseye appears to be spinning, and it takes a minute for the words to fully register. *Cancer?* Tillie envisions this hulking beast eating everything in sight, including her mother, whom she thought was indestructible. She whispers, "Cancer? Where?"

If cancer can penetrate her mother's formidable defenses, then Tillie is vulnerable, too. She props the phone on her shoulder, freeing her hands to make a survey of her body. Her fingers poke and prod. They've developed their own intelligence over the years in shaping clay and other substances, adept at picking out the flaws. A man standing outside the booth, waiting for the phone, stares at her. Tillie realizes it appears as if she's coming on to him. She shuts the door and turns her back.

"Colon. But the doctor thinks he can cut it out."

"Surgery? Christ!"

"The tumor's so big, it's almost blocking my bowel."

"How'd they find it?" She turns around and looks through the door at the square. The man has gone, but she thinks she glimpses the weeping torso, hovering over a nearby canal.

"I started passing out all over the place. The doctor wanted my blood checked. He said I was severely anemic and did a bunch of other tests. That's when they found it."

"Why didn't you tell me sooner? I feel awful! I should've been with you."

"I didn't want to spoil your trip. It's not every day you get to Europe. Besides, the boys have been a big help. And Valentine called his granny. He's coming to see me with his new girlfriend."

Tillie feels guilty that her half brothers are carrying the load. Even her son is showing some responsibility to family. "Has the surgery been scheduled yet?"

"A week from today. I need to get it over with quickly. Sam wants to marry me as soon as I'm better. He's really gone on me, you know."

"No, I didn't know. But I'm glad you've got someone to look out for you."

Tillie doesn't point out to her mother that at ninety-four she might not make it. The chances that she won't make it are greater than that she will. Still, the doctors wouldn't go ahead if they didn't think she had a chance.

The thought of her mother dying gives Tillie an icy chill. Her installation, art, everything, fades in comparison to this actual life-and-death
situation. Her mum could die. No, erase that. Her mum will die one day.
But it could be sooner than Tillie thought. Much sooner. It could be any
minute. Cancer is as unpredictable as life.

"Look, Mum, I've got a few things to take care of here and then I'll join
you. I'll try to get a flight out on Sunday. Can you hang on till I get there?"

"Don't worry about me. I'm not going anywhere. Not when I've finally
found a man who wants to settle down. Besides, I want to see what this
new century's like."

Tillie's chances of getting a larger audience for her work and her new
relationship with Bud are now threatened. She knows it isn't May's fault she
has cancer. These things are random. She tries to suppress her resentment,
reminding herself that her mother kept her after she was born. She could
have dumped Tillie and abandoned her completely. But May claimed she
couldn't give Tillie up for adoption once she looked into her eyes. Tillie
owes her mum something.

The Divine Comedy

Bud has given Tillie her own key to the *pensione*, and she goes there now, wanting a quiet place where she can just think. She enters his pad, closes the door, locks it, and flops onto the bed, kicking off her shoes. It feels strange to be alone in his space. Except for Bud's Mountie hat on the nightstand and his glove next to it, the room doesn't have any distinguishing features. This seems appropriate given his profession—one of them, at least—as a priest. No one thinks of clergy as having a private life or being individuals with feelings, hopes, and dreams. She actually finds it comforting to be in a more neutral place, not pulled by the demands that personal effects place on a visitor to notice them. It allows her to focus inward.

There's so much to absorb, and it's all catching up with her. May is facing the end. Frank has already died and left her his art. Bird is a father. And she's falling for a priest who makes "art" films. He's an artist, too, trying to awaken people through their senses. It's a noble cause. Why should so many people still think of sex as something shameful? It's true that the sex drive can complicate things. Get messy. Look at Tillie, acting like a teenager at her age. Or May, panting after another man when she's dying of cancer. Or Moll, being turned on by Emil. Or Daddy, drooling after Carmine. Even Sibyl is having an erotic dance with Thanatos. There's something arousing and compelling about death.

Since being in Venice, Tillie has developed a greater lust for living, a passionate appreciation of the world's beauty and ugliness. All of her senses seem more finely tuned. She gets rhapsodic about the outlines of leaves against a contrasting background, the way the dawn washes the sky with rosy wisps, the intensity of all colors. Time itself is retreating, and she feels at one with everything, her love affair with life only beginning. It's comforting to know that life on earth continues, even in the face of death. She's beginning to understand what is meant by the fullness of time. She's entering it. Or it's entering her.

Besides death, one constant thing is her work. That she can count on—the ideas, her imagination. The actual work might be ephemeral, but the conceptual part isn't. It enters into some black book in Artist Heaven, existing forever in a kind of cyberspace, taking up its distinctive place. Or so she likes to think.

Propped up on the pillows, she picks up Bud's copy of *The Divine Comedy, Vol. I: Inferno*. She looks at the opening pages, feeling some identification with the person narrating the poem.

> *Midway along the journey of our life*
> *I woke to find myself in a dark wood,*
> *for I had wandered off from the straight path.*

Tillie also feels she's awakened from a kind of sleep, and she too has wandered off, but she's not sure the path she's left was a straight one. For her, it feels the reverse, as if she's been on a meandering course and is now finding one that's more focused.

She scans the first few cantos and realizes why she wasn't able to get into the poem before. A particular theology informs the epic. The first-person narrative describes a Catholic male's descent into hell and purgatory. He runs into guides that eventually lead him out of his dark pit and into paradise. Of course, it's a woman who tries to save Dante's immortal soul and who enlists Virgil's help. Dante owes the entire journey to her.

Though a great work of imagination, filled with literary devices and multiple levels of meaning, it also adheres to Christian dogma, a turnoff for Tillie. She wants to find her own way into whatever mysteries there are and to discover her own guides. She trusts her imagination to take her where she needs to go. Maybe the Black Madonna will be *Tillie's* escort.

Tillie might not resonate with Dante's world, but she does understand now why his work is a comedy. He believed strongly in the Christian myth's happy ending. She believes just as strongly in the happy ending of life's cycles. She pictures them as multiple helixes that intertwine. These cycles do end, the bad *and* the good ones. And people do move on. They sometimes even experience a kind of rebirth. And then another cycle reigns. Time's healing power takes over. Flowers grow from graves. So, for her, a happy ending represents the end of a difficult time. Still, happy endings always have the potential of something darker. Happiness is never separated completely from its opposite.

Lack of sleep catches up with her, and she drifts off, relieved to be free for a while from her thoughts and concerns about May and her looming death. But not for long. Tillie dreams that May has two babies, twins, one a boy, the other a girl. They're wailing, and Tillie's having trouble sleeping. Her mother—much younger—still isn't careful about birth control, willing to have sex with men who don't hang around afterward. These babies are the result. The girl in particular is precocious. She makes her way from the bedroom to where Tillie is sleeping and howls, "I want my own food! I want my own food!" Tillie gives her some milk, satisfying the child for now, and she goes to sleep. But it's clear she won't be satisfied for long.

Then Bud turns up in the dream. He tells Tillie about a secret society she should check out. She goes to the address he gives her, not knowing what to expect. It's located in San Francisco in a Victorian with the usual high ceilings and dark wood trim. The building and the era seem to fit the esoteric group using the building. No one tells Tillie about the organization; everything is to be revealed in stages.

A woman rubs some lotion onto Tillie's skin that causes it to tan. Another woman carves something into the top of her head, working intuitively, not knowing till she's finished what it will be. When the woman tells Tillie it's a maple leaf, Canada's national emblem, Tillie bursts out crying and says, "I'm from Canada," something the carver didn't know. Amazed, Tillie loses her skepticism about this group of women and tells them about her previous dream, wondering aloud if the food the baby was crying for is connected to the activities in this Victorian. Do these women have some special knowledge that the child needs?

Someone's lips are pressing against Tillie's. She melts under their softness and warmth, thinking she's still dreaming.

"Wake up my sleeping beauty."

Tillie opens her eyes and shrieks, forgetting where she is. Bud throws up his arms.

"It's okay! Just me." He takes off his clerical robe and drapes it over her. "The sun's gone down. It's getting cool."

She stretches her arms above her head and yawns. "What a dream!"

"You mean me?" Bud strikes a pose, flexing one arm like a muscle man.

"You are a treasure, an angel, but I meant the other kind of dream."

He takes several bottles of wine, some cheese, and a baguette from a bag he's carrying, setting them on the bureau. "Want to talk about it?"

"The wine?"

"The dream."

First Tillie tells him about her conversation with May and her need for surgery.

"I hate to tell you this, but I have to leave on Sunday."

Bud doubles over, as if he's been kicked in the gut. "Sunday?" He drops onto the bed and grabs her hands. "That's just days away. We must have more time!"

"I wish I didn't have to go, but Mum needs me."

"So do I! I'll die of a broken heart."

She avoids his eyes. "I'm sorry. I didn't plan any of this."

Bud picks up *The Divine Comedy* and chews on the edges, his eyes misting up. "But you're my Beatrice. It isn't supposed to end this way. We haven't reached *Paradiso* yet."

She stares at him. "*Paradiso*? I can hardly find my way across town." Then she blurts out, "Mum's baby needs me, too."

His eyes widen. "Baby?"

Tillie tells him of the strange dream.

"Breast milk," he says.

"What?"

"She needs breast milk. The real thing."

"Well, she won't get it from me."

"It sounds like your mother's passing the baton to you, expecting you to care for this child."

He gets up, loosens the seal on the wine bottle, and extracts the cork. "Our best Chianti." He pours a glass for each of them and hands Tillie hers. Then he sits on the bed next to her, stroking her leg. "The dream suggests your Canadian identity is your crowning glory, my love."

Tillie gets goosebumps hearing him refer to her as his love. She hasn't had a relationship develop with such intensity and speed. Both feel the time constraints they're under, not only in terms of how long she'll be in Venice, but also because of their age. There isn't much time left in either case.

"Yeah," she says, "it's kind of like wearing a brand, 'Made in Canada.'"

Bud sips his wine and looks thoughtful. "Could the baby girl in the dream also be you? Some young version of you wanting her own food?"

"I haven't a clue what it would be."

"It doesn't sound like she'll be satisfied with the conventional solution of milk for long. Does this secret organization have something she needs? What's it about?"

"I don't know. I was browsing through *The Divine Comedy* before I fell asleep and realizing Dante's way isn't mine."

"What would your way be?"

"Not sure. My skin is being darkened in one dream scene. I'll be closer to your coloring. Maybe it has to do with letting go of 'white' or Western consciousness, getting a whole new worldview." She tosses aside his robe and sits up.

"Where would that take you?"

"Not sure, but if this baby wants her own food, and if it has something to do with being a girl, she's going to have trouble finding a truly feminine perspective."

His hand brushes one of her breasts. "You seem pretty feminine to me."

"That's biological."

"It's a good start."

"Maybe. But how do we nourish our feminine selves? How do we even know what they are?"

"Love?"

Tillie frowns. "How can you love something you don't know?"

Bud reaches for the wine bottle and fills their glasses again.

She takes another sip of wine. "I keep hearing the baby's cry, 'I want my own food.' What in hell am I supposed to do?"

"In the dream, you thought the secret organization was the key."

"I know. Reminds me of the women's initiation scenes at the Villa of the Mysteries in Pompeii."

"I've seen those frescoes."

"I wonder if that's why you're the one who introduces me to this secret group."

"Maybe. Pompeiian women had much more freedom than the earlier Roman women. They sold goods, owned property, built temples, acted as priestesses. They even formed and led their own cults. Dionysian cults were the most popular. He's the Greek god most associated with women."

"Why is that?"

"Women always surrounded him, from the time of his birth. He also rescued Ariadne, who ended up becoming his wife and was made immortal by Zeus."

"So I'm being initiated into a Dionysian cult?"

"Maybe. But in stages. By the way, have I told you I plan to retire soon?"

"Retire?" The thought seems foreign to her, and she wonders what it has to do with her dream. She's never thought of retiring. She'll continue to make art until she dies. Why would she give up something she loves? "And then what?"

"I want to travel the world," he says, waving his arms. "Care to join me?"

When Bud asked her that question once before, she was too stunned to answer. Now she doesn't hesitate. "*Assolutamente.*"

They clink their glasses together and take another sip of wine.

Still, she's not sure she can trust him to leave the institution behind. It's his mother and father. And that's Tillie's main concern. How can he have a real relationship with her if he hasn't yet established an identity separate from his institutional parents? He may be such a good actor that he can deceive himself *and* Tillie. Or perhaps she's asking too much of him. At the moment, it's enough to know she has a future traveling companion. As long as they're on the move and seeing the world, permanence may not be an issue. Whether they'll stay together beyond their travels remains another of life's uncertainties, keeping her as off balance as her mother does.

It always returns to May.

Tillie has already called Bud "Mother" a couple of times. Is this her modus operandi, picking men who are similar to her mum in some way? Men who keep her up in the air? Of course, making these problematic choices in lovers keeps Tillie attached to her mother, even now. She was too dependent on May as a young girl to separate from her as an adult. Maybe the baby in the dream is finally ready to leave her mother and find her own food.

Tillie doesn't want to think any more about her mother or anything else. So she sets down her glass of wine, places Bud's on the nightstand next to hers, and pulls him onto the bed, loosening his belt, helping him to shed his shirt and trousers. What she finds there definitely doesn't resemble May or Mary Magdalene.

CARNIVALE BECKONS

Time takes over again, the minute hand moving inexorably forward. Tillie returns to Sibyl's place the next morning after working half the night on the head, hoping to finish it. The flat is strewn from end to end with bits and pieces of brightly colored and patterned cloth, bones, plastic, sequins, foil paper, glitter, thread, feathers, shells, beads, ruffles, ribbons, fur—anything and everything. Carmine and Emil's music floods the place with sound.

Jet zips in and out of the tunnels she has created in the hills of stuff, skidding to a stop in front of Tillie, who is bent over one of the mounds. The cat's greenish-gold eyes fix on the silver ocelot pendant dangling on a black cord from Tillie's neck. Jet flicks at the jewel with a paw. She scoops the cat up in her arms and buries her face in its fur.

"Reminds me of a cat I once had. I called him Spook."

Jet slithers from her embrace and dives under the dining room table, peering out from behind one of the heavy mahogany legs.

"The cat has good taste," Daddy says, eyeing Tillie's pendant.

Tillie fingers it. "Frank bought it for me in Mexico. The Mayans worshipped ocelots."

"You getting over his death?" Sibyl asks.

"Haven't had time to think about it much. I'm sure I'll get whomped when I return to the apartment. We shared it for a while, you know. I mean, it's not like we were serious about each other. Fellow artists, that's all."

"Sounds pretty serious if he left you his art," Moll says, glancing up from some fabric she's working with. "What did your Mum want?"

"She's being operated on for colon cancer in a week."

They all shout, "A week!"

"Yeah. I have to cancel my return flight to S.F. and book one to Calgary instead for the day after our celebration."

"What a bummer," Daddy says. "We were just getting into the groove here."

Moll says, "Your mum's pretty old to have such major surgery."

"I know. But her spirits are good, and she has a new man in her life."

"What about *your* new man?" Sibyl asks. "Will you ever see him again?"

Tillie plucks at her spiked hair and tells of their plans to meet up in a few months and travel. "It's pretty intense and scary. I feel I knew him in another life." She also mentions her concerns about problems they'll face as a couple. "I mean, we're similar in some ways, but we're from different planets in others." She hasn't told them yet about Bud's alias or his extra-curricular activities. She may never do so. He's such a paradox, which, of course, contributes to the attraction.

Daddy peers at Tillie from behind the mask she's constructing. "There's no such thing as the 'perfect' mate. We all have flaws—we're human, for chrissakes."

Moll nods in agreement.

"I appreciate Raleigh more when I'm away from him," Sibyl says, lighting a cigarette and sucking on it, pushing the cat off her lap. "The guy must have some good qualities. After all, he chose me."

"You mean, he puts up with you," Moll says, waving the smoke away from her face.

"We put up with each other," Sibyl says, aiming a smoke ring at Moll. It collapses before it reaches her. "A marriage made in heaven."

"Is there such a thing?" Daddy asks.

"Not in my book," Tillie says, threading a needle. "Sounds boring. Who would want a perfect marriage? The challenge keeps it interesting, don't you think?"

"Not if you aren't on the same page," Moll says, standing up and heading for the kitchen. "Tea?"

Daddy says, "Yeah, I'll have some tea. Herbal."

Moll returns, carrying a tray loaded with a pot of boiling water, cups containing tea bags, and spoons. She sets it down on the coffee table, making room for it amid glue and scissors and tape measures.

Tillie looks at Moll and Daddy. "What about you guys? Any plans after Venice?"

"I'm ready to sign up," Daddy says.

"Sign up?" Tillie looks puzzled.

"You know, the army, the navy."

"Not!" Tillie says.

"There's a Canadian version of the Peace Corps, VSO—volunteers sign on for a couple of years in a third-world area—could be helping with forest conservation, forestry—political organizing—helping promote women's rights."

"Sounds cool," Sibyl says, retrieving a long black ribbon from under the sofa.

"I know," Daddy says. "They have people in Africa, Asia, the Caribbean, Eastern Europe, the Pacific. Plenty of options."

Moll looks morose. "Sounds great, but I can't just walk away from my life in Nelson, much as I'd like to. Jesus, I'm a grandmother! I'm part of the community. I have responsibilities."

"Two years isn't so long," Daddy says. "Your grandkids can wait."

"Hey, I'd like to go too," Sibyl says, smothering a cough.

"And leave this pad?" Tillie says. "Why abandon paradise?"

"Amen," Daddy says. "The pace here is so incredible—no rushing around—shopping at open-air markets—visiting with shop owners. People actually stop in the street and chat. It makes me realize what I'm missing at home—my life!"

"I know," Tillie says. "I feel the same way. You've got it made here, Sibyl."

Sibyl doesn't look convinced. "I'm really stuck in my life. At a dead end."

Tillie blanches at Sibyl's choice of words.

"I don't think VSO would consider you with that cough," Moll says. "You should see a doctor."

"Yeah, yeah. Maybe when I get back." Sibyl gets up, drapes a scarf around her head, and circles the room, shaking her hips and moving to the Gypsy rhythms.

"You got it, babe," Daddy says.

They all jump up and join Sibyl, linking arms, Sibyl taking the lead, snaking through the piles of material they're working on. Jet jumps onto the sideboard and watches. Tillie and the others kick their legs high, laughing and dancing until Sibyl starts hacking again. Then they all collapse in a heap on the floor, disentangling themselves from one another.

Tillie pours some hot water into a cup. She presses the teabag against its side, watching the color darken, and calls out. "Anyone else want any?"

"I'm ready for a beer," Sibyl says.

"Me too," Daddy says, heading to the kitchen to grab them.

Moll returns to her costume, and they all settle in again, working away.

Moll says, "Canadians should have something like Carnivale."

"Bud says it owes a lot to Africa. A form of street theater. They imitate ancient African traditions of parading and moving in circles through villages in costumes and masks."

"I guess the Calgary Stampede comes the closest," Daddy says. "A lot of people get out of their skin for ten days."

"I know," Tillie says. "African villagers thought the dancing and celebrating would heal problems and chill out angry dead relatives who had passed into the next world. They thought it was a chance to be reborn and to grow spiritually."

"I'm all for being reborn," Sibyl says, fanning her face with a flyer announcing their party. "Forget the spiritual part, though."

"Okay, so look at it as a celebration of life and rejuvenation," Daddy says. "I like the idea of the usual order being subverted—everything's up for grabs."

"Bud thinks all the lewd, sexually charged stuff can be considered religious, a dance of the sexes, males and females in a symbiotic embrace."

"Bud thinks that?" Sibyl says. "He's my kind of man."

"Guess that leaves me out," Daddy says.

"Except masculine and feminine are parts of us all," Tillie says.

"You know what I like about Carnivale?" says Daddy. "Joy reigns—the imagination reigns—sensuality reigns—sex reigns. Sounds like heaven to me."

"Yeah," says Moll. "We need more joyfulness in our lives. The real stuff. The church talks of joy, but I've never experienced any in that setting, except when I had the affair with my minister. Hypocrisy kills the spirit."

"I have to say, hanging out with you guys has made my spirits soar," Daddy says. "I'm aware again of the ideals I once had—was going to change the world—fight for equal rights for everyone. How did I give all that up for money and security? Totally forgot what's really important—want to do something of value before I die—make a contribution—not just be a parasite."

Moll nods. "Me too. I've been living in this bubble. Miss Responsible. It's time to break out!"

Tillie's Black Madonna

Tillie leaves the other Muskrateers and returns to the *pensione*, wanting to unveil the head she's been sculpting. Though she hasn't looked at it yet, she senses the head is finished.

She takes a plastic trash bag from under the bed where she's been storing the sculpture and places it on top of the mattress. Her hands shake a little in anticipation, and her fingers fumble with the knot she's tied. She finally loosens it and tosses the cord aside. She almost expects lightning bolts to zip across the sky, followed by thunder. Or is it the other way around? It doesn't matter. All she hears is the crinkling of plastic and her own breathing as she slides the head out and places it on the bedspread.

It's unsettling to be looking into the Black Madonna's eyes, reminding Tillie of the eerie feeling she gets whenever she looks at a doll. The eyes appear to have life, as if seeing something that Tillie doesn't.

But more startling than the eyes are the Black Madonna's features. The face is her mother's as a young woman, or close to it, though the skin color is different. It's a dark-skinned May staring at Tillie from the bed—serene, composed. A far cry from the May she knows, usually caught up in a frenzy of activity. And then it dawns on her why the torso in her visions have looked so familiar: it has been May's younger self she's been seeing.

Carnivale meets Death in Menace

On Friday, Tillie returns to the garden to put finishing touches on her installation, delighted to find it fully intact. With Bud's help, she hooks up the videos and tape recorder. She also attaches the head she's carved to a torso, made from a cast of her own body before coming to Venice. Bud helps her set it up in a small clearing among some cypress trees. The head's weathered appearance almost makes it appear part of the foliage. Head and torso seem to reside over the place. Tillie's grateful May is enjoying some degree of immortality.

She also brings an aquarium for the termites, only to find she must not have tightened the lid on the jar she put them in. They've escaped.

Saturday arrives, and the strains of Carmine and Emil's music float over the canals, melodies in minor key that speak of loss and longing and life, drawing a large crowd to the garden. It's a strange sight, the parade of elves and hobgoblins, hip-hop artists and punk rockers, angels and devils, princes and princesses, Mafiosos and clergy, kings and queens, fairies and witches, wild and domestic animals. People weave through the streets and waterways, wearing new identities that free them from their usual roles, shedding everyday expectations.

The garden at the Palazzo expands to contain the multitudes that appear, everyone liberated from customary constraints, time suspended. Carmine, Emil, and their group of Gypsies form the heart and pulse of this throng, wearing their traditional dress, black masks covering the upper half of their faces. Encouraging others to join in, their voices rise in song, feet following the music's ancient and intricate patterns. The beat infectious, young and old dance frenetically, abandoning themselves to the music and spirit of the occasion, switching masks, roles. Hands touch and testify to the joys of erotic play and the flesh. All is spontaneous, everyone swirling in a frenzy of desire, giving themselves over to their instincts.

By the time Tillie and Bud arrive, the celebration is in full swing. Tillie wears a Harlequin costume, pieced together from a full palate of colors that make up irregularly shaped patterns. Bud has come as Pan, with the hind legs, ears, and horns of a goat. They flit among the revelers like bees pollinating flowers, casting a spell, performing ribald satires in corners of the garden.

The other Muskrateers merge with those gathered. Daddy turns up wearing a nun's habit, and her mask resembles a bird. Moll has come as a bear. Sibyl—hips rotating, shaking her bones—wears a skeleton costume she put together and does a flirtatious dance with another skeleton that has been pursuing her.

The women's Canadian roots and mutual history—the memories they all share, the values and expectations they grew up with—still bind them. Something has happened between them in Whistler and Venice that they all feel but none can articulate clearly, connecting them more deeply. And they have helped each other enter an exhilarating and scary new age.

No one knows what the twenty-first century will bring, except everything seems to be speeding up, even time. The earth and its inhabitants appear out of control, rushing towards some unknown destiny. Venice has offered a neutral place from which to mark this passing, a place outside time, remote from the ultramodern future.

Gypsy music weaves together the celebrants. The haunting sounds affirm life and the passage from life to death and back. With everyone in costume, the distinctions between the dead and the living are no longer apparent, the veil between the worlds perforated.

Tillie thinks she sees Frank fading in and out of the crowd, first dancing with Sibyl and then with Bud, the dead the only ones who don't need a costume. All the great Northern Italian painters have turned up: Titian, Giorgione, Veronese, Tintoretto, Tiepolo, Bellini. She flings herself into their midst, whirling like a dervish, passing from one to the other, hoping their greatness will rub off on her. Even Marco Polo has been drawn to the event, followed by an entourage of lords and ladies.

The music lures all within hearing distance.

Not to be left out, the termites have also joined the celebrants, line dancing, kicking their legs in unison. Later, they feast on Tillie's installation, ignoring the flowers and bushes in the garden. As they devour the work, piece by piece, leaving only remnants of the Muskrateers' torsos and legs and the other objects there (though miraculously ignoring May's head), the installation becomes more interesting to the art lovers in the crowd. They find it one of the more ambitious projects the Biennale has presented this year, giving Tillie the exposure she's hoped for.

That evening, reeling from all the dancing and drinking, Tillie stumbles into the clearing where she and Bud installed her mother's head, needing to recollect herself. She's never been a Harlequin before, and she finds it particularly freeing to play a clown. All she has to do is approach someone and the person laughs at her, even before she opens her mouth. No matter which way she moves or what she does, it evokes hilarity, everything having a comic edge. The costume draws out her humorous impulses, making her limbs seem fluid, almost weightless, her motions resembling a puppet's. She pretends she can't stand alone, flopping all over the place, limbs like rubber, defying her age.

It doesn't take long for her to discover she isn't alone in the glade. Bud, masquerading as Pan (or is it Pan masquerading as Bud?), has been luring maidens to this place. At the moment, he's chasing a sweet young moonbeam around the statue. She doesn't put up much resistance, letting him catch her before he's out of breath. It could have been a scene for one of his art films, his fly unzipped, penis exposed, except he is Pan in name only.

He can't will his organ to stay erect. The girl giggles and runs away, leaving him standing there. Her laughter lingers in the grove.

He looks up, his eyes meeting Tillie's. They stare at each other for a long moment, strangers for all their intimacies. She can't help feeling sorry for him, his making of art films clearly a compensation for his decreasing sexual powers. Still, Pan—the impersonal aspect of the sex drive—can be problematic if out of control. He upsets things, his animal nature not contained in civilization and its discontents. It's worrisome. She's not sure how much Bud resembles Pan. Or maybe he's come dressed as the wrong Pan. Peter Pan may have been more fitting.

Yet Tillie has been encouraging herself and the other partygoers to follow their instincts, to loosen restraints and embrace their sexual impulses, temporarily banishing the consequences. Maybe she, too, is compensating, trying to cling to youthful potency and to step outside the usual moral restraints. A bohemian drifter, living on the fringes of society, critical of the "adults." She's always wanted to experience what Daddy did when she lived on a commune, flinging aside convention and giving herself over to free love.

Has Tillie set herself up for another betrayal? Can this boy/man grow up? Or are dalliances so much a part of his nature that he can't help exploiting women under the guise of returning to a more earthy spirituality? Is subverting the church's authority through eroticizing all of life any better than viewing sensuality as a sin? Extremes cancel each other out. Paganism presents problems, too.

Tillie can't return to some innocent pre-Christian time, if there ever was such a thing—a nostalgic idealization that keeps her from growing up, flitting around without a real home of her own to return to. It's a '60's notion she's carried around and polished, expecting it to yield some truth. It reminds her of wanting to rub Bud's bald head. She had hoped he was a genie and had the answers. But she knows the answers are within her. All she needs is help uncovering them.

First, though, she feels she must embrace the real spirit of the '60s by breaking away from received ideas and descending into the black hole.

Alice found a new world waiting for her there; maybe Tillie will, too. Of course, Alice had the rabbit for a guide. Tillie has to make do with the Mad Hatter.

The spell of Carnivale descends on Tillie and Bud again, throwing them into each other's arms where they can temporarily forget the everyday world and its many problems. Speechless, both toss their masks aside, relieved to see each other's faces, clinging throughout that long night to the unfulfilled promise of the other.

—— THE END ——

DON'T MISS FLING!
by Lily Iona MacKenzie

Sneak peek below

Is it possible to come of age at 60 or 90?
Is it ever too late to fulfill your dreams?

When ninety-year-old Bubbles receives a letter from Mexico City asking her to pick up her mother's ashes, lost there seventy years earlier and only now surfacing, she hatches a plan. A woman with a mission, Bubbles convinces her hippie daughter, Feather, to accompany her on the quest. Both women have recently shed husbands and have a secondary agenda: they'd like a little action. And they get it.

Alternating narratives weave together Feather and Bubbles' odyssey. The two women head south from Canada to Mexico where Bubbles' long-dead mother, grandmother, and grandfather turn up, enlivening the narrative with their hilarious antics.

In Mexico, where reality and magic co-exist, Feather gets a new sense of her mother, and Bubbles' quest for her mother's ashes—and a new man—increases her zest for life. Unlike most women her age, fun-loving Bubbles takes risks, believing she's immortal. She doesn't hold back in any way, eating heartily and lusting after strangers, exulting in her youthful spirit.

Has Bubbles discovered a fountain of youth that everyone can drink from?

PROLOGUE TO *FLING!*

Isle of Skye, 1906

Malcolm—Heather MacGregor's grandfather on her mother's side—told anyone who was willing to listen that his granddaughter hadn't been born the usual way. She'd danced right off one of his paintings, landing in the family's potato patch, except the land was too barren to produce much by the time she came along. It wasn't a promising beginning.

She made the best of it. At least it hadn't been an onion patch.

The family and villagers had heard the story so often they were sick of it. Yet no one doubted Heather's origins (or Bubbles', as she was later known). The Scots, reputed to have a sixth sense, know unpredictable things happen, and there's no telling when something out of the ordinary will occur. They give lip service to Christianity, but the old religion hasn't gone anywhere.

She grew up knowing that the sea was the province of Manannan mac Lir, King of the Land-Under-Wave. And the Tuatha De Danaan, the supernatural race, lived in the glens, appearing to mortals as birds or animals. In front of the hearth, while stirring the broth, her granny sang to Heather from the time she was a babe in a cradle:

> *Wisdom of serpent be thine*
> *Wisdom of raven be thine*
> *Wisdom of valiant eagle . . .*

The prayers didn't help her much—at least her granny didn't think so. Granny thought that wisdom would appear as good sense and judgment. As she told Heather's mother, after whom Heather was named, "Maybe it will just take longer for wisdom to reach her in Skye."

And what of Feather, her only daughter? She didn't visit Skye until she was a middle-aged woman, accompanying her mother there to meet the remaining relatives. Yet Feather also seemed infected by the Scots sensibility, expressing through her art's underworld. It permeated everything she did or created.

Get your copy now or read the first chapter FREE at
www.Pen-L.com/Fling.html

ACKNOWLEDGMENTS

For their inspiration, good care, and thoughtful comments, I would like to thank the following people:

Duke and Kimberly Pennell, for their courage to run a small press in today's economic environment and for their belief in *Fling!* and *Freefall: A Divine Comedy*.

Joan Fornelli, an early reader of *Freefall* and my first fan.

Hugh Cook, a fellow Canadian who offered wise editing advice.

Victoria DeMara, who read *Freefall* in its early stages, resonated with its characters and themes, and made valuable suggestions.

Members of my online writing group, whose perspectives are always cherished.

Laurie Ann Doyle and Mark Willen, for writing wonderful blurbs for *Freefall*.

Eva Zimmerman, for her valuable marketing advice.

As always, my husband, Michael, and my son, Leo, for their continuing encouragement as I navigate publishing's treacherous waters.

And anyone else I've forgotten!

Discussion Questions

1. How does your understanding of Tillie evolve over the course of this novel?

2. How would you describe the relationship between Tillie and her mother?

3. What role does the Black Madonna have in *Freefall*? How does she differ from the Biblical Madonna?

4. What do Carmine and Emil contribute to this narrative given their Gypsy heritage and music?

5. Why are events such as Carnivale important in *Freefall* and for a culture?

6. What do the four women's Carnivale costume choices tell us about them?

7. What do you think has transpired between these four women during the course of the novel, both in Whistler and Venice?

8. In what ways is *Freefall* a "divine comedy"? What might the humor reveal about Tillie and life in general?

9. Describe how the '60s penetrate these women's lives and contribute to the narrative.

10. Masks have an important function in *Freefall*. How do the characters use their various masks to conceal and reveal themselves?

11. Art and art making is woven throughout the narrative. What have you discovered about art from reading these pages?

12. How is death aligned with beauty?

13. Death permeates this narrative. What is Tillie trying to work out here in terms of her relationship with death?

14. Bud has a significant role in *Freefall*. In what ways is he an important character and why?

15. How do the main settings for this work—Whistler, B.C., and Venice, Italy—contribute to the overall narrative?

16. What changes for the women after their encounter with the grizzly in Whistler?

17. How are magical realistic elements woven into this narrative?

18. In what ways do Tillie, Frank/Bird, and Bud enlarge your understanding of art and artists?

19. How do Tillie, Sybil, Moll, and Daddy reflect and enlarge one another?

20. Do Tillie's reflections on death alter your understanding of it?

About the Author

Lily Iona MacKenzie has published reviews, interviews, short fiction, poetry, travel pieces, essays, and memoir in over 155 venues. Her poetry collection, *All This,* was published in 2011. *Fling!,* her debut novel, was published in July 2015. *Curva Peligrosa,* another novel, was released in September 2017. She has taught rhetoric and literature at the University of San Francisco for over 30 years. Currently, she teaches creative writing at the University of San Francisco's Fromm Institute of Lifelong Learning.

VISIT LILY AT:

www.LilyIonaMacKenzie.com

Dear Reader,
If you enjoyed this
book enough to review
it for Goodreads, B&N,
or Amazon.com, I'd
appreciate it!
Thanks, Lily

Find more great reads at
Pen-L.com

Made in the USA
Middletown, DE
30 July 2019